The Enemy Mind

The Enemy Mind

Jonathan David

iUniverse, Inc.
New York Lincoln Shanghai

The Enemy Mind

iUniverse, Inc.

For information address:
iUniverse, Inc.
2021 Pine Lake Road, Suite 100
Lincoln, NE 68512
www.iuniverse.com

ISBN: 0-595-30053-7

Printed in the United States of America

Some of the cumulative theories and principles based on centuries of research and hypotheses from many reputable scientists have been combined and made available in "Unveiling the Edge of Time" by John Gribbin.

The day the darkness fell…

Crandall Cady turned the acorn over in his small hand looking at its unique shape. How smooth the rounded edges were that led to a razor sharp point at its base. And on top of the curious looking 'seed' was a brown cap that looked more like one of those silly little hats a painter wears what with the small stem at its center.

"C'mon, shrimp," his friend, Ben yelled. "Hurry it up, will ya?"

Crandall looked up to see his friends each carrying handfuls of acorns across the lawn. Frowning, he dropped the acorn in the palm of his left hand and atop the pile he had collected before rushing to catch up.

Ben was carefully stacking his acorns in a line upon the surface of the asphalt. "If we make a line, there's no way a car can miss 'em. It sounds really cool to hear 'em pop when they get run over and stuff."

The others jumped in and began lining up their acorns in-line with Ben's, and soon they had built a stream of acorns that stretched the length of the right lane.

"Guys, there's a car comin'!" Gary shouted. "We gotta hide!"

Together, the group of boys gathered behind the tall bush beside the road, peering through the leaves at the road as the heavy pickup sped by. Rolling over the acorns, a few short pops ringing out before the truck sped away, the boys all jumped from their hiding place shouting and laughing, pumping their fists in the air.

Crandall looked around with a small grin on his face, but slowly noticed that the others were congratulating one-another, yet he stood at a distance, nobody around him.

It was like this most often. He was a part of the 'gang', but at the same time, he was the party's outcast. Being the youngest and the smallest made him more often the punching bag than anything else, and forever was he looking to gain favor and earn a rank among his friends.

He looked at the road, the line of acorns split in two places, the small corns smashed into the pavement. Honestly, the sound had been exciting when the truck ran them over…

Looking down at his feet, he saw he was standing in a patch of acorns beneath the old tree towering miles high over his head, the sunlight unable to penetrate the layers upon layers of leaves. Bending down, he began to scoop the acorns into his hands, using the loose lower half of his T-shirt as a receptacle to pile them into. The other boys were busy talking among themselves as cars rushed by, crunching one or two acorns here and there. Some would blast their horns or pass an obscene gesture, and Ben and the others would return it. Crandall just continued to pile the acorns into his makeshift basket, hurrying to gather as many as he could so the idea could be his; no one else could claim credit. For once, he'd be the coolest…

"Whatcha doin', shrimp?" Ben asked, seeing the littler boy rapidly piling the acorns into his shirt.

Crandall ignored the question, and instead realized that now was the time if he was to stay ahead of the rest. He stood up, his joints stiff from crouching so long, but he made his way to the road.

"That's a lot of acorns," someone mumbled from the pack.

"What's he doin'?"

Crandall stepped onto the asphalt and crossed to the center of the lane, a car rising up over the hill and bearing down on him. He released the basket he had made of his shirt and hundreds of acorns tumbled to the road where they bounced and rolled in every direction, spreading all over the pavement.

"Lookit 'em go," Ben said from his perch beside the road.

The car was coming closer, and Crandall had to hurry to shake the remaining acorns from his shirt. He looked over at his friends with a sheepish grin before running off the road, his friends wide-eyed with excitement even as the car charging them slammed on its brakes, the heart-stopping sound of rubber screaming on pavement.

The car, some late-model Toyota, hit the acorns and rolled over them, traction stolen from beneath the vehicle's weight, the frightened-eyes of the female driver white with terror as the car to spin. The vehicle's passenger locked eyes with Crandall, a look of disappointment and fear blending his emotions.

Crandall's devious grin of triumph slipped quickly as he saw the car losing control with the road, the popping of acorns muffled by squealing tires. He felt his stomach turn, a fear of dread building in him while knowing that this was his fault.

The car continued to spin until the tires suddenly locked with unmolested asphalt, and it lurched forward off the road into a tall oak on the other side, the driver's side front end crunching forward like tinfoil, the sickening sound of shattering glass and collapsing metal reaching Crandall's ears like laughter.

He cringed and suddenly wished he could take it back. Throwing a glance toward his friends, they were all turning and running away, pumping for speed, leaving the scene as fast as they could.

Crandall looked back at the wreck and though about going to help, but all he could do was stand and watch, his hands trembling with fear, his eyes leaking, his feet locked with the ground.

The car settled along with the silence, the shattered remains of what had once been a vehicle now a twisted mess.

* * * *

"So, do you regret your actions? Do you feel any guilt for doing what you did?" She loomed closer, her beady eyes digging into his, her wrinkled lips curling into a grotesque form, the dark lipstick hideous against her pale, white skin. "Now do you understand why your parents tried so hard to raise you right?"

Crandall shrunk against the couch, his blue eyes fixated with the demon across from him. She was his psychologist, but he didn't rightly understand how she was helping him through the terrible dreams he was experiencing as a result of the accident.

"Your little game has cost the life of a twenty year-old girl," the demon continued. "Imagine her parents, her brothers or sisters. Imagine what they're going through right now."

"I didn't mean it," he whimpered.

"Didn't mean it?" The hag cackled. "Well, that makes everything hunky-dory, doesn't it? Takes it all back and wipes the slate clean, so to speak. Erases the fact that you killed someone because you were playing a game. A stupid little juvenile game, and you robbed someone of their life."

He felt it coming, and he tried like heck to hold them back, but the tears came anyway, slowly trickling over his cheeks and dripping to his lap, his lip uncontrollably curved downward.

Why was she making him feel so guilty? He felt bad enough as it was.

"Go on and cry for a little while," the witch said, standing and walking across the room. "Cry like a little baby, Crandall. Don't worry, I won't tell anyone." She turned and winked, an evil twinkle in her eye. "But God saw you do it, you little shit."

Crandall leaned over the edge of the couch, his stomach lurching, thick liquid rising up his throat and out his mouth where it splashed and splattered on the rugs beneath him. The witch started screaming at him, but he stood and ran for the door, his sweaty palms having trouble finding purchase until the knob finally turned and he was released. His legs carried him down the hall, the fancy lights overhead mocking him as he raced beneath them and away, one door after another all becoming one, the world uniting against him as he became imprisoned by the building stretching forever like endless arms.

All around, the ghosts opened doors and pointed, laughing at him and yelling, grotesque breath smelling of rot as long tongues lashed out and bound his wrists, yanking him back.

Kicking and screaming he was flung to the ground, the tentacles tearing into his arms, shredding the skin, the pain searing and unbearable.

"Now maybe you'll feel regret," he heard the echoing call of the psychologist. "Maybe now you'll shape up, young man."

* * * *

The lights were bright as he jolted upright, a scream tearing his lungs, his hands and feet restrained even as the veins stood out on his neck.

Doctors were all around him, their faces and hair hidden behind baby-blue masks. Only concerned eyes watched him, and they tortured his soul as the restraints dragged him back down to the hospital bed, a trickle of blood leaking from his nose.

"It's okay, Crandall," a doctor whispered.

Another cast a look of doubt.

"What the hell's the matter with this kid?" a second voice came.

Something sharp stung him in the arm, and Crandall relaxed, sleepiness coming quickly and dragging him into the darkness.

There in the black, the witch waited and cackled, her fingers drawing closer, her breath smelling like decaying fish.

"Guilty!" she hissed, her hands wrapping like ropes around his neck, and she squeezed. "God saw you do it, you little shit."

CHAPTER 1

He was no longer an agent.

The idea in itself was unfamiliar and made him wonder what was next. Had it been a rash decision to quit after only nine years in? With a family to support and bills to pay, would this decision come back to bite him?

Tomorrow. There would be a tomorrow—there always was, but tomorrow wouldn't be anything like he'd known over the past decade.

At the age of thirty-three, it seemed like such a backward move to start over. Jesus, what had he been thinking? Sure, he'd hated being an insurance agent, but he was his own boss—to some extent—and he made a stable if not guaranteed living. There would be enough money to put Angela through college and the mortgage would be paid.

Still, he hated that place. The smell of the moldy carpet that he never could solve, the sound of his secretary clipping and filing her nails even when she was on the phone, and the maniacal silence that drove him to playing endless hours of Solitaire on his PC as he waited for a customer to walk in or telephone. On top of it all was the overburdening expense of his health insurance for himself, his secretary and his wife who was in and out of the hospital almost monthly to treat her schizophrenia, manic depression and diabetes.

As a college professor, his health insurance would be covered by the university, and he hoped that it would help ease the stress that was causing his hair to fall out. Under bright lights, he could already see his scalp beginning to show through the crown of his head where there used to be only dark hair. The hours at the new job would be shorter so he could spend more time with his wife and daughter and keep up with the Jones' in terms of yard maintenance. The paycheck would be significantly smaller, but they had savings, and it would last so long as they were careful.

His hands were shaking as he popped the white lid off the orange plastic bottle and dumped two white pills onto his tongue. Swallowing them dry, he popped the lid from another bottle and shook two more, cringing as the dry beasts slowly rolled down his throat. Shaking the bitter flavor, he turned the key and his Jeep responded. Consistency was what Crandall Cady needed now more than ever. Things he could depend on to remain the same, leaving him having to deal only with the small issues that came up from time to time. He could handle that.

Looking at his hands, he saw that they were still trembling. It usually took a good ten minutes for the effects of his medication to settle into his system, but he worried about his driving when he was this way, and the wait seemed too long.

Crandall felt afraid; afraid that he wouldn't be able to make things right for his wife, Emily. It was difficult. Her sickness, that is. It placed such a burden on the family and his marriage. When he had told her of his plans to become a college professor so he could be home more, she had accused him of conspiring against her, meaning to kill her with all his extra time.

More neuroleptics for her, more anti-depressants for him, and eventually they both calmed down.

He pulled out of the parking lot for the last time and turned home. Emily and Angie would be waiting, dinner on the table as usual. They'd talk about his day and then theirs, and things would be normal all the way up until he switched out the light to go to sleep where he'd be left alone in the dark to entertain his worst fears: What if he failed?

God, now that it was real, he didn't feel so good about it.

The light up ahead turned yellow, and the driver in front of him accelerated, blatantly running the red light before slowing down. Crandall slowed to a stop at the intersection, cars whizzing past him from either side. Sighing, he scanned the radio dial and found nothing interesting, his eyes darting from the digital display to the people crossing the walk in front of him, his patience wearing thin as the light refused to turn green.

He bolted forward when the light changed, charging into the intersection.

Someone stepped into his path.

Crandall panicked, his foot hitting the brake, the tires locking, his body thrown forward, his heart racing, the squealing scream of his Jeep trying to stop, the rubber shriek was enough to cause those on the sidewalks to stop and turn. The Jeep rocked backward as forward motion stopped, Crandall bouncing back and forth inside, his heart pounding against his ribcage, the adrenalin making him feel faint. The man in front of him turned his head slightly, his eyes hidden behind dark shades. He stopped walking as he looked down to see the Jeep's bumper brushing his slacks, and he was suddenly interested in the vehicle that sat humming in idle boredom, the man behind the bug-stained windshield a wide-eyed and well-dressed gentleman whose fingers were locked in a death-grip with his steering wheel.

Crandall slowly began to relax, as he realized what might have been a disaster had ended up okay.

*I didn't hit him, I didn't hit him...*he thought as he drew a deep breath.

The spectators along the road resumed, still mannequins becoming pedestrians again, chatter resuming, and they swarmed like flocks in parallel to his Jeep. The sun dipped behind the tallest building and the shadows began to fall, stretching like an erection over the streets and the people.

The old man rounded Crandall's vehicle and approached the window, smiling from behind his black shades, missing teeth gaping tunnels into darkness, his long white hair brushing against his neck in the afternoon breeze. He made motion for Crandall to roll his window down and Crandall did without thinking twice.

"Jesus, are you okay?" Crandall asked, chucking apologetically. "I didn't even see you coming."

The man leaned in the window. He grinned. "Nice ride, mister. Had us one of them, whatchamacallems? Close encounters."

The cars behind Crandall began to honk as the traffic around him resumed.

With trembling fingers, the old man pulled a cigarette from a crumpled pack, tenderly pinched it between his lips and offered one to Crandall who shook his head. "Don't smoke. I've got a daughter."

The man nodded, flicking the Bic and pressing the flame against the tip of the cigarette, sucking in, his cheeks retracting over the bony cheeks and stretching, the cigarette's tip glowing orange. He exhaled a cloud of smoke, adjusted his glasses and grinned again. "It's only a matter of time afore they catch me again, so I'm enjoying the day while I've got it."

"Catch you?"

"I escaped, but dollars to beans says they'll come looking." He leaned over, lowered his glasses to reveal his eyes, and winked. "Incidentally, I knew you weren't going to hit me."

Crandall checked his rearview mirror and saw the driver behind him lifting the universal sign of 'fuck you' at him through his windshield. He became antsy to press on, but the old fellow didn't seem the least disturbed. "And how's that?"

Shrug. "Clouds ain't right for an accident today." The man stood up and dragged on his cigarette.

The cars behind him were honking in unison, a terrible blare that carried for blocks.

"I wouldn't worry about them," the old man said, grinning again.

Crandall smiled. "To be honest, I'm worried I'm going to piss my pants out of relief. I thought that was it. Thank God for reliable brake-pads, eh?"

The man looked at Crandall though his black glasses. "You got that timid look that suggests anxiety yet carefully hides behind an arrogant 'things are okay because that's just the way things are supposed to be' look that's manifested from years of close calls you'd take for granted. Suddenly, you break into a cold sweat at the selfish prospect on how your life would have changed had you run me over."

Crandall frowned.

The horns continued to blare.

The man leaned down again, into the window, his cigarette leaking a thin string of smoke that pressed upward, a bit of ash dropping into the Jeep and onto Crandall's armrest. "Like I said, I wouldn't worry about them."

Crandall checked his rearview and saw the man waving his hands, his face exasperated with frustration. "And why is that?"

The man in black clothing grinned. "I imagine," he began as he leaned out of the window and straightened, dragging on the cigarette and pulling it from his lips, a stream of gray smoke racing into oblivion. "They can't take the pressure."

Patting the door, the old man walked away, took the curb, and disappeared into the crowd.

The insatiable honking continued, and Crandall touched the accelerator, his Jeep driving through the yellow light overhead only to have it turn red once he'd passed, the traffic behind him screeching to a halt.

He played a million thoughts over in his mind, and at the end of every possibility he continued to draw blanks, not having the slightest clue as to what the man had meant.

Crandall pulled into his driveway and parked in the garage. He shut the overhead door and grabbed the briefcase from the passenger seat as he always had. Grunting, he climbed from the Jeep and shut the door behind him, careful to wipe his feet on the mat before entering the air-conditioned home he had lived in for nearly ten years.

"Welcome home, dear," Emily said from where she stood by the sink. She always said that in the same exact tone from the same exact place. *Welcome home, dear.*

He put his things down, kicked off his shoes, made his way into the living room and plopped down in front of the news the way he had for years and years. He knew exactly how the day was going to end. Even though his day would change, and his office would change, and the people he reported to would change, and his itinerary would change, and the weather would change, and his favorite gas station would change, his days would always end the same way.

Consistency was what he craved.

Welcome home, dear.

He knew *exactly* how the day was going to end, and the thought made him smile.

Today.

Tomorrow.

Next week.

Next month.

He knew exactly how the day was going to end.

Exactly.

CHAPTER 2

"Where are you going?"

Crandall looked over at his wife and smiled softly. "I'm just getting up, honey."

"But it's Saturday."

"That's true, but that doesn't mean the sun won't come up." He leaned over and kissed her on the forehead. "I thought maybe I'd make you a nice breakfast before we go up and see Mom."

Her sleepiness was instantly forgotten. "We're going where?"

Jesus. Here we go again. "Honey, we talked about this last night. We're going up to see your mother today. The doctors said she's doing much better and could use the company."

"You're not going to institutionalize me again, Crandall. I won't allow it." She swung her feet over the edge of the bed and rocked back and forth, her head lowered, hair hiding her face.

Crandall reached over and touched her shoulder, but she shrunk away.

"Come on, baby," he whispered. "We're only going up for a visit, then we're coming home. I'm not going to institutionalize you."

"You did before!" she shrieked, jumping from the bed and backing against the wall. "You had them tie me up and shoot me up with that…that *shit*, Crandall!"

"It was Risperdal, Emily. The same supplements you take every day, but they had to use a syringe because—"

"You were trying to kill me!"

Crandall stood from the bed and put his back to her, hands on hips. It was going to be one of those days. She was worse than usual. Approaching the nightstand beside her place on the bed, she darted to the side only to see that he wasn't coming for her. Instead, she watched as he dumped her prescription on the tabletop and began counting the small pills.

Nineteen. "Goddammit," he whispered, pinching his eyes closed. He scooped the pills into his palm and returned them to the orange container. "Why haven't you been taking your medication?"

She slid down the wall into a sitting position. "You're trying to poison me..."

Crossing the room, he brought the bottle with him and sat down beside her, smiling softly. He turned the label to where she could read it. "You see that?" he asked softly. "Dr. Hammond prescribed it. He's a good doctor, Emily. He's been your doctor since you were twenty, and he's never prescribed you anything that would hurt you."

She looked at him, doubt in her eyes. "You didn't switch them?"

He wrapped his arm over her shoulder and hugged her close. "When I say that I love you, do you doubt me?"

Emily shook her head.

"Good, because you know in your heart that I would never do anything—anything to ever hurt you. Will you please believe me?"

She softened, her breathing beginning to calm.

"Risperdal makes you better, honey. Please take one? For me?"

She nodded, and he kissed her lightly on the cheek before reaching into the bottle and pulling out a tablet that she accepted and placed on her tongue.

"There's my girl," Crandall whispered, squeezing her arm with affection. "Would you like some breakfast?"

Emily nodded. "I should do something with my hair first."

"Tell you what. I'll make breakfast while you do your hair. How's that sound?"

She offered a smile. "Thanks, honey."

He released her and left the room, trotting down the stairs, his hopes high that maybe things would be okay after all.

His smile faded when he saw his old Labrador, Charlie, its big, brown eyes looking at him sullenly from where it cowered, lying in a pool of urine.

Sighing, he made for the kitchen and where Emily kept her paper towels.

Yep, it was going to be one of those days.

* * * *

"I'll just need to see your IDs," the man said with a timid, pleasant smile. He was fidgeting from where he sat, his rubbery chin moving as he jiggled. "For, you know, security reasons."

Crandall pressed his driver's license against the window, and the man leaned forward, squinting through his glasses as he adjusted them, his mouth hanging open slightly.

"Yeah, okay. What about her?"

"She's my mother," Emily answered.

"Yes, well, we'll just need to see about that, dear."

Emily held up her ID. It was an expired driver's license as she hadn't been able to drive since she had been diagnosed as both schizophrenic and with bipolar disorder, and she had lacked the courage and ambition either way.

"Got anything more recent," the man asked, reading Emily's information through the glass. "That card's expired."

"We were just here two days ago, Mike," Crandall answered. "We went through this then, the same way we have for the past six months upon our weekly visit."

The man sat back down, insulted by the jest made at his expense. "Can't be too sure these days. I've got a responsibility to the patients in our care here, you know. I can't let just anybody through them doors."

Crandall hardened, his patience thin. "We're here to see my wife's mother, Lucille Akers."

The man behind the desk nodded, crossed his hands over his chest and looking across his counter and beyond the couple. "What about the kid?"

"That's our daughter, Angela," Crandall returned, his voice dark.

The man nodded again. "Cute little girl." Sighing he reached over and grabbed a sheet of paper that he slid under the window. "Fill this out, please. I'll have Ms. Akers prepared for your visit. Thank you."

Crandall held his tongue and corralled his family backward into the waiting room where they sat down, and he began to hurriedly scribble the necessary gibberish he'd filled out every week for the past half year.

"I don't like that guy," Emily whispered, mistakenly thinking she was out of Angela's range. "I think he might be one of them."

Crandall shook his head. "I had him checked out," he lied. "There was a full FBI inquiry, and Mike checked out. It's okay. He's with us."

Emily relaxed a bit and sat back, though her eyes continued to scan the room and return frequently to where Mike sat behind his desk, answering his phone and adjusting his glasses.

Angela lowered her eyes, her legs swinging under her chair.

The door opened and a nurse greeted them with a practiced smile, but Crandall noticed that her lipstick was smudged. Just a bit.

"Ms. Akers will see you now," she said.

Crandall returned the plastic grin as he herded his family through the door and handed her the clipboard. "Thanks."

He slipped through, and the white light greeted him along with the smell of decay.

* * * *

Crandall looked around. He was bored out of his mind. Emily was talking with Lucille, but the conversation had digressed to a kindergarten level.

"Have they been serving you good food, Mom?"

"I had mashed potatoes yesterday. And gravy too."

"Gravy too? Wow. I'm so jealous!"

Crandall hated age, and even more so the degradation a person goes through as they revert back to the fetal position, their minds returning to that of a child. He hated to have to entertain it, and he hated having to play a part in it. He just wanted to go.

"You won a game of Bingo?" Emily's eyes lit up. "What did you win?"

Lucille smiled, her face as wrinkled as a prune. "I won front seat at movie night."

"Mother, that's wonderful!"

Angela yawned, and Crandall related. He stood up. "Ladies," he began, donning a smile. "I need to use the restroom."

He mightn't have said anything at all for Emily and Lucille just kept on babbling about nothing, though Angela looked at him with forlorn eyes. Crandall didn't like leaving his daughter in an obviously uncomfortable situation, but he figured that after he relieved himself, he would come back and save her too. In the end, he didn't want his nine year-old daughter roaming the bathrooms of this 'hospital' on her own. He wanted her safe—or as safe as she could be expected to be—with Emily and Lucille.

He made his way past the rows upon rows of beds, all carefully aligned beneath a large window, all carefully adorned by a vase filled with silk flowers on the sill. The sheets were white to match the bedclothes to match the floors to match the walls. Pushing his way into the bathroom, he stood beneath the blinding fluorescent lights and stared at the hollow eyes staring back from the reflection in the mirror.

Crandall ran cold water and doused his face, wishing he was anyplace but Clear Haven. The bleached scent alone was enough to make him sick, and he had to concentrate to keep from gagging. He pulled the orange bottle from his pants, yanked off the lid and dropped three tablets of Effexor into his palm. Downing them with water from the tap, he stared at the man in the mirror. "Hey, buddy," he whispered.

The paper towel dispenser was empty, so he resorted to using his sleeve to dry his face and hands, all the while mumbling to himself.

A drop remained on the countertop and looked out of place. Crandall felt the urge to wipe it off, dry the counter and return the room to its serene perfection, but there was something down deep that told him to let it alone. The room was supposed to be perfect. The sheets were all supposed to be straight, the flowers dusted, the shades lowered exactly fourteen inches.

The drop of water just sat there, mocking him and looking insanely out of place, and he was drawn—almost magnetically—to it, wanting to right what was wrong.

Straightening, he forced himself out the door, refusing to look back.

"Is it open?" an old man asked, his hands trembling as he pointed, his back hunched.

Crandall smiled and nodded. "Bathroom's all yours, pal." He patted the old man on the shoulder and continued on.

"I wasn't referring to the bathroom," the man returned.

Crandall looked over his shoulder, something in the man's voice familiar.

"Your mind, son. Is it open?"

Crandall eyed the man up and down, took in his physique, the hunched back, white hair, withered hands. "I know you, don't I?"

The old man grinned, chuckled, stepped forward and suddenly lunged, his eyes wide, the whites engulfing the lifeless pupils. "Screeeeeeeeeeeeeech!" he shrieked, baring his claws. "Bam!" He laughed. "Not…so…fast…"

Had us one of them, whatchamacallems? Close encounters…

Crandall relaxed, making the connection.

The old man winked, waving a knowing finger Crandall's way. "Nothing is coincidental."

Crandall grinned. "I remember you now."

"I certainly hope so," the man snapped. "You nearly made road kill outta me."

As if things weren't bad enough. Now he was stuck in a man-made hell called Clear Haven with his doped up wife, her doped up mother and a doped up man who was remembering—in a rare moment of clarity—his own clash with death.

It was serving. The old man should be in a place like this. He was clearly out of his mind, his own existence a danger to those around him.

"I'm sorry," Crandall said. Finally.

The man smiled. "No you aren't, and I can't hold it againstcha. I wouldn't be sorry neither. It was a moment that changed two lives. In one moment, your brakes made a decision to either perform or fail. They chose to perform. It could have gone either way. In simple terms spoken by a brilliant man on the subject of death: that's life."

Crandall grinned, but he didn't feel any humor hanging in the air.

"The thing is," the old man went on, "your brakes could have chosen to fail, and at this very moment you would not have been stopped as you make your way back to your wife and your daughter. In fact, taken one step further, dollars to beans says you wouldn't even be here as an investigation would still be ongoing. Maybe it's ironic, but that just isn't very sexy."

Crandall looked out over the sea of beds and saw the only disruption to the white color at the far end of the room where Emily and Angela sat on the edge of a dying woman's bed.

The old man was shaking his head when Crandall looked back, and he was fumbling for a chair, his strength waning. Sitting down heavily, he breathed a heavy sigh, his eyes shut, his lower lip raised with bare pride. "I was once your age, my young friend. I remember what it was like." He opened his eyes, and there was a twinkle of knowledge. "I remember feeling a loathing and lust for life, both at the same time. Know what I mean?"

Crandall could have nodded and walked away, but where would he have gone? Back to Emily and Lucille? Back to the same stench? What did it really matter if he stood here or sat there?

He nodded.

The old man chuckled. "Course you do. You got all the answers by now."

Crandall felt like laughing, felt like striking back. Where he stood was imposing enough to the world of this man and the other patients, but he felt like them. He felt intruded upon, imprisoned. It was like this was his home as well.

"Have a seat," the old man said. His voice was pleasant but firm. Like a father about to spread a wealth of knowledge to his son on the boy's twenty-first birthday. *Have a seat* was more an order than an offering, and Crandall, having lost his grand-father years ago to an automobile accident, obliged.

"You play cards?" the old man asked, whipping out a deck, his shaky fingers clumsily shuffling them.

"What's the game?"

"Blackjack."

"I'm game."

"What you got to wager?"

Crandall grinned, taking the man for a joker, but the old eyes returned to him as cold as the room. Pulling a twenty, Crandall dropped it on the tabletop. "You?"

The old man grinned. "Wisdom." He snickered. "Christ, I wish they'd let me smoke in here. You got a cigarette?"

Crandall was about to answer when the old man shook him off. "Never mind." He pointed to his head. "The old ticker ain't right. I almost forgot. You got a daughter and all."

Crandall remembered the old man leaning into his window, his eyes hidden behind black glasses, a stolid grin upon his leathery lips.

"Name's Spoon. Benjamin Spoon. Ben Spoon. Ben. Benny. Call me as you see fit, and I may or may not answer." He shuffled. "I could see it in yer eyes. The question, that is. That isolation you've built around us because you don't know who I am any more than I know who you are." He winked. "See, they locked me up on account of how dangerous I am." He chuckled. "Dangerous. Me. Go figure."

Ben was dealing.

Crandall checked his card. Ace. Hearts. He eyed his crumpled twenty lying on the table.

Spoon looked across the table. "What's your play?"

Crandall wasn't sure how he should respond. There were so many different ways to answer that question that he became confused as to the direction of Ben's inquiry. "Hit me."

Spoon dropped a card, face down. "Know why they put me here?"

Crandall shook his head. "No idea."

"I know too much, see."

"Is that so?"

Spoon looked around, assuring maybe only himself that they were out of earshot of anyone else. Turning back, he leaned on the table, scattering the cards. "I can trust you."

"What makes you so confident?"

Spoon grinned. "Because I know who's dear to you."

Crandall stopped, his humor lost, his eyes darting across the room to where Emily and Angela sat and back again. "You threatening me?"

"Absolutely..." A wink. "...not. I'm just an informant."

"For who?" He turned over his card. Six of spades. Six and eleven made seventeen. He called, taking his chances.

The old man chuckled, nodding over Crandall's shoulder. "You see that?"

"What?"

"Up at the screen, jackass. The commercial."

Crandall turned around, casting his attention toward the ceiling and the hanging television that played silently. The commercial was familiar, and Crandall turned back. "What about it?"

"What about it, indeed. What's it about?"

Crandall shrugged. "A new medicine. Ask your doctor."

The old man leaned in. "Spies, my friend. Spies. A new medicine to do what exactly?"

Crandall looked over his shoulder again, and the screen returned smiling faces, stories of triumph, the name ZayRhran suspended at the bottom of the screen.

Spoon took a card and eyed it carefully. Smiling, he placed the three cards down, face-up, crossing his hands and leaning back. "Nineteen. I win."

"Congratulations."

"Some new damn procedure. Like we need another one," the old man answered in reference to the commercial as he rounded up the cards and began shuffling the deck. "The latest and greatest in technology. Welcome to the twenty-first century again and again and again. Blah, blah, blah, understand? They'll catch this cancer before it starts and that cancer before it ends. Blah, blah, blah." He looked even as he dealt. "Bullshit." He snorted as he laughed.

"So?"

"I'll bet you dollars to beans that they just want you taking their glorified Computerized Axial Tomography—I'm using their language against them, see?"

"Glorified what?"

The old man was talking in riddles. "Cat Scan, pal. They read your brain. They're not scanning for cancers; they're learning about you."

Crandall looked at his card. A six of hearts. "Hit me, old man."

Ben threw down a card. "Course, they can't make it that obvious."

"Why would they?" Crandall was willing to play along. His two cards added up to fourteen. "Hit me again."

The old man tossed the card. "No reason."

Crandall turned the card. A king of diamonds. He sighed and dropped his cards. "Why would the government want to read our minds?"

"A million reasons, maybe more," the old man went on. "But who said it was the government?"

Crandall shrugged. "Well, you know. Big Brother and all."

Ben was grinning. "The government couldn't afford such a risk. Dollars to beans its private investors." He picked up the twenty-dollar bill and pocketed it. "But I guess this means I don't have to talk anymore."

"I figure if you wanted to talk you would whether you won or not."

"You'd figure wrong."

Crandall licked his dry lips, and the stink of the clean room was on his tongue. "Guess so." Standing, he was about to excuse himself when the old man grabbed at his arm and yanked him back.

"You can't just walk away like that!" Ben hissed. "They'll see you!"

Crandall knelt down. "Who will?"

Ben struggled, but his resolve was weak—just as his opponent had predicted. "The powers that be don't want me out there," he whispered. "'Cause I'm dangerous."

"So you say."

"Damn right I do. I know all about their weather experiments. I know about their goddamn magnets."

Magnets?

"I was a spy," Ben said, his lip quivering, his eyes darting to either side. "Not for the government, see, but for a private organization. I can't tell you who. They'd kill you if I did."

Crandall was intrigued, and he returned to his seat. "They'd kill me? Who would?"

"The government. They're watching, you see. Even now. Even here. They're watching."

Looking around, Crandall saw only a few doctors and a lot of mentally disturbed patients. "I don't see anyone watching, Ben."

"That's the way they want it, see? Government's a self-actualizing entity, a living thing that's dependant on its own secrecy. I know. I worked as a spy."

"You were a spy against the United States Government?"

"Sometimes. Sometimes I worked for the government. I was a spy. I had inside information, the underground kind, see? There's a network of us, but I know how things worked. I know how it still works, but I can't get out." He pointed. "You can."

If nothing else, Ben Spoon was more amusing than Lucille, so Crandall stayed. "How does it work, Ben?"

Spoon looked to his side and hunched forward. "Stays between us. If you see Mario, you tell him the password's Atom Heart Mother. He won't kill you then."

"That's a Pink Floyd album."

"So? You think I just made it up? You think this network was created yesterday?"

"Network?"

"Goddamn right, network. You see, we figured out, and when I say 'we' I mean the United States Government, a way to finally beat them sneaky Russian bastards."

Crandall looked over Ben's head to where Emily and Angela were. His daughter was staring back, a 'save me' look all over her face.

Soon, honey. Soon.

"I didn't realize we were still at war with Russia."

Ben shook his head, chuckling as if to say, 'oh ye of the naïve world'. "Where you been, man? We been at war for eighty years with 'em. Papers don't cover it 'cause the G-ment don't allow it. Dubya, dubya IV, if you get it. Not a cold war, but a silent war. We, we as in the citizens of our great US of A, don't know we're fighting, and they, they as in the inbreeds of Russia, don't know we're fighting, but I'll guarantee ya that our military knows we're fighting."

Crandall grinned. "You're a conspiracy theorist, aren't you?"

"There are clues," the old man responded. "Mad cow disease. It hits Russia in January, and it hits the states in March. A Russian commercial jetliner goes down over the Pacific, and six weeks later a U.S. jetliner plunges into the same place. Same exact place. Within ten miles. Coincidence?"

Crandall shrugged. "Maybe."

"Coincidence is having a cavity in the same tooth as your wife. Coincidence is getting into your first car accident only to find out you smacked your best friend from grade school. Coincidence is discovering your high school sweetheart married a man by your same first name. Coincidence, my friend, isn't two mysterious airliner crashes within six weeks."

Crandall frowned, playing along. "So it's a conspiracy."

Ben pointed, a toothless grin cast Crandall's way. "And do you know how they did it?"

"Did what?"

"Crashed two planes in the same spot?"

"The same spot, though ten miles apart?"

Spoon frowned. "This ain't apples and oranges. It ain't cats versus dogs. It ain't as simple as black and white."

"You have a fixation with things in three's," Crandall answered. He was enjoying himself.

"Things come in three's," Ben retorted, un-amused. "Major league baseball. Three strikes. Three outs. Three bases. Football. Field goals equal three points. Three downs and punt. Basketball. Three-pointers. Hockey. Hat trick equals three goals in one game." He lifted his brow. "Deaths come in threes. You'll never see a renown name pass without two following on his or her heels. Twelve months in a year, divisible by three. Three hundred sixty-five days to a year. Sixty is divisible by three."

"What about the five?"

"Both are odd numbers," came the quick reply. "We digress."

"We most certainly do," Crandall said, unable to hide his cynicism.

"It's the magnets," Spoon growled.

"Magnets?"

"You mock me. Just like the rest of them did. You're why I'm here when I should be out there."

Realizing his mistake, Crandall sobered, taking an active interest in the cards again, scooping the deck and shuffling. "I don't know anything about the magnets, Ben. I apologize if I'm naïve."

Ben wasn't sold, but he wanted to talk; that much was obvious. Leaning forward, his put his hand over Crandall's, bending the cards down. "You know nothing about the magnets. You're a child."

An old woman wandered by their table, knocking on the wall opposite them with every step. She'd stop, press her ear against the drywall and listen for a few seconds before moving on. Another knock, another pause, another step.

"She knows they're here too," Spoon whispered. "She's trying to find 'em, but she's sloppy, and when they catch her, they'll punish her. I'm much more discrete."

"I agree," Crandall answered, holding a straight face.

"She's a lunatic," Ben said, his eyes gray. "You're a parasite. Gonna ride my coattails? Don't think I'm that easy to win over. I'm not crazy." He pointed at the old woman. "Not like her. She's listening for rats. Rats and mice and bats, the little devils of our world; sneaky little spies that are trained to report back to their masters. But there ain't no rats here. She's nuts thinking that there are. Mike puts up fresh traps each night. The spies can't get in, see?"

"Sorry. I was just being agreeable," Crandall said, his face flushing. "You're right. I'm naïve here. What do you want me to do?" It was a game. He felt somewhat bad to be playing with the old man's mind, but this was more fun than a sitcom or a group of commercials. It was more fun than talking about the crap Clear Haven served at mealtime, and it was more fun than having to listen to it.

Ben looked over his shoulder and leaned in. "You have to be very careful with this information. I need you to get it to the American Embassy in Argentina."

"I don't think there is a—"

"It's there, believe me. There's a man by the name of Smith. Tell him I sent you."

"Smith?"

"Don't make me repeat myself. We're on a short chain, my friend."

"Okay, fine. What do I tell him?"

Ben gripped Crandall's wrist and tightened his grip. "This ain't a game, mister. Same page?"

Cady nodded. "Sure."

"The Russians have retaliated. Can you remember that?"

A nod.

"They have similar technology. There was a leak. Four years ago. One of our own defected. A man by the name of Smith."

"Another Smith?"

"Pay attention."

"Right."

"They copied our technology and used it against us."

"What technology?" Crandall was concerned because Ben hadn't loosened his grip, and considering his age, he had a bitch of a grip.

"Magnets. You know how a magnet works?"

"Sure."

"You're an idiot. Magnets either attract or repel one another by exerting forces. This is basic science. These magnetic forces react upon each other. Distances don't matter so long as you know how to control the force, see?"

"So what?"

"The Russians have a magnet as big as ours."

"How big is ours?"

"Thirty-thousand tons."

"That's a big magnet."

"Magnets at either sides of the earth, in direct opposition can be used as weapons. You can control weather-patterns and completely destroy negative energy. A moving charge will experience a force. You oppose that force and you control everything in between. Magnetic forces cause charged particles to change their direction of motion. Basic goddamn science, mister. The year twenty oh six. We plugged a stake into the North Pole as well as the South. They sent an electromagnetic charge between the both of them and created a charge of ions so strong that we were able to erupt weather patterns. We bent, literally *bent* forces by controlling the mass of particles and creating a field, an electric field into Russia."

Ben grinned, shaking his head. "They…were…pissed to say the least." Sobering, his smile melted downward. "They mastered our technology and returned the charge. They learned how to manipulate magnetic fields through loops of wire to construct currents." He shook his head. "We're at a stalemate. Whenever we sent a tornado their way, they counter with a hurricane."

Crandall liked this man. He was probably a man of extreme power at one time, but his mind had melded into mush, confusing facts with theories. However, considering the intensity of Ben's words, he was unwilling to let go. "We control the weather?"

Ben cast a look of exasperation, his hands spreading. "What have I been saying? Take a look around. We're sick of Californians, so we sent them a five-year drought. The bastards are fleeing like rodents. We sent snow to Texas to keep them sober in winter, and we keep our Mid-western residents on their toes by keeping their lives lively with tornadoes. You don't think we can't do the same to our enemies? It's a matter of control."

"Wow. This is all so sudden."

"I know." Ben lowered his voice. "Sorry. You couldn't have known, but you must now understand, see? We're building, literally *building* diamagnets, which, in turn, produce eddy currents to seek and destroy our enemies attempts to wipe out our databases, electricity, communications, the works. That's our defense—this so-called magnetic levitation—our leverage so-to-speak. Now that we have magnetic monopole control, we're…Dammit, I'm talking too loud. This information is so dangerous that both of our lives are now in danger." He leaned in. "We must be careful to control the Curie temperature. If we lose control, we're finished. Our enemies can walk right in and take over."

"This is pretty intense," Crandall said, maintaining balance. Ben was a trip.

"We must regain control," Ben continued. "The only way to do that is to capture the electromagnetic induction by applying Lenz's Law. We can accomplish this by *channeling* the direction of the induced current so that the magnetic field, the field we've created, see, becomes the result of the induced current opposing the change in the flux that *caused* the induced current." Ben shook his head, biting his lip, his eyes distant. "I don't think the big wigs in Washington understand this simple formula, and they are, indeed, panicking."

"I don't follow," Crandall interjected. "How can we control weather patterns using magnets?"

"Where the hell were you born? Dipshit USA?" Spoon shook his head with disappointment. "Lightning. What is it? Electricity. Electricity is what? Charged electrons. A magnetic field that exerts a force on a single moving charge and also exerts a force on a current can, in theory, become a man-made collection of moving charges. Magnetic charges. Under this principle, ions are accelerated to a given velocity; then those ions are passed into separation based on mass. Once you control mass, you control everything based on mass. Everything is based on mass, therefore we control everything." He sorrowed. "Or they do. Whoever crosses the finish line first wins, my friend."

"You're right. I didn't see it coming."

"Damn right you didn't. Listen, you need to get this information to the president. Now, I know you won't get within a mile of the man himself, but you can get to those around him. He'll know what to do with it. They won't shoot you. Not with the information you have, but they will be skeptical. Expect your life to change. From this moment forward, things will never be the same."

"I understand."

"I'm not sure you do. We need to control the heavier ions traveling in a circular path of the planetary radius. Without them, we're finished, see?"

"I'll do my best," Crandall replied, taking the man's hand and squeezing. "I won't let you down."

Ben nodded, sighing with relief. "See that you don't. The fate of the free world rests on your shoulders, friend. Make haste."

"Will do. Take care of yourself."

Crandall tried to get away, but Ben caught him by the hand, pulling him back. "You won't just leave me here, will you? You'll return? Update me on the status of the war?"

"Sure I will. I promise." In all truth, he'd have to come back with Emily to visit Lucille on a weekly basis, so he might as well pay the crazed old man a visit and learn of any new conspiracy theories that are, if nothing else, entertaining.

"I expect an update within the week," the old man grumbled, his eyes drifting away. "The bastards'll come looking for me. I must protect myself."

Crandall kneeled down. "I'll make sure you're guarded, Spoon." He figured addressing the old man by last name alone would add a confidential emphasis. "Top secret. They'll be posing as doctors or even patients, but you'll be protected twenty-four, seven. Understand?"

Ben nodded. "See to it." He lifted his blood-shot eyes. "You're a good man, whoever you are."

Crandall smiled. "Crandall," he offered. "Crandall Cady. I'll deliver your message."

Ben smiled, stern but appreciative. "Good. I knew I could trust you, Cady."

Walking away, Crandall felt a tinge of guilt, but he also felt good. By his own standards, Ben had an important purpose. He was the courier of information. The fate of the free world rested on his shoulders. That knowledge may even be strong enough to keep him going, keep him alive.

Crandall refused the guilt and took his deed as positive. Returning to Lucille's bedside, he sat down, a soft smile on his face.

"Mother is tired," Emily whispered. "I think she needs to rest."

Even better.

Together, as a family, Crandall, Emily and Angela stood, but not before Emily gave her mother a kiss and Angela gave her grandmother a hug and Crandall squeezed his stepmother's withered hand with tenderness.

"We'll come back in a few days," Emily whispered, and Lucille nodded, closing her eyes and shifting into the fetal position.

She's waiting to die, Crandall observed before dismissing the thought, dismissing the idea that someone would actually wait to…die.

They passed, as a family, through Mike's door, and the large man sat up, adjusting his glasses, licking his lips and squinting to be sure that the three people leaving Clear Haven were only visitors and not patients.

"Have a nice day, folks," he said in a cheery voice. "Come visit us again."

Crandall waved, but he never turned back.

Angela did, and she stuck out her tongue.

CHAPTER 3

She was crying again.

He could hear her even from where he stood at the living room window. Though she was in the bedroom on the second floor with the door closed and, no doubt, buried under her covers, Emily's sobs sounded like the irritating whine of a teakettle boiling upon the stove. Crandall winced as he stared absently through the dirty glass at the driveway across the street where two little boys were playing with their toy trucks. The Johnson's were on the front lawn, the missus reading a book while looking up every few minutes to see that the boys were careful of cars. Mr. Johnson was trimming the hedges that accented the precise cleanliness of his rancher.

Crandall was ashamed of the condition of his own home. He did his best to keep the place up, but given the hours of his previous job and the full-time occupation of caring for his wife and daughter, the time he had left to devote to the home just wasn't enough. It was only early July, but there were already patches of dead grass in the front yard, and the hedges were out of control. Even the window he was staring through needed cleaning from the outside. Emily took care of tidying things inside, but she was afraid of confrontation and rarely stepped foot in the public eye of their neighborhood.

She was still sobbing.

It wouldn't do any good for him to try and comfort her as that would only make a bad situation even worse. She'd accuse him of conspiring against her or worse—attack him as she'd done before—eyes wild, a knife in hand, her throat emitting screams high enough to cause him to remember even in his sleep.

He winced, a bit of a tick just beneath the skin below his left eye, but he lacked the ambition to scratch at it as he stared, seeing nothing through the dirty glass.

Angela was at her friend's. Crandall had insisted she leave at the onset of her mom's episode, and Angela had been more than happy to oblige leaving him alone to deal with Emily. He was tired of playing the responsible adult, always doing the right thing, always calm and in control. In his mind, Crandall was fed up with this whole scene. He hadn't signed on to be married to a woman with Emily's condition. He had married a bright, green-eyed girl with an insatiable giggle and a loving heart. He missed that girl terribly and only saw glimpses of her on Emily's good days. But even now, despite her illness, he loved her as much, if not more than on the day he'd said 'I do'. It just wasn't easy.

She was still sobbing.

He needed to get away—even if it was for only an hour or so—just a little time away. It was too much to handle twenty-four, seven, and he needed a little while to feel normal.

"I'm going out," Crandall called, though he knew it wasn't loud enough for Emily to hear. It wouldn't matter. She would never even know he had gone. Her 'episodes' generally lasted several hours, and this was—

He checked his watch.

—in the midst of hour number two.

Emily was shrieking, trashing the room, the sound of her charging back and forth like elephants stomping overhead.

Just an hour. Maybe less…

He grabbed his keys and made for the door, careful to lock it as he left. The door was always locked, day and night. Her paranoia was easy to identify, but difficult to control.

Crandall shook the thought and briskly took to the sidewalk, his head lowered so he wouldn't have to look his neighbors in the eye. He wouldn't have to speak and talk about how beautiful the day was. Instead, he concentrated on the cement paving under foot, one step after another and how they carried him out of the neighborhood, away from what lay behind him.

A few of his neighbors called 'good morning' as he passed them by where they watered their bushes or cut the grass or washed their cars or cleaned their garages, but he ignored them, hoping they'd forget about him and return to whatever it was they did. Sometimes they'd give chase—just to ask how Emily was doing so they'd come across as concerned friends.

Bullshit. They wanted to take part, know how bad things had gotten, live that separated moment before returning to their clean life where they could have something to talk about around the coffee machine on Monday morning. Bullshit. Not today.

The neighborhood, Autumn Lane as it was, gave way to Port Henry, a four-lane straightaway through the heart of their small community. However, a block away, an old two-track had gone unattended for decades, overgrown with wild flowers yet remaining unique and popular as a path to the residents of Peyton, Michigan. That was the path most easily chosen for a lonely man to walk, and Crandall took it, wanting to get away from the noisy traffic, wanting to absorb himself in the silence of nature.

Absorption was achieved, and Crandall felt himself relax as the soft sounds of crickets and other insects sang to him in company with birds from their perches in the tall maples and oaks. Time seemed to slow down for him as the crunching gravel underfoot reminded him that a simpler life was out there, begging to be found. The weeds, tall and unattended, were beautiful, though most garden enthusiasts would just as soon see them yanked and discarded.

The path was his. No one else was around. The path ahead and behind was empty, save that of mid-summer greens and the off-colors of wild flowers. Only the sky broke, occasional clouds hanging around as if to observe or maybe just too lazy to continue drifting. Crandall had walked this path so many times that he could have done it blind-folded, yet every time was a new experience, a new retreat that he'd savor long after the light went out at night and he lay staring straight ahead into the digital display of the radio alarm-clock, one minute flicking, licking to the next. Off to his left was an old farmhouse, the roof long collapsed, the exterior in shambles and a dangerous play-station for the children who liked forts and castles. The tall barn in the backyard was still intact for the most part, even the traditional red paint giving a good fight against the gray poking through, the green roof blotchy but stable.

Crandall walked on, one step after another, enjoying the afternoon, when he suddenly stopped and looked at the antique farm and barn. He had never ventured from the path to live the life the old farmer must have enjoyed prior to his death. How many people had traipsed through the timeless capsule since? What was the fascination?

Crandall broke tradition and stepped into the tall grass, the snake-like greens whipping and wrapping around his legs, desperately trying to hold him back. His heart was giddy, and he felt excited in the way he hadn't been since a child when he'd dared to skip class or TP a neighbor's home. He felt like he was doing wrong in a perfectly innocent way, and the feeling was gripping him, wringing and jerking him. He was free.

The porch was old, and by the looks of it, unsafe. Beyond the open doorway he saw only shattered remains of what had once been a home and was now only a memory. Taking the first stair, the wood beneath his shoe groaned and warned of give but held in spite of its weakness.

"This is insane," he said aloud, chuckling at the sound of his own voice. He felt like a kid exploring areas he knew to be forbidden, yet he was unwilling to turn back. Just for a moment, he wanted to sample a farmer's life where the burden of provisions and the means of attaining them were in the fields surrounding his home.

The ceilings were collapsed, drywall and gray timber making a mockery of what was once a living room, the rotting furniture smashed beneath the weight, the happy sun trickling down. He was wrong. Apparently, the kids hadn't taken to the abandoned home, or if they had, they had left things be for the farmhouse seemed to have gone untouched for years. There were no piled up walls of debris to make a handy fort, and there was no graffiti to claim a teenager's territory. No discarded pop or beer cans, no litter. Even the old floor-standing radio stood in its corner, the surface peeling, the knobs rusting. The home might as well be visited upon for the first time in fifty years by the looks of it. Crandall's confidence was somewhat overshadowed by his sudden hesitancy to move forward. He felt like an intruder upon someone's grave.

He looked over his shoulder to see an empty yard stretching back to the two-track, the grass overgrown, the tall weeds dull beneath the heat of the summer sun.

Nobody was looking for him.

He moved through the doorway into the main living room, careful to sidestep the fallen debris, everything breakable cracking underfoot as he cautiously moved forward, testing each step to ensure the floor wouldn't collapse.

The once white walls were stained from moisture and mold, the once clean carpet ruined from rain, snow and animal waste, but the feel of the room—the feel of what was once a home remained.

Crandall stepped over rotting dolls and broken lamps. Into the kitchen where the stove still stood proud and the refridgerator hung open—exposed, the inner contents frozen in a waxy state upon each shelf, thousands of ants somehow finding worth in what remained. He turned on the faucet, but only a dead moth fell out.

Life begins and ends. Crandall observed the cycle.

He moved to the dining room where an antique table was crushed beneath the collapsed ceiling, two legs still strong, the table at a slant, a clock on the wall was silent, the brass pendulum green from exposure.

The bedrooms were similar—items of a former life giving way to the present, giving way to the future. What was once a magnificent king-size bed was reduced to rot, white sheets tattered and overrun with mildew. An oak dresser was in pieces, its contents admitting that people had once made a life here.

Crandall turned away.

The basement door swung open, its hinges snickering at him and revealing the hole that lead down into the darkness. The stairs leading into the black appeared sturdy enough, protected for the most part from the weather, and curiosity alone drove him down.

God, how he loved the smell of old basements. The antique aroma was something he cherished from childhood when his parents had purchased an old home in the country, the coal-bins in the basement still full, a pair of boots beside an old shovel. This place was similar, thought the coal rooms had been made to be pantries to store homemade canned goods from the fields, the Ball jars filled with black slime.

A makeshift washer was in the opposite corner, the washboard at its pit. A furnace, the likes of which Crandall had never before seen, stood at the damp room's center. The coals at its hearth were as black as the night sky and as cold as Hell.

He looked around the room, noting the stored treasures that were once the building blocks for a lifetime of memories. Two rusty bicycles, collapsing books and magazines, boxed clothes that lay spilling to the floor, a welcome home for the mice that raided the lifeless basement.

Crandall smiled sadly, thinking quietly to himself that life comes and goes, and memories are soon forgotten. Everything before him lay naked and exposed except for the door directly across from him that stood firmly closed, cobwebs carefully strewn from the handle to the floor, an array of insects captured and long forgotten by the web's absent owner. He'd already gone this far, so what was breaking and entering of a forgotten room?

Crandall turned the handle, disrupting and finally rupturing the web as he pushed the heavy door inward. The room was dark. Darker than the others as there was no outlet save that of the minimal light trickling in over Crandall's shoulders. The room was dusty, undisturbed and moist. Mice scattered, making for their holes, the spiders mocking him as he stepped in, the Salticus jumping and hiding. The cold air, cooped up for months upon months slowly began to seep past him, the smell of age delicious and sinister in its own right.

Crandall took a look around, seeing the rows upon rows of books. Hardbound, the type you'd see in a museum or foreign library, the kinds of books that were long lost and, for the most part, forgotten. Many were scientific, old manuscripts used fifty years earlier for college study. Old magazines, old recipe books, old methods for farming...old.

The surface underfoot cracked with a sickening crunch, and he looked down to see a sea of dead beetles, feet up, bodies curled into rotted shells.

Pulling a book from its shelf he scanned the pages, mystified by the old methodology, thought processes. Things went from old to ancient—obsolete yet fascinating. Crandall grinned as he flipped through the yellow pages that wrinkled and crackled, breaking as he read.

A mouse raced over his shoe, a spider dropping in liquid motion from the ceiling to his shoulder, snickering in his ear.

Something was offset.

Crandall leaned closer, his eyes finally adjusting to the dark and peering between the gap left by the book he'd pulled and the back wall that became suddenly visible. It wasn't so much a revelation as it was a passage into something even darker than the gloomy room he already occupied. Frowning, he reached forward and pulled away the books about the gap, opening the hole even wider, the evidence beyond something curious. The wall was gone behind the books, a bleak emptiness sifting endlessly beyond and out of sight.

Crandall frowned. A hole?

It was so dark that he couldn't see into it, but instinct alone led him to believe that the hole went on for ages. The possibilities were numerous. Maybe it was the breakdown of a hidden bomb shelter as the house was old enough to be a part of the cold war, or maybe it was a closed off room that had become unstable, unclean for the residents that once lived here. It might have been only a pocket of air. Whatever its mystery, the hole was as interesting as the history of the house. The hole was a part of him, a part of his escape from reality.

He saw Emily beyond the hole, her tear-stained face hissing back, her eyes red with hatred and accusation. Angela was beside her mother, her head lowered, hands folded.

Crandall timidly reached forward into the hole, expecting the worst, expecting to be bitten, expecting his arm to be ripped from his shoulder the way it would have been in a traditional horror movie, but nothing happened; his hand found only empty air, cool and moist. Groping, his fingers found the edges of the cold brick, tracing its worn and broken tips.

What was he searching for? Crandall frowned, his fingers searching, thinking, actually knowing that something must be back there for if the brick wall was the end of the line then the long road would be a disappointment, a melodramatic climax not worth the price of admission.

But there was nothing there. Only empty air that made him sad that he had intruded upon a life lost, and he withdrew, guilty by his own charge. He had expected something more, something mysterious, but he had found only the ugliness of decay, the ugliness of forgetfulness.

Crandall ascended the stairs and vacated the house, taking a look back, seeing not a face but a dead home that was lost in time, forgotten by life. Making his way back to the two-track, he considered venturing further into its heart and decided against it. Instead, he turned for home, realizing that his window of opportunity was closing. Emily would eventually open her door and come down the stairs only to find an empty house. She would panic and do something…

…something completely irrational.

The dirty tracks led him back toward civilization. Away from the soft buzz of life within the weeds and back into the irritating smell of exhaust and honking horns, pavement and the blur of people racing this way and that toward their respective destinations.

The road was alive. People whipped by him, absorbed in conversation, cars gunning their engines, racing yellow lights, the drivers merely mannequins behind the wheel, the living city somewhat dead with redundancy.

It was the typical Sunday-afternoon blur.

His mind shifted to his priorities as he continued toward home. Tomorrow marked the first day of the rest of his life. In spiritual terms, it sounded glorious, even biblical, but in reality, it was a Monday and he would have no place to go or anything to do. School didn't open for another five weeks.

Jesus. He was imprisoned until then.

People were bumping into him, passing him by, their steadfast pace leading them home—wherever home might be, yet home was where Crandall was headed, and he hated every step that brought him closer. He was shuffling, dragging his feet, delaying the inevitable, his eyes planted squarely upon the paved walk he trod.

Here he was normal. Life was normal. He was among normal people leading normal lives where back home—1156 Autumn Lane—was anything but a home. The idea of another dinner at a silent table with Emily staring straight ahead, her knife gripped in one hand and a fork in the other was too much.

If he were weaker or didn't feel the guilt that kept him awake long hours during the night, he might not go home again—ever again. He might just keep on walking. He could just keep on going until the sun had set and risen again. Start a new life. Get a new job.

He wanted so badly to hate Emily, yet he loved her enough to round the bend and turn onto Autumn Lane. He was going home.

A dog rushed him, barking and salivating, teeth bared, eyes wild, and Crandall recoiled, taking a step backward into the road, a car blaring its horn as it swerved to miss him, its lights flashing as it raced past, the dog suddenly yanked back as the chain about its neck reached its limit. There was a sharp yelp, and the dog nearly collapsed, but he righted and came back, snarling at the end of its chain, its upper lip quivering and revealing sharp teeth still white with youth.

"Sparky!" a woman yelled, trotting barefoot across the lawn. "Calm down!" She reached the dog's side and slapped it upside the head, turning an apologetic smile Crandall's way. "Sorry. He's just a pup yet."

Crandall looked down at his feet, his heart racing, his mind wanting to yell, his legs wanting to carry him away.

The woman dragged Sparky away, the dog's tail between its legs.

Crandall stopped.

One foot down, one poised in mid-stride, something curious lay at his feet. Settling down, he studied the object and frowned.

The door slammed at his right, the woman having fully corralled her dog, the event ending.

And there was this matter about a small disk at his feet. Kneeling down, he picked up the disk, blank on both sides, at least in terms of a label, so his guess was as good as the next as to what the disk might hold.

Curiously, he looked at each side and determined by the discoloration that one side indeed held something—be it music or video. Documents maybe. Looking around, he saw no one staring back, no one looking for a missing disk and no one accusing him of anything. No one. Period.

My lucky day, he thought as he continued homeward.

The scratches didn't appear deep enough to render the disk useless, so he figured he might as well find out what was on it. Maybe it was some sleazy porn or something interesting that he could enjoy once Emily and Angela lay down for the night. Either way, it mattered little. He'd determine the contents or he'd pitch it.

"Evening, Crandall," a man called from his porch.

Crandall looked up to see old man Levy waving from his porch. Acknowledging, Crandall continued on, not wanting a conversation.

"Everything all right?" Levy asked. He wasn't accustomed to being ignored.

The day went on, and on. The road beneath him was soggy, soft due to the heat that clawed at him, drawing his shirt to him like static-cling, the humidity a summer disaster.

His house was in sight, the sorry thing standing apart from the rest, the only one with a tan lawn and unkempt shrubs in the neighborhood. Taking the driveway, head lowered, he pulled his keys and slid one into the lock to open the gateway back into Hell.

An hour hadn't been enough.

The door clicked shut behind him and it came drifting toward him—a sound as strong as a repugnant stench, and enough to curl his stomach and make him turn back for the door, his hand centimeters from the knob. He was going to leave, but something inside told him to stay.

Despite the sound.

Crandall stood in the foyer, his heart pounding, his eyes glinting from beneath slanted lids, his lips curled slightly downward.

The sound continued like a beacon against the fog, like a head-beam racing against the night, like a rabbit caught in the jaws of the cat.

She was still sobbing.

CHAPTER 4

"Did you have fun playing at Stacie's?" Crandall asked as he bit into the dry chicken. He ripped the meat from the bone and gnawed, up and down, until he felt confident that he could swallow without regurgitating.

Angela glared at her father from across the table. She knew what was going on, and she hated it. "Yeah. Tons of fun, Dad."

The two shared a moment, sad eyes interlocked from across a great divide until the girl looked down at her burnt food that her mother had cooked. Crandall was helpless from where he sat, noting his daughter's sarcasm, casting a suspicious eye toward Emily who was blank-faced as she chewed her food, oblivious to the conversation. He looked back at Angela to find that she had lowered her eyes, concentrating upon her meal, her sadness resonating about the room.

Crandall sat back in his chair, his appetite lost. Part of him wanted to be mad, obscenely irritated with the company at his dinner table, another part of him angered at himself for not knowing how to react. "So what did you do?" he asked. It was a stupid, untimely question, he knew, but he was grasping at straws.

Angela lifted her eyes from her chicken, her lips greasy. "Played computer games."

He smiled and nodded. It was a part of the conversation.

"God told me you were evil, Crandall," Emily said, her eyes as distant as a star. "I guess He might be right, but I'm giving you the benefit of the doubt."

Crandall looked at his daughter who looked back. Both were upset, concerned and selfish at the same time, and both understood.

Angela dropped her chicken leg to her plate, and she pinched her lips, holding back the choke. "May I be excused?"

"No," Emily responded, almost hurriedly. "This is a blessed meal, given by God. Be grateful."

Angela looked to her father, but Crandall only lowered his eyes and gnawed at his flavorless chicken bone.

Angela sucked in her pride and stayed put. She continued to be a part of the family. As a trio, they were a picture perfect family even though her sad eyes gave her away as she searched across the table for her father's help.

Crandall felt like vomiting. His eyes continued to well, and he blinked away the tears, afraid to look his own daughter in the eye. "Mind your mother, honey," he whispered. Angela did because that was the way she had been raised, but she was sad anyway.

The meat was dry and tasted terrible. The vegetables were overcooked and bland, much like her life. Everything was bleak.

Nothing would change.

He just knew.

* * * *

The house was silent. Emily and Angela were asleep so far as he knew, the world his domain. Despite his fatigue, he knew these were his few moments of solitude that he could claim for himself.

The television spattered on about the evening news. Another murder, another fire, another disease, another cure and another commercial that turned the clock past eleven to eleven 'o one. Another brand of soap, another barbecue sauce, another insurance agency, another car.

Another life. Start over.

Crandall blinked.

The world aside from the television was silent.

Experiencing baldness? Tried every solution? Well, you haven't tried Lotsahair! We're the leading brand in-

He punched the remote and the screen blipped to the next channel.

Lose those ugly carbs today! No exercise required! No painful diets! Just-

Click.

Sparkle Mist! The new energy drink brought to you by-

Click.

Carl's used cars! Chevy's, Ford's, Saturn's, you name it, we got it!

Click.

Tired of the same ol', same ol'?

Crandall punched the power button and the screen flickered, died and crackled, a soft light left over. The room resonated in darkness. Yes, he most certainly was.

I'm dying here, he thought.

He paced the living room, enough light spilling in from the street to guide his path. He didn't want to go to bed. Didn't want to go to sleep. Most of all, he didn't want to wake up. Right now, here in the darkness, things were better. Things were clear.

Click, and the television illuminated again. *Click*, and he switched to the sci-fi channel where a monster in a rubber suit was slowly eating its victim.

Better.

He paced.

He smiled as the low-budget and insanely innocent science-fiction film returned him to level state of consciousness.

Stay tuned for the exciting conclusion of Godzilla versus the—the television barked.

Commercials. More commercials.

Click.

Crandall continued to pace, the room bloated with darkness. He held his eyes centered at the room's core, his focus lost in the oblivion of his mind. His fingers collapsed around the bottle of Jack, and he brought the neck to his lips. He used the liquid to wash down two more pills from the orange bottle, and he winched at the burn in his belly. He would feel better soon.

Click.

The television again illuminated, a friendly face laughing at him, mocking him, enticing him to buy Crest toothpaste.

Crandall fell to his knees, the house falling with him, the bottle jarred against the abrupt fall, the inside contents sloshing around against the inner walls. His fingers barely held the bottle upright, and finally, he let go.

His mind went to the disk, and he recognized the fact that he was alone. As alone as he could imagine he could ever be, both Emily and Angela were gone, lost in their dreams, hopefully clean, hopefully safe.

Crandall pulled the disk from his rear pocket, inspecting each surface, top and bottom for scratches. There weren't many. He opened his player and dropped the disk in place, his mind sinisterly hoping for something pleasurable, something dirty, something worth stealing.

The drawer slid shut.

Rolling the dial on his receiver to "CD" he waited, but the contents did not load, and no sound came from the speakers. It was a format unrecognizable to the command.

Crandall frowned.

He rolled the dial to DVD and punched play. This time the disk spun and played. Switching on the television, the screen slowly brightened, gaining in strength, the illumination tackling the darkness.

The picture focused, but it was choppy.

At once Crandall sat forward, leaning toward the screen, his heart stopping, the world around him stopping, the idea of present, past and future stopping, the idea of life magnanimously and ultimately—without judgment or recourse—stopping.

Stopping.

The night became old as he watched.

*　　*　　*　　*

The picture was of him.

Scenes of him. Images.

He was walking through his backyard, playing with Angela who was smiling and laughing, holding a Frisbee over her head, tossing it away, the dog chasing after it, his tail wagging back and forth as he corralled the circular toy.

"Buddy's got you, hon," Crandall grinned as the dog ran circles around his daughter.

"He's just a dog."

Buddy came back, his tail wagging, the Frisbee clenched between his jaws.

Something was wrong. Where was Charlie?

Crandall didn't even own a dog named Buddy…

*　　*　　*　　*

Angela was just standing, dressed up like a doll, her eyes sad. She was doing her best to be strong, her cheeks shining under the soft light, the camera dancing around. She stared straight forward, her eyes pointed away from the camera.

"I miss Mom," she said.

The camera went dim.

"So do I, hon."

* * * *

She was sitting at the table, her eyes lost, all nine candles dancing and flickering against her face though her expression was sad. Lifting her eyes, she seemed embarrassed.

"Make a wish, honey," and the voice was unmistakable. His own.

Angela leaned forward, drew a breath and blew, the candles flickering and extinguishing, columns of gray smoke pilfering away. Her eyes remained sad.

"Won't come true," the girl whispered, the camera dangling each way, dancing, unfocused.

"How do you know that?" He was talking away from the camera's eye.

"Cause she's already dead."

* * * *

The camera focused in on Crandall walking, one slow step after another. He was completely unaware of the camera, head lowered, face gray.

A dog barked in the background, and a baby cried.

* * * *

A scene with him frantically scanning the front yard, or what looked like his front yard. His face seemed concerned and wary.

* * * *

Crandall watched the feed from his living room and frowned. *What is this?* he wondered. *Some kind of perverted joke? Some kind of game?* He shifted with unease from where he sat. His eyes darted from the television screen to the windows experiencing that icy feeling along his neck that made him feel as though he was being watched.

But he found only black panes of glass returning his reflection.

Jesus…

He went for the windows, dropping the shades, closing the blinds, sealing himself within his home before returning to the television, sitting lightly upon the edge of the coffee table and scooping the remote, pressing play.

* * * *

"I'm so sorry," she whispered, leaning in, but Crandall stepped back and his neighbor felt the distance. She drew her bleary eyes to him. "I'm so sorry that things were so ugly for you." She turned away, and the camera turned to a casket. A smaller casket this time.

The screen faded.

* * * *

Crandall was in his bedroom, face buried within his hands, sitting, waiting, the clock over his shoulder calling out one second after another.

He lifted his eyes.

* * * *

He watched the video, wondering where it had come from. These were images of him, but not him. The events were falsified—manufactured. Emily was still alive, Angela still alive, Charlie still alive. He could prove it now by walking into their rooms. This farce was made to mock him.

* * * *

He was standing at the edge of the pier, the waves breaking over the rim, crashing twenty feet high, the beads of water splashing down over his head, dousing him with innocence. He stood firm, the brisk wind whipping the slacks about his legs, the loose shirt flapping with the breeze, his hands planted firmly in his pockets, his face poised against the storm.

* * * *

He was grinning, pacing quickly along the walk.

He was in the park. It was obvious for the trees around him were a dead giveaway. Everything was familiar, yet unfamiliar. The words coming out of his mouth—not his mouth, but his mouth on the disk seemed foreign. The scenes were fakes—had to be.

He was walking, head lowered, alone, face as white as a man in January, eyes as intent as a man in Hell.

* * * *

He was mowing the grass, Buddy following at his heels, tail wagging against the wind. Crandall's face was gray, emotionless, expressionless, lifeless. He was doing his duty because that what was expected.

The clippings flew.

* * * *

"What the hell is this?" Crandall whispered. He felt angry and violated. Looking around, he found the draped windows of his home not enough to quiet his unrest. Crossing the room again, he peered out from the side into and the night where he saw the empty road dividing his neighborhood. Frowning, he returned to the table, and his attention was returned to the screen where images of himself, completely unfamiliar, were playing in the past tense.

* * * *

He was walking along the streets amidst a crowd, fishing his way for advantage, having to push and vi for position. Crandall stopped at the curb, life revolving around him, all around him, among him.

Crandall turned and seemed to stare directly back at the camera, in a sense, staring directly at himself. Then he just looked away.

* * * *

"This is a joke," he whispered. His hands were trembling, his stomach queasy, his head a mess.

The remote tipped from his fingers and fell to the carpet, bouncing to a rest.

* * * *

The sky was gray, the background surreal. It appeared to be a playground. No, something else. An amusement park.

"Hello, my friend."

The film jerked, lines running across the interface, the image becoming distorted.

"You've finally made it," the voice said.

The image flickered. Two people, one standing over the other. The man looking up was wild-eyed, fearful, surprised, faint with dread.

"How does it feel?" the hidden voice called.

The stranger's eyes were sad with confusion—absolute despair. A gun dangled loosely in his right hand as he paced back and forth, a body at his fee. The man on the ground was wearing a T-shirt with his blue jeans, his black hair disturbed, his back turned to the camera, a blotch of red sitting on top and soaking through the shirt.

"What just happened?" the old man asked in small voice. "Everything's different."

The hidden voice was chuckling. "This was your doing. Enjoy it."

The old man didn't know how to react, his hands trembling.

Laughter.

"It's not my fault," the man whispered, turning to the camera, his teeth bared, eyes flashing. "Turn that fuckin' thing off."

The eye of the camera danced away, seeing the bleak sky before dimming and going black. The square display collapsed into a tiny yellow dot that died, Crandall's television screen going black and leaving him to fend for himself against the silent night.

He could only sit in silence, his mind absorbing what he had seen—images of himself that he had not experienced—images of his wife and daughter, both gone, images that hadn't occurred.

It was a cheap trick, a joke at his expense. That was his best explanation; the disk was a forgery.

The room around him was perfectly silent, the blue screen from the television the only light that glossed his face.

His mind raced at a lethal level, his mind crazed but focused. Whoever was playing this game was seriously disturbed, and it angered him to think someone would make a video where his wife and daughter were dead before planting it where Crandall would find it.

He felt sick, his pride challenged as much as it appeared that his family was being threatened.

Who the hell was the man behind the camera?

Christ, he felt so weak, and he was stunned, coerced to watch the video again.

His blood was boiling, his pulse racing, his eyes twitching, his heart pounding. Clenching his fists, he leaned in, studying the images, memorizing the background, taking it all in, all of it. A woman was grinning at the edge of the lens, a small boy laughing, a little girl crying.

He clicked *power*, and the television flickered and died, enveloping him in darkness.

The only sound was that of his own breathing, his heart bleating against his ribcage. Clenching his fists, he fought for control, his focus rejoining him, tears streaming down his cheeks, his resolve lost. Who was he?

A small man raped by the dark.

He smiled bashfully, the art imitating life a mockery of what he had achieved.

And everything else was just a masquerade.

Crandall watched from the edge of the fire, his face sullen at the sight of so many laughing faces.

He turned away and vomited.

CHAPTER 5

"I'm sorry, Mr., uh-"

"Cady," Crandall spat, impatiently filling in the blank.

"Right. Mr. Cady." The woman looked up from her desk, folded her hands and smiled. "I'm sorry, sir, but I'm not sure what it is you want me to do here."

Crandall pinched the bridge of his nose, frustrated yet holding back from saying something he might later regret. Drawing a breath, he exhaled and slowly counted to five. Opening his eyes, he had calmed. "I would like for you to help me out. You are, after all, a police officer whose mission statement is to serve and to protect civilians."

The woman noted his sarcasm, but she felt somewhat bad for him anyway. The man opposite her looked like he hadn't sleep in a week. Returning her attention to the disk that lay on the desk in front of her, she picked it up, studying it. "Look. No crime has been committed, Mr. Cady, which isn't to say that we only react to situations, but this disk contains neither a crime nor a threat. It's obviously a prank meant to upset you, and I dare say that the intent was achieved."

"How can you say there's no crime?" Crandall asked. "At the end of the recording there's clear evidence of a dead man shot with a gun. For God's sake, the old man's gun is still smoking if you'd just watch the goddamn thing."

"Relax." Officer Brennan sipped her coffee, taking a moment to compose her best argument. "We'll watch the video, and we'll try to verify its authenticity. However, there is another matter we need to discuss."

"Which is?"

"If, and I'm not saying you did, but if we determine that you, in fact, manufactured this disk as some elaborate hoax, you will be liable for all man-hours devoted to your case."

Crandall spread his hands. "You're implying *I* did this?"

"I'm not implying anything at this point, Mr. Cady. All I want is for you to be aware. I want to give you an out *now* before it's too late." She grinned. "In the unlikely event that this disk was created with an ulterior motive."

Crandall felt like laughing and screaming at the same time. "This is a disk showing me that my dog, my wife and my child are dead. Then it graphically depicts a murdered man and his killer. For all I know, this is some crazed man who intends on killing my family, and the goddamn disk is his way of making it some perverted game!" His voice was rising along with his blood-pressure. "And you're going to sit here and accuse me of making this disk because I have some kind of ulterior motive?"

"Mr. Cady, if-"

"What could I possibly accomplish with this disk? What would I stand to gain?"

She didn't answer right away, and by the small grin that she unsuccessfully tried to hide, she wasn't convinced. "Perhaps an alibi?"

The comment caught Crandall completely off-guard, and all he could do for several moments was stare at Brennan in shock. He couldn't believe she'd say such a thing. When he did find his voice, he found all of it and all at once. Leaping forward, he lunged halfway across the desk, his fists coming down and pounding the desktop, papers scattering from his fury, the cop's eyes growing wide as she leaned back.

"Fuck you, bitch!" he shouted, his face red, spittle flying from his mouth. "You want to accuse me of murdering my family?"

"Mr. Cady, I-"

"Fuck you, pig!" he repeated.

Heads were turning in his direction, all commotion around the office having stopped, the ringing phones going unanswered.

Brennan hardened, her lips pinching tight, her eyes glowering from where she sat.

"If they die, it's your fault, Brennan!" Crandall shouted.

She didn't respond.

"And wipe that goddamn smug look off your face!" he finished, swiping the disk from Brennan's desk and turning to leave. They weren't going to help him; they were going to try and blame him.

The other cops in the room lined up to glare at him as he stormed toward the exit, his comments an inflammatory attack on not only Brennan but also against every badge in the department. Crandall didn't care. His mood was sour, his blood racing. Even though he knew the consequences, he'd fight back against any cop who tried to restrain him, and he'd enjoy the better part of the year behind bars for doing so.

Kicking open the doors, he trotted hotly down the steps back to his car where he climbed behind the wheel, took a moment, and slugged the dashboard two or three times, screaming obscenities, a rush of tears suddenly falling over his face. He clenched his fists, desperately trying to regain his composure, his knuckles bruised as he collected himself. Looking over at the disk that lay on the passenger seat, he felt suddenly sad. Hoping that Brennan was right, he was clinging to the idea that the disk was meant to scare him, though he could think of no one that truly disliked him—especially enough to go to this extent. The entire idea was preposterous.

Crandall turned the key, shaking his head and turning for home.

Preposterous, but he tried to convince himself anyway that it *was* all a scam, a joke. Something his buddies had dreamt up. Tony and Steve were always trying to get his goat. Just a year earlier they had managed to break into his garage, push his Jeep onto the front lawn where they proceeded to prop it up on blocks and take the tires as a good-humored April-fools joke. This was a bit more elaborate, but it wasn't beyond them to try and pull such a stint…

Pulling into his driveway, Crandall didn't feel any better, but he had relaxed somewhat, the anger slowly settling. He even tried on a smile to see if it would fit, the concern of alarming his family the motivation.

He was home. For better or for worse, he was home where his wife and daughter would be waiting for him, wondering where he'd been, hoping he was okay. He'd deal with Emily's outbursts and love her even stronger. Maybe he and Angie would take Charlie for a walk after supper.

The disk could be used to his advantage. Instead of looking at it as a negative, maybe he could take it as a warning to appreciate what he had while he had it. After all, Angela wouldn't be living at home forever, and Emily was only going to get worse as her disease progressed. Right now, today, was as good as things were going to get, and he needed to take the time to appreciate it.

And there was his daughter now.

Angela came running from the garage toward him, and he smiled, glad she was so happy to see him.

Except she wasn't happy.

Her face was flushed, her eyes stained and puffy. She wore a smile upside down, her appearance soggy and downtrodden. Crandall pulled the Jeep into the garage, but Angela was already hanging onto the window, her face streaming with tears. He quickly killed the engine, his eyes frantic as he opened the door, his thoughts going to Emily.

"What's the matter, Angie?" he asked, ready to bolt for the door.

She was shaking her head, struggling to come up with the right words.

He gripped her by the shoulders, not intentionally gripping her so hard. "Is it your mother?"

She continued to cry, but she was shaking her head. "Charlie," she managed. "Charlie's dead."

He relaxed instantly. The dog. The damn dog. "Oh baby, I'm sorry," he whispered, and pulled his daughter close to him, hugging her, thankful he could still feel her alive against him. "It's okay, honey."

Angela sobbed, hugging him back, and he forgot for a moment all about the disk.

* * * *

He wasn't going to get another dog, no matter how much his daughter pleaded. The image of the little yellow lab answering to the name of 'Buddy' was enough to persuade him to wait.

Crandall hadn't, nor did he have any intention of telling either Angela or Emily about his find. The contents alone would be traumatic enough, and until he verified that it was a hoax played upon him by either friends or enemies, and he'd had sufficient time to adequately kick their collective asses, he didn't plan on telling anyone.

Instead, he and Angela buried Charlie in the backyard, and even as they stood over the fresh grave, his little girl was asking if she could get another dog. In her defense, Charlie had been her best friend as he had watched over her as closely as a parent since the day she had been born. Even so, it was a bit shocking for Crandall to see his daughter healing so fast. "We'll see," he answered. It was the best answer he could provide.

"The Johnson's just had puppies," she had replied quickly.

"We'll see," he repeated.

No more dogs. There was too much activity going on as it was. He needed time to think and lay things out. Crandall was a man of detail, and he needed the whole picture to plot his next move. And if he were being completely honest with himself, he wanted to prove the disk wrong.

Yet, two days later, Angela had brought home one of the Johnson's puppies just to 'see if he'd fit in'. Crandall knew that the moment the dog crossed the front door's threshold he wasn't going home because Emily was suddenly smiling and laughing and uncommonly happy.

The yellow puppy was all wags and licks as he danced between Angela and Emily, begging attention from both and receiving more than he could handle. Rolling onto his back, the small dog just wriggled and grinned, and Crandall watched, knowing that the dog looked like the one from the video.

His own eyes were untrusting and he watched with an attitude, upset with his daughter while realizing he shouldn't be. She was an innocent participant.

"Can we keep him, Dad?" Angela asked as she cuddled the puppy that was squirming in her arms. "They said he's almost potty-trained already."

Emily looked up. "We still have all of Charlie's things, dear. We could let him stay the night just to see how things go."

Crandall knew he needed to shake his head, but it was already too late. The dog was staying whether Crandall liked it or not. In all honesty, he didn't mind so much. He loved dogs, always had, and the loss of Charlie was hard enough without Angela's pleading eyes and the little furry package in her arms. Things could go back to normal, and a fight wasn't going to help anybody, least of all himself.

His mind went to the disk and the vision of Angela playing Frisbee with a yellow puppy named Buddy. Crandall knew he could win both sides of the coin if he were careful. They could keep the dog, but name him something different.

Kneeling down, he pet the puppy on the head, and the little guy responded by licking his hand, his eyes twinkling as if he already knew he'd found a home. "He can stay the night," Crandall said.

"Thank you, daddy," Angela smiled, leaning over and kissing her father on the cheek.

"We'll have to come up with a name," he said softly as he scratched behind the puppy's ears. "I'm thinking something like Ditka after my favorite coach." He grinned. "Whatdya think, pal? You like that name?"

The puppy liked everything.

"The Johnson's already named him," Angela argued.

Crandall looked up. "Well, he's young enough yet. We can name him whatever we like."

"I like the name though," she countered. "So does Mom."

Crandall looked to his wife, and Emily was silent, just quietly smiling. He sincerely doubted if she cared one way or another.

"He answers to Buddy," Angela said, and the puppy licked her on the face, bringing a giggle. "Don'tcha, sweety?"

Crandall froze. His eyes went from his daughter to the dog to his daughter to his wife.

"Like that name, huh?" Angela was loving the puppy more than she had loved old Charlie.

Crandall felt sick to his stomach, but he didn't know how to respond.

"I like that name," Emily said softly, touching her daughter's hair, and for a moment, the old Emily was back, the family reunited. But to Crandall, the night was deteriorating, and he was confused, something in the pit of his stomach telling him this was all wrong.

He got up, leaving the room, heading for the kitchen.

"Is that okay with you, hon?" Emily called.

Crandall yanked open the cupboard over the refridgerator and with shaking hands pulled down the bottle of Jack and another orange bottle of pills. "Fine," he answered, though his voice didn't sound fine. He already had a clear glass that he dumped two cubes of ice into, watching them spin around the bottom before the yellow-brown liquid chugged from the bottle and floated the ice.

Three Prozac.

He had every intention of returning to the living room, but he only stood at the sink, staring down his hollow expression in the dark reflection of the window before him as he sipped the liquor. From the living room he could hear his wife and daughter playing with the puppy, giggling and laughing, over and over calling him by the name of Buddy.

Crandall felt violated—as though he were staring into a one-way mirror where he only saw himself, and someone, beyond the dark glass, was watching him. He didn't want to believe in the contents of the digital disk, but how could he afford not to? It could just be a coincidence—the death of Charlie and the introduction of the blonde puppy. After all, Charlie had been old, arthritic and falling apart. The writing was on the wall. Or maybe the hoax could be taken only so far. The Johnson's must have known about Charlie's death, and ironically, they had a litter of puppies they didn't need. Buddy wasn't an uncommon name for a dog…

No, he didn't want to believe in the contents of the digital disk, but judging by the way he was slurping down the Jack without the slightest flinch, he figured he was already sold.

I can stop this, he told himself. The disk wasn't his future, the contents not a blueprint for his life. How could anyone predict the future? It wasn't possible. The whole thing was a scare tactic—maybe co-workers from the office making a prank video as a sendoff to his new job. Maybe an old enemy he'd pissed off. Maybe a lot of maybe's. Anything was possible if the right person had the proper motivation. Maybe it was Craig or Joe. Neither of them liked him much. Maybe it was Sandra. She was a fanatic about computer stuff. She had once made video of herself where she overlaid her face with that of the First Lady's as a spoof for the company Christmas party. This video certainly wasn't beyond her talents. Maybe she was playing a part…

Maybe a lot of maybe's.

"Honey?" Emily called from the living room. "Are you coming back, dear?"

Crandall swallowed the last of the liquor, and dumped the ice into the drain. He wanted more, but he was afraid if he opened the Jack again, he'd never get the cap back on. He needed to focus. Concentrate. He needed to stay in control or the whole thing would drive him mad.

For his family—Angela, Emily and…and even Buddy—he needed to keep his mind clear.

Whoever was responsible for the disk was going to fail in their task—whatever it might be. He was going to keep his sanity and do his duty as a husband and father. He would be there to protect them. A disk was not going to decide the fate of his family.

"I'm coming, Em," he answered, his control returning, his confidence building.

Killing the kitchen light, he returned to the living room, a calm grin on his face, and he sat down between Emily and Angela, reaching out and scratching the puppy behind the ears, the wriggling creature grinning madly as he rolled onto his back and asked for more.

"I like the name Buddy," he said. "Fits him fine."

They were a family again, whole and complete.

* * * *

He turned into the driveway and grinned at the sight of Angela running and laughing with Buddy, the small puppy dancing at her heels, its tail whipping back and forth. She had a Frisbee in her hand and she tossed it, but the puppy continued to chase her, barking with its small voice.

She tripped and somersaulted, laughing as Buddy jumped on her, lapping her face with his little tongue.

Crandall pulled into the garage and Emily came out to greet him, smiling hello and heading for the rear of the car where he popped the trunk so she could get to the bagged groceries.

"Saved over twenty-dollars in coupons today," he said happily.

"That's why I clip 'em," she answered with a smile. "Thanks for doing the shopping, hon. I just didn't feel like being around strangers today."

He looked at his wife and smiled, honestly feeling good about himself. "I love you Emily. I mean that. This was my pleasure."

She blushed, and for a moment she was the girl that he had once married. Turning, she looked out from the garage to the sunny afternoon and the front yard where their daughter was playing happily. "I'll take of this, Crandall. Why don't you go play with your daughter?"

The invitation was tempting, but Crandall wanted to keep things nice and serene the way they were when Emily was having a good day. "Are you sure? I don't mind helping."

Emily only grinned. "You always put things away in the wrong places anyway. Seriously, the garage is your domain, but the kitchen is mine."

Crandall didn't argue. Instead, he kissed his wife on the cheek and winked before making his way toward his daughter and her little buddy.

Angela was giggling on her back, trying to push the puppy away that came back for more, his tail on autopilot. "Help!" she shrieked happily.

Crandall sat down, grabbing the puppy from his daughter's chest. "Where's that little bugger?" he asked.

Buddy wriggled, his tongue hanging out, his little paws working as though he were trying to swim.

"Lemme get the Frisbee," Angela said, scrambling to her feet and chasing down the toy.

Crandall looked the puppy in the eye and couldn't help but smile. He was so small, so happy, so innocent. There was no ploy.

"Catch, Dad!" Angela called, and the Frisbee came spinning his way. Crandall dropped the puppy, jumped and caught the disk while Buddy yipped at his feet.

"Right back atcha!" he said, and the Frisbee went Angela's way, the puppy racing across the lawn, it's tail a propeller behind him.

The Frisbee spun and smacked the ground, rolling through the grass like a tire, his daughter and the dog chasing after it. She caught it a second earlier, lifting it over her head, the puppy jumping and missing. Angela laughed, taunting the dog and dancing away, Buddy on her heels.

"Buddy's got you, hon," Crandall grinned.

"He's just a dog."

And everything stopped.

The grin vanished from Crandall's face, his eyes going cold.

Buddy's got you, hon.

He's just a dog.

Jesus, those were the exact words from the…

His eyes went wild, scanning the yard, the neighbors' yards, the street, parked cars, bushes, trees. He looked for shadows, figures, people that didn't belong. He looked for a camera, a strategically placed object that could hide a camera, anything out of the ordinary.

"What's the matter, Dad?" Angela asked, the concern on her face as she walked toward her father.

"Nothing, Angie," he said, his forehead breaking into a cold sweat.

A bird took flight from a nearby tree, and his attention jerked that way, feeling instantly deceived. A car came down the road, its motor little more than a soft idle as it puttered closer, but it was Mrs. Fernandez in her old Buick. A cat jumped from its perch from a porch across the street, meowing as it went.

"Dad?"

His heart was pounding as he spun slowly, his eyes focusing on the small details of the neighborhood, searching, scanning. A branch was waving in the breeze, a woman shaking her rugs over her railing, a man mowing his lawn. Everything seemed normal and unconcerned with him, everybody role-playing life. He peered through the bushes beside the house next door, certain he had seen a shadow move, but after a long moment, he saw that there was nothing.

"What's wrong?" Angela asked. She had reached her father's side, and Buddy was wondering why the game had stopped so suddenly.

"Get in the house, Angie," he answered coolly.

"But, I don't-"

"Now," he said with quiet stern.

His daughter looked on for a few seconds before scooping Buddy into her arms and heading for the house.

Crandall stepped forward toward the street, his eyes going back and forth. He had promised himself that he wouldn't allow the disk to control him, but he wanted to be sure, just be sure in order to satisfy himself. The man mowing his lawn lifted a hand to wave, but Crandall looked the other way, his eyes searching for movement of any kind, finding nothing to calm him down. He stood in the center of the street, slowly turning circles, his brow lowered, his eyes aimed for the shadows, and around him he heard the serene rustle of leaves and whisper of wind. Pale faces began to poke out from their windows, expressionless faces staring at the man in the center of the road. Emily and Angela watched from their respective perch, noticing all of the attention suddenly focused on their father, their husband.

Crandall was far from satisfied, but he could find nothing out of the ordinary, nothing suspicious. Silently cursing, he returned to his yard, pounding a path to the porch where he whipped open the front door, turned to see his family staring back at him, and bolted for the basement where he locked himself down in the cold, arid room, away from the light and away from the suspicious eyes. Crouching into a ball, he masked himself with dark, afraid to go back up. He didn't want to admit his fears, not even to himself but mostly to his family.

He sat in a hunched ball until the knocking stopped from the upstairs door and the basement's bleak lighting grew even dimmer as the sun set from beyond the small, dirty panes. The control he had wanted so bad to hold was lost.

He was lost.

Finally he stood, his mind awash, his legs rubbery. It was absolutely unbelievable. The entire scenario was a Saturday-morning cartoon, completely unreal, a fabrication of the truth. This wasn't happening. Not to him. Not now when things seemed to be somewhat falling into place. Just couldn't be. Not now.

Crandall made his way up the stairs, unlocked the door and stepped into the kitchen that was dim save that of the small nightlight beside the sink. His shadow loomed large against the opposite wall, bigger than him.

Where was he going to go? What could he do? He had no leads, no evidence, nothing. If only he had seen something when he'd turned to look earlier that afternoon. If only…

The house was silent as he made his way into the living room and to the entry-foyer's closet where he kept the disk hidden in his old work-jacket. He had to find the discrepancies that must be there. Somewhere. Something wrong with the film. Something wrong.

The television illuminated the dark room, and he killed the volume so as not to wake his family, and he told himself over and over to be careful, watch slowly, ignore the foreground and look closer.

The image came into focus, and he saw himself crossing the lawn to play with Angie, Buddy all over her, his happy tail wiggling.

Jesus Christ, this was déjà vu.

Uncomfortably, he shifted but did not divert his attention from the screen.

"Where's that little bugger?" he was asking from the disk.

This wasn't possible. How could it be a fake? How could its engineer have known he'd say such a thing?

"Lemme get the Frisbee."

Something caught Crandall's attention, and he reacted, sitting upright, grabbing the remote and hitting pause. Leaning closer to the screen, his heart stopped.

27 July, 15:37:48

The date was small, and nearly absorbed by the background, but it was there and legible to someone willing to pay attention. The timestamp was current. Dated today. This afternoon.

Crandall sat back, his respiratory system playing tricks with him. It wasn't possible. He had found the disk two days ago. The contents had been filmed prior. It wasn't possible.

Looking over his shoulder, the drapes were hung high, the outside world looking in on him, prying in, and he was caught off guard.

He could have gotten up, crossed the room and shut the blinds, but it was too late. If someone was watching him, they'd already seen what he had seen, they knew what he knew, and it was his anguish that sparked the film.

Scooping the remote, the zipped through the scenes, the images flying past until he came to the final frames, an old man leaning over a body, blood on the old man's face and hands, the gun in his hand trembling slightly.

It's not my fault.

Whose fault? What was the man talking about? Who was he talking to?

Frowning, Crandall pressed pause, the screen flickering a moment before locking into a perpetual freeze, the old man glaring into the camera, his eyes frigid, almost familiar by feeling.

Crandall looked to the corner of the screen, and the date recorded there.

27 August, 17:29:59

The screen went blank, the video ending. The disk stopped spinning, the room coming under control.

Crandall looked down at the remote in his hand. He recognized his position and how he weighed in on things. He had the power to replay the disk, but he lacked the authority to change it. Didn't matter. He was where he was, and he had to deal with it from where he sat. There was no room for self-pity or remorse. Things would move forward. Now.

He punched play, and he was playing Frisbee with Angela and Buddy again. Watching the disk he looked for discrepancies, but the scene seemed authentic. The angle was from behind him, so it had been shot from the Lewis' yard or thereabouts.

Buddy was happy, his daughter happy.

He turned at the last moment, a look of hysteria on his face as the screen faded.

Crandall clenched his fists, the knuckles turning white as the screen brightened again, a picture of Angela standing at the foreground, her eyes sad. She was dressed in her Sunday best, and her cheeks were shining beneath whatever lights loomed over her head. Suddenly, she looked away.

"I miss Mom," the little girl said.

The camera went dim.

"So do I, hon."

He punched pause, his eyes going to the corner of the screen as he leaned forward, squinting at the date.

7 August, 11:13:58

Twelve days away. He had twelve days to figure it out. Twelve days to prove the disk unauthentic.

Clicking stop, the screen went blank, fading to black, the image scorched on his memory. He stared on, not moving, his mind intent. It was coming. The end, whatever or whenever that was supposed to be.

He pressed the power button, and the image dwindled to a yellow dot that slowly faded leaving Crandall alone in the dark.

Right where he wanted to be.

CHAPTER 6

"I just thought I'd go for a walk," Emily complained. "I feel all..." She tried for words, using her hands to emphasize. "Cooped up here."

"But I can't go with you?" he asked.

She shook her head, her eyes closed, the veins showing out on her forehead. "I need to be alone. Can you appreciate that?"

Normally, Crandall would be all for her taking a walk by herself. He'd be all for her getting air out there, somewhere beyond the perimeter of their yard, but this was just an invitation to get her away from him. It was an open invitation for disaster.

"I just thought I'd spend some time with my wife," he answered truthfully, grinning. "You know, the way we used to? Walking on the train tracks, prodding each other with awkward questions that are somehow tastefully funny?"

"I miss those days," Emily answered with a girlish grin. "Things weren't so..." She shook her head. "...so clouded." She raised a hand to her face, pinching her eyes closed.

Crandall went to her, wrapping his arms around her and drawing her close, reminiscing on the familiar scent of her hair, her breath. She was still his Emily, his wife. He still loved her so intensely that he thought he'd choke at the thought of her loss. "If you don't want me to go..." he said, knowing his words weren't necessary.

She squeezed his hand. "Of course I want you to go."

Smiling, Crandall led Emily toward the door, but his wife stopped, holding him back. "What about Angie?"

He smiled, an unaccustomed confidence in his voice. "She'll be just fine. Trust me."

Emily nodded and allowed her husband to lead her to the door.

* * * *

Crandall was beside himself, sitting at the center of the lawn, his daughter and the dog playing at his right, his wife weeding the flower garden over his left shoulder. His eyes were as alert as his ears. He was waiting for something to happen as though it would at any second. He was obsessed, and he knew it, but he couldn't let his defenses down. Either he was losing his mind or he wasn't, in which case he should just relax either way because his problems were over. In the end, that's all he wanted—to forget and move on. There was guilt all over him, laid out for everyone to see, bare-naked and exposed. The shadows were shallow, revealing nothing, and he looked at his watch.

7:56 p.m. 1, August.

In the end, it didn't matter what he was supposed to feel or expect. He was here to protect his family whether they knew it or not.

A car came from the opposite direction, and Crandall stared down the driver who waved politely at first before frowning and shrinking as he passed. Crandall didn't flinch as he continued to stare, eyeballing the license plate, memorizing it just in case. If August the seventh was the next entry, then Emily had to pass before then, and he'd be damned if would happen on his watch.

"I think we'll have Mom's pasta salad for dinner," Emily said over his shoulder.

Crandall nodded, but he didn't turn.

"I should get started before it gets too late."

He didn't respond, and the storm door slowly closed over his shoulder.

Angie was still playing in the yard, Buddy on her heels as she dodged and went the other way, her voice that of an angel as she laughed.

The door opened again. "Hon, I need you to go to the store. We're out of olives."

"We don't need olives for a salad, dear," he answered coldly. He hated the way his voice sounded.

"It just isn't a salad without olives. I'll go. The Corner Mart is just down the road. Olives are on sale this week."

Cursing under his breath, Crandall stood, turned and smiled. "I'll go."

Emily smiled softly. "No, that's okay, dear. You've been out all day. I don't mind. Actually, I'd like to see old Ike and shoot the breeze a minute."

This wasn't good. "We'll go together." He practiced his humor. "Dear."

Emily frowned. "What's wrong, Crandall? You don't want me going out on my own?"

Catch-22. He told himself to stay calm, talk smooth, be himself. "I just thought we might go together. We never shop together anymore." We never shop together anymore? How stupid.

"You're afraid I'm going to fuck up the olives?" Emily shouted.

Angie stopped, Buddy running circles around her legs, and she turned.

"Of course not." He tried his best. "I just want to spend time with you."

"I can handle buying olives, my dear husband," she remarked with sarcasm. "I wouldn't be so sick if you wouldn't keep me drugged up all the time. I still have a mind of my own, you know."

Crandall approached her, casting sideways glances at their daughter, trying to spread the hint. "Honey, you're fine. You're perfect. I just want to go with you."

Her face was sour. "You're crowding me, Crandall Cady. I'm not a goddamn patient in a mental hospital."

"I never said-"

"Don't talk down to me like I'm some kind of wrinkled old bag that needs a new daisy every day to feel worthwhile. God's watching you, you know."

"I know. God's watching me. I can feel it. I'm not pulling any stunts, baby. I just want to go shopping with you."

Emily looked from Crandall to Angela, back to Crandall and back to Angela. "What about Angie."

"She'll be fine," Crandall answered. "This a good neighborhood, hon. We've got the Neighborhood Watch program thing going on. She'll be fine. Trust me."

Emily shook her head. "You're always saying that, but how do you know?"

"All I'm say-"

"You don't know shit, Crandall. What are you doing? Trying to set her up to get raped? Is that what you want? You're little daughter? Your own flesh in blood?"

Christ. Here we go.

"You're our worst nightmare, Crandall. You're more dangerous to me and her than the scum out there!"

Mr. Johnson lifted his hand in a timid wave from across the street, but he was perplexed and ashamed to be seen where he was, and before Crandall could return the wave he had retreated into his home.

"You want me committed, don't you? This is all a conspiracy against me, isn't it? Well, I'm not going down because you feel intimidated by what I know!"

Crandall lowered his head, sighing, a headache coming on.

"Mom, I don't think he-"

"What do you know, Angie?" Emily snapped. "You're an innocent girl, corrupted by your father to believe what he's told you to believe. You don't honestly think the world is so cozy out there do you?"

Crandall slightly shook his head at his daughter, hoping she'd recognize his signal not to argue.

"Dad's not the enemy, Mom," Angela answered, not giving in.

"What did you say to me?" Emily shrieked. "Are you calling your mother a liar?" Her face turned red. "Angela JoAnn Cady, you are indefinitely grounded, young lady! Go to your room!"

"Emily, your daughter meant-"

"You shut the fuck up, you anti-Christ of a man. You're not my husband. My husband would stand by me. He'd protect me, not imprison me."

The neighborhood was taking notice—a few stepping onto their porches to see as well as hear. They looked on like gapers at the sight of a car-accident, wide-eyed as though they'd help but moreover fascinated by the destruction of a human mind. Crandall wanted to fight them all, knock in the mocking faces, destroy their holier-than-thou expressions, but he felt subdued, sullen and soft. Saddened by his own weakness in the wake of his unhealthy wife, he wanted to fight no one.

"Let's go shopping together, Emily," he said in a soft whisper.

Emily stopped short of a scream, composed herself, and stood tall, tears streaming down her cheeks, her mouth curved south, her eyes sad. "I would like that too," she said finally. "Just us. Again."

* * * *

God saw you do it, you little shit.

The sun came up.

Of course it did.

Crandall's eyes slowly adjusted to the light, blinking lightly at first then becoming accustomed. His eyes felt crusty and stiff, his breath sour.

The morning was humid, the air around him stale, and he pushed away the covers, his sweaty body exposed to the cooler air and bringing a chill. Rolling his legs off the edge of the bed he rubbed his eyes and scratched his scalp, yawning and sighing into relaxation.

Morning.

August 2nd.

His hands went for the plastic bottles, knocking two of them over where they rolled off the edge of the nightstand and tumbled to the carpeted floor. He grabbed the three still standing, scooping them into his fist and drawing them close where he popped the lids, and drained two or three from each into his mouth.

Paxil, Prozac and Desipramine were the morning's flavor, and the little bit of warm water left over in the glass beside the bed was barely enough to wash them down.

Five different doctors, five different prescriptions.

He turned to his wife who lay sleeping, her back to him.

No need to wake her, and he made his way down into the kitchen were Buddy jumped up at the first sight of life, his tail going wild, his tongue dropping out as if on cue, his eyes shining.

"Morning, bud," he said without bending down to pet the puppy.

Crandall doused his face with cold water and dried himself off with a towel, the house uncommonly quiet.

Something was wrong.

He let the dog out and allowed the backdoor to shut behind him, returning to the hallway that led to the bedrooms. Quietly opening Angela's door, he heard her breathing quietly, her eyes flickering in dreams behind closed lids as she slept. Satisfied, he pulled the door shut and returned to the empty hallway.

Only the clock ticked and tocked from far away, its happy rhythm enough to calm his nerves, a sad slave to repetition, a beat that wouldn't change until it unwound the way all things did. Sooner or later.

Still, there was something else that he felt deep down. Something unsettling. Sunday mornings were never this quiet. Buddy was whining at the back door, scratching just they way they had spanked him not to.

Crandall returned to the master bedroom where Emily still lay on her side, the blankets pulled up to her chin.

What the hell? What was it that made him so uncomfortable? He was about to leave the room when he noticed the silence. There was no soft breathing as there had been with Angie. There was no sound except for the silk curtains rustling against the morning breeze, the only window he'd allowed to remain open through the night.

Crandall frowned and stepped forward. "Emily?"

She didn't stir.

Of course she didn't. This was a horror movie where she had become a vampire and would lash out at him as soon as he nudged her.

But Jesus, it felt so real. Kneeling down, he looked at her face, so soft and white under the new morning light. Her face was innocent, child-like, her lips small and youthful, the way they had been the first time he'd kissed them.

He touched her shoulder, lightly shaking her. Her body rocked slightly, but her eyes didn't open. "Hon?"

Emily was as still as the quiet morning, Crandall suddenly alarmed. "Honey?"

August 2nd. Plenty of time for a funeral. Plenty of time for Angela to miss her mother.

Fuck that. No. Not today. He shook her by the shoulder. "Emily? Wake up, dear. You hungry?"

Nothing.

He pulled the sheet away, froze, felt his stomach regurgitate acid, and stumbled back, falling into the wall, knocking his head. The smell and sight of blood stole his voice, brought tears, pinched his heart in a vice.

Emily's wrist rolled over the edge of the bed, the deep wound still oozing the burgundy liquid, though it had begun to coagulate, the sheets beneath her body soaked with what had been her life and had become her death.

He didn't accept it. Wouldn't accept it.

Angela was just down the hall, sleeping soundly in her cozy little bed, Buddy at the back door eagerly scratching to be let in, waiting on his family, the neighborhood around them waking up to a new day, a new hope.

Death wasn't a part of this picture. Just wasn't. Just…

Oh hell.

Oh God.

He curled into a ball, not knowing how to deal, not knowing how he'd adjust, not knowing how he'd tell his little girl, not knowing how he'd live on. What had he done to deserve this? What had he done to come across his wife's body in their bed when only a few days ago things were normal? Jesus Christ, that had only been a few days ago…

His eyes were bleary as he lifted them to the bedside where his wife lay, her face peaceful, the sheets around her soaked red, the stench of blood now reaching him, released from its secret.

How was he going to tell Angie?

Tears began to flow freely from his eyes.

It just wasn't fair.

He wasn't even thinking about the disk. Not even concerned that the second scene was coming true. It was only a matter of time, and according to the disk, time was limited to twenty-five days.

Anyone sane would probably crack.

Crandall did.

The end had begun.

* * * *

Angela took it pretty well, considering. Better than Crandall, she had only asked to say goodbye. He had expected her to go hysterical—the way he had wanted her to. He felt a need to show her that he could still be a strong father even though he had failed his wife, but Angela deprived him of that. Instead, he had had woken her up, and his gray face must have given him away because she didn't smile or say anything.

Crandall had held off calling an ambulance because there really was no point to it, and he didn't want the sirens and slamming doors and oh-so-friendly faces riddled with concern to be the first things she saw and heard.

"Hi, honey," he said softly.

Angela was working things over in her mind. Why had her father woken her up? Why hadn't he shaved? What could be wrong? Why couldn't she hear her mother…And she suddenly knew that something was wrong, but she wasn't alarmed, only saddened. Her eyes rimmed with tears and she asked, "What happened?"

Crandall hadn't expected her to understand so quickly. Most children her age would hardly even understand the concept once told—let alone before a word was said. Then again, Angela hadn't grown up in a traditional environment. She was maturing faster than he wanted her to, and it saddened him more deeply that she simply accepted what he told her rather than behaving the way most little girls would at such horrible news.

"Can I see her?" she asked, her lower lip trembling but under control. "Before *they* come for her."

Crandall didn't want his daughter to see the blood stained sheets, and he tried to get around it by asking if he could move her from the bedroom.

"Don't move her, Dad," she said softly.

Seeing the pain in her eyes, he softly smiled and nodded. "We'll go to together."

* * * *

Angela sat down on the floor beside the bed looking softly at her mother's peaceful face, the gruesome reality hidden under the blankets where she wouldn't see. She sat there for a long time, thinking silent thoughts all the while holding her dad's hand. She didn't cry or even frown. She just sat, recognizing that these were the last moments they'd all have together as a family again.

There was a peaceful presence in the room, or maybe Crandall was only imagining it, hoping for it. The soft breeze parting the curtains had a new-morning scent, and the neighbor's dog was barking cheerfully, the slow troll of a passing car a reminder that life goes on even when it seems to abruptly stop.

* * * *

He didn't want to approach the casket even though he knew he must. He was donning a soft smile, doing his best to hold his composure, doing his best to present himself as 'healing' and doing 'okay'.

The place was called Hourglass Funeral Home, but if someone asked him where he was, he wouldn't have an answer. Everything had been a blur. Three days of constant phone-calls to relatives, friends and various institutions specializing in the art of handling bereavement. Emily was dead, but the government had to make it official.

He had gone through the motions in a mostly numb state, driving here and there, getting Angela to soccer practice on time—always remembering to warn her to be careful when crossing the street or when approached by strangers. If he lost her too…

A hand was on his shoulder. "I'm so sorry, Crandall."

He turned to see someone he recognized but couldn't place. She was probably a relative, but Crandall's mind wasn't working right. He couldn't concentrate. All he could see was the open casket at the far end of the room, it's lid open, surrounded by several colorful flower arrangements. Chairs with accessible boxes of tissues nearby, soft music and even softer carpet underfoot. Everyone was dressed for the occasion, and Crandall only felt worse.

Angela was sitting by herself in a chair at the back of the room staring out the window, her cheeks flushed with restraint as though she were trying to hold her breath to keep from crying.

The chatter around him was quiet and forcibly chipper as everyone said nice things and tried to smile as they stared at the board with so many pictures, so many memories of his wife now lost. In fact, the only audible crying came from the tiny old woman on the sofa, three people trying weakly to console her, Lucille a mess while dressed in her Sunday best. Tissues surrounded her like feeding pigeons, as even in her disillusioned state did she recognize the loss of her daughter.

The woman who had offered her kind words finally wandered off, embarrassed.

Crandall had already heard it a thousand times. *I'm so sorry; sorry Crandall; Oh, Crandall, how awful; Don't blame yourself, dear; How did it happen? Oh, God. I'm so sorry.*

So sorry.

He looked at the casket again, but he didn't want to approach it. He knew that the casket would be closed for tomorrow's service, and the doors were going to close in twenty minutes, the final visitation drawing to an end. He'd have to take Lucille back to the nursing home and get Angela to bed.

Focus, Crandall. That was his game plan. If he could just focus on the things he needed to do, he could distract himself from the pain of life would go on even when it seemed to so abruptly stop.

Turning, he looked over his shoulder and across the room to where Angela sat by herself. He knew that this was his chance to be a strong father, but he felt weak. Two days of visitations, and he had lacked the strength to even once go up the casket's side. Now, seeing his little daughter by herself made him regret his weakness more than ever, and he crossed the room, side-stepping the people who were careful to give him space, eyeing him as he went. Crandall sat down beside his daughter and took her hand. She didn't turn to look at him, and he could tell she was trying to control her tears.

"There's nothing I can say or do to make this any easier for either of us, hon," he said softly. "I wish there was." Drawing a breath, he realized he was talking as much to himself as he was her. "You know, kiddo, we're still a family, and your mother is still with us…Just in a different way."

"I don't like all these people here," she whispered, a tear finally allowed to escape, and she wiped it away with disdain. "I can't say goodbye to her."

So she was feeling the same as him. "What do you say we pretend that none of these people are here, and we go up together?"

Angela turned lightly, her eyes pink. "You'd go to?"

He smiled and stroked her hair. "Dad hasn't said goodbye to Mom yet either."

"They'll watch us. They'll see me cry."

Squeezing her hand lightly, Crandall shook his head. "Nobody's going to see you cry, honey. Nobody except Mom, and she'll be glad that you love her enough to miss her so much."

The girl considered his statement. "You think she can see us?"

"You think your mother would ever leave you alone, even for a second?"

Angela grinned. "She hated that, didn't she?"

Crandall smiled, nodding. "Now she can watch you at all hours of the day and make sure you stay safe." He nudged her arm. "*And* make sure you finish your homework on time."

His daughter blushed lightly, knowing that's exactly what her mother would do if she were around, and the thought brightened her.

"What do you say we go up there and say goodbye the way she would have wanted us to?"

She nodded, and as father and daughter, the two rose and made their way to the front of the room, the chatter dying down as the people turned to watch with surprise. Most of them had been there for the two-day visitation period and had noted, with some despair, that neither Crandall nor Angela had made it to the casket, and they were suddenly shocked that in the final moments the two went as a family.

Crandall felt awful looking down at his wife. Her face was made up, and he knew how she hated makeup, her hands folded neatly over her stomach, her fingers swollen. She wore a dress he'd seen her in only once, and one she hadn't particularly liked. He had heard everyone commenting on how beautiful and how peaceful she looked, the disease finally ridden from her mind, but she didn't look peaceful. She looked like she was holding her breath under water while pretending not to.

And Angela did cry. She touched her mother's hair, drawing back immediately, her little shoulders trembling. Crandall pulled her toward him and reached out, gently closing his fingers one last time around Emily's, shocked at how cold and lifeless they felt. So different than they had been when they courted. So different from when she was laughing and giggling, her smile wide and bright. So different, but he held on, afraid to let go of his wife.

Goddammit, he was going to cry too.

"I miss Mom," Angela said.

He had a hard time answering, but he hugged her harder, forcing himself to speak and speak steadily. "So do I, hon."

*   *   *   *

Lucille had been difficult as usual, but Crandall was focusing again, his tasks allowing him to concentrate on something else. Get Emily's mother home before five so she wouldn't miss her supper.

Considering all the expenses that went into funeral arrangements, a free meal that his mother-in-law refused to eat was cheaper than a paid-for meal she refused to eat. And thank God the funeral was done and over with. It had been a cloudy but dry day, which was, as far as Crandall was concerned, perfect weather to bury a spouse.

Both he and Angela had done better. Neither cried at the funeral, something they had both silently promised themselves to save for after hours when the lights were out and the doors were closed.

"These floors are too clean, Crandall. Don't you think they're too clean? They never clean the floors unless someone new is coming to live with us."

Crandall held his tongue, tolerating her babble, being pleasant, a basic need within him just to get through the day, the last day of this nightmare when tomorrow things would be as normal as they would ever again be. "Yes, Lucille. They certainly do look good, but Clear Haven keeps this place pretty clean every day."

"Not this clean. Don't they look exceptionally clean to you?"

The man behind the desk smiled through his coke-bottle glasses, squinting as he eyed the approaching guests. "I'll just need to see your IDs," Mike said with a timid, pleasant smile.

Crandall pressed his driver's license against the window, and Mike leaned forward, his mouth hanging open slightly.

"Yeah, okay. What about her?"

Crandall didn't need this. Not today. "Lucille Akers, Mike. She's a resident here, remember? We went to her daughter's funeral today?"

Mike chuckled. "Just jokin' with you. I 'membered. It's called humor, mister. Try it on for size."

Humor. Right. Beautiful timing, jackass.

Mike buzzed them in, and the door opened, a nurse there to greet them with a pleasant, understanding smile. "Good to have you back, dear. Dinner will be ready in a few minutes. We made you're favorite tonight."

"I don't have a favorite," Lucille mumbled sadly.

"Sure you do. We made-"

"Thanks, Crandall," the old woman snapped as she walked slowly through the door. "For bringing me back to my cell."

He didn't want to have to deal with this. Not today. Not now.

The nurse cast him an understanding frown, but he waved her off, following his mother-in-law in, only planning on staying long enough to get her situated. They crossed the room at a snail's pace and Lucille collapsed on her bed, sighing and sucking in deep breaths of air.

"Guess I never said," she mumbled after a moment, her old eyes lifting to him, her mouth in a crooked downward grin. "I never approved of your marriage to my daughter, Crandall. I should have known you'd be the death of her."

"Mrs. Akers, that's a terrible thing to say," the nurse said, her voice soothing as if it wasn't the wretched woman's fault.

Crandall held the nurse at bay. He wasn't going to fight. Lucille's daughter was dead and that ended his relationship with her mother. He looked to the nurse, smiled softly and said as kindly as he could: "Take good care of her. Emily loved her dearly."

"We'll see to it," the nurse said with a sympathetic smile.

Crandall crossed the room, glad it was done and over with. Angela was at Stacie's tonight, a slumber party with all her friends, an event organized by Stacie's mother, and considering the times, it probably wasn't a bad thing. He'd have the house to himself, and the liquor store was on the way home.

"Is it open?" came a voice to his right as he strode past, and Crandall turned to see Benjamin Spoon staring at him.

Looking ahead, Crandall saw that the exit out was indeed open, guarded by a nurse, and he returned his gaze to Benjamin. "Door's open, Benjamin," he said.

"I meant your mind, son. Is it open?"

Crandall felt like leaving and staying at the same time. His eyes went from the old man to the nurse at the door and back again. "I was able to deliver your message," he said referring to conversation he'd shared about magnets only days earlier. "The President is aware."

Benjamin nodded impatiently. "I know it, Crandall. You were right."

"About what?"

"The guards you sent me are posing as doctors. See that pretty blonde nurse by the door?"

Of course he did.

"She's a man in disguise. She's one of my bodyguards posing as a nurse. I thank you for your due attention to the urgency of my message."

Crandall looked again to the nurse and saw that she was anything other than a man, but the old man was nervous, careful to appear like the conversation was one in passing.

Crandall suddenly felt like staying. The room, this nursing home offered him a comfort, and he felt he might be able to lose himself within the lunacy of others. Maybe he was crazy too and the nurses might take care of him. Maybe Benjamin truly did have all the answers. Seeking refuge, he sat on the bed, and the old man immediately became uncomfortable.

"I need to know something, Ben."

But the old man was already shaking his head. "Shouldn't talk here. This is bad. Real bad. Meet me by the television in two minutes. Go."

Crandall frowned, shifted, stood and walked away. The television. The only television was in another room, its audio cut off by the thick glass in between. Several people were inside the small room, situated in their chairs, eyes trained on the screen while not really seeing the flickering images in front of them. Instead of arguing, he entered the room and took a seat near the back, the door behind him clicking shut. Nobody turned. Either nobody heard or nobody cared.

It was a toothpaste commercial. A woman showing off her shining teeth, a few people in the audience picking at their gums as they watched.

Ben sat down, his eyes on the screen. "Don't be foolish, Crandall. They're watching, you understand. But this is a safe room. They have no cameras in here or microphones. But we must remain inconspicuous, understood?"

Crandall nodded. "Yes. I'm sorry. I was careless."

"A word slips out here and there, here and there, and the right people find out about it, and suddenly you're a dead man. You're erased, your whole family's erased, your entire past is erased. Gone. Hopefully…" Ben looked casually over his shoulder and then returned. "Hopefully no one noticed. Let that be a lesson."

It felt so good to be there that Crandall just accepted and nodded. Here, in the simplicity of this ward, he forgot about Emily and his responsibilities back home. Death wasn't a word to these people. They existed, and when they passed, they were just gone to everyone else. No one had to remember.

"Now," Ben said, his voice relaxing as he crossed his arms and watched the screen. "What was your question?"

"It'll sound ridiculous."

"Most theories do, my friend, but you know what?"

Crandall frowned. "What?"

"That's why they're usually true. No one is willing to believe in them. That's what makes them possible."

"Well, I've got a whopper of a conspiracy then, and I need some help with it."

"Don't look at me when you talk and try not to move your lips. There might be cameras outside, or maybe one of these posers anticipated this move. You never know."

Crandall obeyed. In a way, he was a child again, playing a game. Ben had returned him to his youth where everything was a forbidden secret just begging to be told. "I found something," he said.

"Don't tell me where," Ben said quickly. "I don't want to know. Then I can't be made to talk. Be careful with your details. Tell me only what you must to ask your question."

"It's a disk," Crandall whispered. "A video on disk. Like a movie of sorts. It seems it was filmed a few weeks from now. It's about me."

"Is it authentic?" Ben asked, his hand slightly trembling.

"I don't know. I mean, it's not possible, right? How could the disk be filmed in the future? How could it have gotten here?"

Ben turned, his eyes darts. "Why are you telling me this, Crandall? You're jeopardizing the whole fuckin' thing."

Crandall shrunk. "What *thing*?"

"Our resistance. Dollars to beans says they're going to know you know."

"Who's they?"

"They! They as in the government or an agency. They. You know, you refer to 'they' when you say *they* robbed me or *they* arrested me. They. What if *they* hear us?"

"You said this was a safe-room."

Ben thought a moment, shook his head and relaxed. "Like I said-"

"Right, right," Crandall interjected. "Never be too careful. I got it." He looked around the room and found only old people, most of them off their rocker, staring madly at the screen. The sound of trickling water reached his ears and he looked along the isle to see an old woman sitting with a complacent smile on her lips, urine dripping to the floor from the seat she sat on.

"So what do you think?" Crandall asked without turning back. "Tell me I'm crazy."

Ben chuckled. "You want to know crazy? I'll tell you all about crazy, and believe me, my friend, you'll only find the tip of the iceberg in this place."

Crandall nodded. "I'm waiting."

Ben grinned, his yellow teeth glaring against the white light. "You're an impatient one, my young apprentice. We'll start with mathematics. What do you think about mathematics?"

"I'm not interested in mathematics, Ben."

"I asked you a question, Crandall. Answer it or get out."

Crandall sat, frozen in his seat. The old man wasn't joking around. His voice was solid and bitter, pragmatic in its own right. Ben was pissed.

"I guess I've never given much thought to mathematics, Ben."

"Try."

Crandall shrugged. "Math is useless beyond college. It's used as a tool to teach logical thinking. In the practical world, it has no value given our technological accomplishments."

"Do you realize almost all rules are based around the principles of mathematics?" the old man grumbled through clenched teeth, stale air wafting Crandall's way. "Mathematics are considered to be the only true universal language. It doesn't matter if you're a slug, an extraterrestrial or a human being, mathematics are the same. One plus one always equals two. That's the theory that makes us reasonably confident that should the chance meeting with another civilization arise we could find a way to communicate. Ones and zeros, zeros and ones. You've got your platform set for any language. Mathematics are the *key*, Crandall, do you understand?"

"Right. One plus one equals two."

"Exactly. Except that it can not be proved in every instance."

"I don't understand."

"That's because you're consumed with physical attribution. Everything you see and hear and touch is explainable, attributable in your mind to a finite explanation simply because you can see and hear and touch it. Mathematics are precise in your mind. One plus one indeed equals two."

Crandall grinned, but did not turn. "I get the feeling this will eventually get me somewhere, but you sound like you're stalling Ben. What about the disk? Is it possible?"

"Ever heard of Kurt Godel?"

Crandall shook his head.

"Of course you haven't. You're a puppet to their game, carrying on about your business and accepting things as they are because you can justify them with your opened eyes and your learned knowledge. Knowledge attained within the public school system, captivated in theory, when in reality you have absolutely no idea what's happening out beyond the edge of your crystal…clear…vision." Ben licked his lips, and it was disgusting. "Don' t look at me."

Crandall felt uncomfortable, and his eyes jerked to the screen where a black and white episode of the Three Stooges returned, the protagonists immediately slapping one another across the face and whopping the other on the head.

Ben pulled his deck of cards and began to shuffle them without really thinking about it. "Kurt Godel argued that mathematics can have faults. One plus one doesn't have to equal two," he went on. "By his own hand he showed that arithmetic was incomplete. His incompleteness theorem states that it is possible for areas of mathematics that we take for granted to be neither true nor false. In short, we cannot prove that one plus one equals two."

"I don't understand."

"You're such a child, Crandall. Think about it. Consider the statement 'this statement is false'. Godel pointed out that if it is true then it must also be false. This idea is no more complex than a basic double negative. In the English language, a double negative is something along the lines of, for example, I didn't see no flowers. While it is mistakenly conveyed that the speaker is trying to say they saw no flowers, the double negative is, in fact, stating that he or she actually saw flowers. If no flowers were not seen, then flowers must have been evident. The same holds true in mathematics. A double negative, as proven by Godel shows that a negative, negative one is actually a positive one. You've got the double-negative, the Law of Noncontradition and the Law of Excluded Middle to show just how flawed the universal language of mathematics can truly be."

"The Law of Noncontradiction?"

"It's like saying the not of A plus the not of A is actually true. It takes everything we consider to be a given in mathematics and makes them false, or in the case of false, true."

"I'm lost, Ben."

"Which means specifically that you are not ready to understand your finding. You can, at this point, merely observe."

Crandall leaned closer, though keeping his eyes on the screen that spat black and white images. Three idiots on stage danced around. "That's not good enough. My daughter's life is in danger. I need to know."

Ben turned his eyes slightly. "If you cannot comprehend Godel's theorem, how could you possibly fathom anything else I have to offer?"

"All I want to know is about the disk. I want to prove it a fake, but more than that, I want to know how it came into my possession."

"Inevitably, Crandall, it came into your possession because it was determined to do so. They were watching, and they liked what they saw of you. However, to answer your question as to whether or not a disk could have been filmed a few weeks from now only to wind up in your past comes dangerously close to the definition of time travel. As to whether or not time travel is possible, the answer by today's standards is unequivocally 'no'. We lack the technology."

"How do you know?"

"I worked with them and against them. You're making me repeat myself, Crandall. We've been over this."

"Sorry."

"If you were actually sorry you wouldn't apologize. Double-negative. You're not sorry."

"You're right, I'm not. I think you're talking out of your ass."

Benjamin grinned, his eyes gleaming as they were aimed at the screen. "You have no idea what you're getting yourself into, my friend. My best advice is to let it alone. You have enough to worry about what with all the roaches."

"The roaches?"

"Fuckin' roaches everywhere at night here. I kill one and it's replaced with two. They're spies, you see. That's how they get past the guards you sent me. Worry about the roaches, and then we'll talk."

Crandall looked around the room, and in the darkest corner he did see an ovular shadow that moved an inch forward before stopping.

"Dollars to beans he knows you saw him," Ben whispered. "You're best bet is to get out now while you still can."

Crandall grinned, but Ben turned away.

"Now."

Shrugging, Crandall was tired of the game anyway. What had his intentions been? Humiliate the old man? Try to relate? The whole idea of the disk was preposterous anyway, and what could a lunatic in a nursing home know about his problem anyhow?

He made his way to the door, thought better of it and sidestepped to the corner where he squished the roach with the heel of his shoe before exiting the room. In his mind he was making a mockery of Ben's statements, proving that he was above such stupid theories. After all, a roach was just a roach, and while he was reasonably sure Ben was off his rocker, there was a part of him that felt awkward, and the killing of the bug wasn't just a measure to ensure the cleanliness of the nursing home; it was a precaution.

Just to be sure.

Chapter 7

Angela's birthday.

Just two days after he buried daughter's mother, and he was supposed to celebrate her ninth birthday. Angela was supposed to celebrate.

He bought her a few gifts, more than he should have, but he felt better spending money, expressing his love for her the way dad's did, and he thrived on the feeling by bringing her home a new bicycle, cookbook—because she loved to cook—and a doll that talked and cried when thirsty. The doll even asked to use the bathroom two hours later according to the synopsis on the back. Sally Sister was the closest Angie was going to get to a real sister anyway. The doll might as well pee.

But his heart wasn't into wrapping, so he just left the items in the back seat of his Jeep. He'd bring her out to the garage after Dominos delivered her favorite pizza. Hopefully the day wouldn't be a complete ruin. Crandall even had a cake—one of those store-bought things on special because it was more than a day old. *Freshness guaranteed!* yet at half the price, so what the hell? What did he care if it had two racecars positioned upon a frosted track? He took out the Hershey's syrup from the fridge and clumsily squirted, *Happy 9 Angie!* He was quite certain this was already a birthday she'd never forget.

He sunk the candles deep into the soft breading before sticking the cake into the oven where it would be hidden. Making his way into the living room, he saw his daughter draped over the chair, staring out the window, buddy beside her and happily asleep. She must have been there a long time because the dog was dreaming, kicking every few seconds, but she didn't notice.

"Happy birthday, Angie," he said softly.

Buddy raised his head, his little tail thumping lightly.

She did smile, making an effort of it by cooperating. "Mom said she was gonna take me to the mall today. It was gonna be our secret."

"Do you want to go to the mall? Just you an me?"

The girl shook her head. "No."

He tried smiling and approached her. "I thought we'd order a movie and a pizza tonight. All the pepperoni you want, and whatever movie you'd like to see. The movie-guide came with today's paper."

Angela smiled. "Sounds like fun, Dad. I'd like a break from feeling sad."

That was his little girl. She always did her best to make those around her feel happy. She always looked for the best in any situation. He rustled her hair and pulled her from the couch. "Let's order up, shall we?"

* * * *

Two slices of pizza remained in the box, and the cake was glowing, all nine candles shimmering, making the girl's face glow, though her eyes were somewhere lost behind the tiny flames.

"Make a wish, honey," he said, trying to be positive, trying to be…

It just seemed futile.

Angela leaned forward, drew a breath and blew, the candles flickering and extinguishing, columns of gray smoke pilfering away. Her eyes remained sad.

She had liked her gifts and expressed gratitude, but it wasn't the same. Her mother was missing, her eccentricities and all. Emily was missing.

"Won't come true," the girl whispered.

Crandall froze. Something sounded familiar. His thoughts raced to the disk and what he had seen. Same scene, same dialogue, same atmosphere. The words were on his lips. He remembered what he was supposed to say, and he almost said it—

How do you know that?

—but he held back. The disk was wrong. If for no other reason, he would make it wrong by denying it its destiny. He would interject a Ben Spoon double-negative.

Pinching his lips tightly shut, he abstained.

Angela looked up, expecting her father to say something in return, but he sat quietly nodding but saying nothing. "She's already dead," she continued sullenly.

Crandall sat for a moment longer before jerking from the chair, spilling it to its back, his eyes frantically searching the room.

The camera had been close, and he began to pull cushions from the couch and pillows from the chairs. He dumped books from the shelves, looked behind curtains, opened cupboards and peered madly inside.

"Dad?"

He spilled the decorations Emily had carefully adorned the cabinets around the dining room as he looked, searched.

"Dad? What's wrong?" Angel's voice was scared.

"Not now," he whispered. "They're watching us right now."

Crandall peered through the branches of the artificial vine tracing the wall, dumped magazines from their perch, scanned the walls, corners, every shadow, nook and cranny he found.

"What are you looking for?" Angela asked.

He double and triple checked, silently cursing, racing to the front door and bolting to the porch where he searched both ways, looking for something—anything—out of the ordinary.

Nothing.

"Dad?"

She was right behind him, and he softened, turning, donning a smile. "It's nothing, hon. I thought I heard something, that's all."

They returned to the dining room that was in upheaval and Angie, bless her heart, started to clean up, but he stopped her, insisting they continue with her birthday celebration.

Celebration.

He cut the cake, but neither felt like sugar.

* * * *

After Angela had gone to bed, Crandall dug out the disk, switched on the television and zipped through what he knew, the images of Buddy and the funeral racing by.

Stop.

"Make a wish, honey," he heard himself say, and Angela was across the table, her eyes sad.

She shook her head, her brown hair dancing lightly against the glow cast by the candles. *"Won't come true,"* she answered.

Crandall leaned forward.

How do you know that? he heard himself thinking. He was waiting to hear his voice cross through the speakers. After all, the recording couldn't change. It was a forgery. Nothing could predict the future as it was undecided.

How do you know that?

Crandall waited, but the Crandall Cady on the disk did not answer and Angela frowned. *"She's already dead."*

His blood froze, his eyes welling with fear and anger.

It changed.

The goddamn disk changed.

Simply because he had willed it to.

He punched the 'fast-forward' button on the remote and skipped through the images, hitting 'play' upon instinct.

"You've finally made it," an unfamiliar voice said, the recording at the end where the unnamed old man stood over a fallen corpse. The same as it had been before, the mystery alive and well.

The ending, as unfitting to the rest of the video as it seemed, remained unchanged, unaltered in the least.

He knew exactly how the recording was going to end.

Exactly.

Chapter 8

Crandall didn't know what to do or how to react. Figuratively speaking, he had a jigsaw puzzle in front of him that wouldn't assemble. He couldn't even figure out the frame and work his way inward.

The library was of no use. There were books upon books discussing the possibilities of time travel as that was the only logical way he figured the disk wound up in his possession. Logically speaking, time travel wasn't logical. It wasn't even possible. Most of the books were fiction and held little merit, but even the ones written by reputable scientists were dated from the early nineteen hundreds and before. The principles weren't realistic to achieve, and he didn't have the time to read them even if they were. According to the disk, he had only a few days to figure the mess out and reverse the course being laid before him.

Crandall hated the idea of not controlling his destiny, but more than that, he hated the story the disk had told. His hope was that since he'd altered the content once, he could do it again. He just had to be smarter about it—more prepared.

Slamming the book shut, he leaned on his elbows, running sweaty fingers through his hair. There must have been ten books alone on his desk, each containing more information than he could absorb. There was just too much information. Sitting back he saw an old woman staring at him with a scornful look from across the library. Adjusting her glasses, she went back to her reading, shaking her head lightly with disgust.

Crandall changed direction. It would get him nowhere to learn how to make time travel work. At this point, all he needed to know was whether or not it was possible. If the consensus was no, then there had to be another explanation. Considering the absurd idea of the whole H.G. Wells' *Time Machine* fantasy, he was already leaning that way, but he had no other ideas. The disk was far too detailed to be a hoax, but he had no explanation—everything eventually leading him back to science-fiction movies and ridiculous contraptions allegedly capable of jumping through time. Benjamin Spoon didn't seem to think it was possible anymore than Crandall, and considering the old man seemed to believe everything was a conspiracy, Crandall felt like an idiot for believing in it. Surely there was someone else he could talk with such as a legitimate scientist. The problem was, Crandall didn't know any scientists. He didn't even know somebody who knew somebody who knew somebody who knew a scientist. His ring of acquaintances was limited to the small suburb outside of Peyton.

Stacking the books into a pile, Crandall returned them to the front desk, smiled a thank you to the librarian and was on his way, exiting the library and entering into the bright sunshine of the afternoon. He felt so useless. He had failed Emily, and he already felt as though he had failed Angela.

Maybe he should just keep Angie indoors for the next three weeks. Once the final date had expired, the question behind whether or not time travel was possible would be irrelevant.

God, he was going nuts…

He lowered his head, shoving his hands into his pockets and continuing his slow pace along the sidewalk.

A dog barked in the background, and a baby cried.

*   *   *   *

I'm so sorry. I'm so sorry that things were so ugly for you.

Crandall hit pause, and the screen in front of him froze, the woman on screen beginning to turn, the television version of Crandall's face solemn.

He climbed off the couch and approached the screen, his hand reaching out and wiping the dust off from the lower corner where the date hung suspended.

15 August, 11:33:48

Four days away, yet it had taken a full three days to arrange Emily's funeral. It was only logical that if something was going to happen, then it should have already. But there was nothing. He felt and heard nothing, and as he considered this, he panicked because it meant he also couldn't hear his daughter.

"Angela!" he called, jumping to his feet, nearly jogging down the hallway to her room where he barged through the door only to be greeted with silence. Her window was slightly open, a summer breeze shuffling the curtains, but the room was empty.

"Angela!" he called again, turning away from her room and trotting through the kitchen. Maybe she was in the back yard. He yanked open the back door, jumping onto the back porch. "Angela!"

Buddy, who had been laying in the shade on the porch, jumped to his feet, tail wriggling as he approached, licking his nose as he came. Crandall called out for his daughter again, but it was obvious she was neither in the house nor the back yard. Had she said she was going somewhere?

Stacie's. He closed the door, leaving the dog abruptly shut off from the attention he had assumed was coming. Grabbing the phone, Crandall punched the speed-dial and impatiently paced as the incessant ringing bled through the tiny receiver.

"Hello?"

"This is Crandall Cady. Is my daughter around by chance?"

"Oh, hi, Crandall. Sharon." Stacie's mother. "Sure. Just a second."

He was still pacing, but he began to calm as he listened the rustling of the phone on the other end being covered while Sharon called for Angela.

Absently, Crandall checked the clock and saw that it was twenty minutes past two in the afternoon.

"I'm sorry, Crandall," Sharon said. "She and Stacie must have gone down to the river again. You know how much those two like the water. I would think they'd be back in a couple of hours. Do you want me to have her give you a call?"

Crandall was already hanging up, racing for the garage, swooping his keys from the counter as he flashed past. He didn't bother to lock up as his possessions suddenly meant little to him. He started the Jeep and squealed the tires as he punched the gas, the automobile reversing down the driveway. The tires left black marks on the asphalt as he slammed the brakes and shifted into first, his foot smashing the gas pedal, the Jeep leaping forward.

He was cursing under his breath. Why hadn't he checked the video before now? It was a perfect setup. If there was someone out there making the events of the disk come true, here was the perfect opportunity.

The Jeep rolled through a stoplight, horns blaring at either side, but he only accelerated faster, dropping the transmission into overdrive. He'd never forgive himself if something happened when he could have prevented it. Never.

The houses and trees blurred as he raced past them, the engine responding with confidence. He turned into the park, zipping through the rows of parked cars until he reached the front. Without really noticing, he pulled into handicap parking, killed the engine and hit the pavement running. People stood aside and watched with both curiosity and concern as he pumped for speed toward the beach. Crandall hurtled an occupied park bench and sank deep into the sand, his balance temporarily lost. Agitated voices were yelling at him as he scrambled to his feet and scanned the sand, hundreds of oiled bodies glazing under the sun.

Sweat rolled into his eyes, and he fiercely wiped it away, walking toward the people, laughing children and common chatter filling the atmosphere, the stench of sunscreen thick like ozone around him. He saw two girls playing and laughing, building a sand castle, but neither face looked familiar.

He swore, exasperated, his labored breathing making him feel faint, the blaring sun burning him where he stood. Not giving up, he began to traipse through the staggering sand, searching the faces of all the young girls he saw. How could that woman be so irresponsible with two little girls? How could she let them go to the beach by themselves? Goddamn her to hell. He'd kill her if anything happened to his Angela…

The thought stopped him.

Would he? Was he capable of killing another human being?

Still scanning the sea of faces, he was alarmed to find that he was. His rage had manifested itself as cold sweat soaking his entire body, and his fear squeezed his lungs and heart.

Angela wasn't there.

It was redundant to go back through the crowd of beach goers. He knew he could pick his little girl out of a million faces, and she wasn't anywhere on the beach.

Turning around, he made his way back to his Jeep. He tried to hurry, but he was exhausted, his body drained though he pushed it. Age was really taking its toll on him. Ten years ago he'd have been ready for more, but the soft life of Suburban America left him sluggish.

Crandall drove to Stacie's house, hoping against the odds that Sharon had merely been wrong and Angela would come rushing out to greet him. Pulling into the driveway the door opened, and ironically, as if written into a script, Angie did come rushing out to greet him, her face beaming though a little timid.

"Stacie's mom said you sounded worried on the phone," she said as she reached the Jeep.

Sharon came out on the front step, tentatively waving hello, her face embarrassed. Crandall couldn't help but glare back, his obvious disapproval in the way she kept watch over the children evident in his dark eyes. "Get in the Jeep, Angie. We have to go."

The girl whined. "But why? Stacie and me were gonna go get ice-cream."

"Because I'm your father, and I said so," he returned without snapping.

Angela's shoulders sagged, but she didn't argue further. Instead, she turned to Stacie who stood on the porch with her mother. "I gotta go," she said sadly. "Maybe tomorrow."

Stacie nodded, but didn't say anything. Angela climbed in, pouting as she crossed her arms.

"Seatbelt," Crandall said as he backed out of the driveway.

She obeyed, but unhappily. "I didn't do anything wrong, Dad."

"I know you didn't, honey. I'll make it up to you."

"Then why did I hafta go?"

"Don't argue. I can't explain it right now."

The girl shook her head and looked the other way at the passing houses. Crandall didn't particularly care that she was upset with him so long as she was safe. Driving home, he made sure he obeyed the speed limits, stop signs and lights. He watched the other traffic, weary of mistakes the other drivers might make. Angela wasn't out of danger until he got her home and into the house. She wasn't going anywhere until the recording ended. Stacie could come over, but they would venture no further than the front porch or back yard. The disk would be wrong, her fate changed. He was the instrument to her salvation.

The Jeep rolled into the garage, and Crandall switched the key, the engine clicking as it cooled. Angela climbed out without a word and stormed into the house, slamming the door in Crandall's face.

Let her be mad. At least she was safe. He'd calm the storm later.

He closed the large garage door and locked the entryway behind him as he entered the house, his fortress. Let them come and try to take her now.

Peering through the large glass windows at the front of the house, he scrutinized the neighborhood, interrogating it for clues and finding none.

Bring it, he thought, his eyes dark. *I'm ready.*

* * * *

He sat staring straight through the dark and out into the quiet streets. In his hand he held his grandfather's baseball bat, hand-carved two generations earlier. For decades it had been a mantle-piece ornament, but it was solid oak, and a hell of a weapon.

Crandall felt he had already averted whatever it was that would have taken his daughter's life, but he wasn't taking anything for granted. Maybe she would have been fine at the beach and the ice-cream parlor. Maybe it was a nighttime robbery where his little girl became the victim of a kidnapping or accidental murder. He wasn't taking chances.

Emily had been a paranoid schizophrenic, and Crandall imagined he was starting to behave like one as well, but he felt confident enough that he was thinking clearly to continue on his mission.

His fingers locked around the cool grip of the wooden bat as he sat in silence, listening to the rhythm of his own heartbeat.

Everything was so still that he figured he could hear a mouse laughing from the other room. The floors and walls were done settling, the neighborhood quiet, the lonely street lights buzzing softly beyond the range of his hearing from where he sat barricaded in his house. All doors locked, all windows closed and latched. Buddy was at his side, silently sleeping, but the puppy had put on seven pounds of strength since they'd taken him in, and Crandall knew the dog's loyalty.

The silence and darkness engulfed him, surrounded him, swallowed him. His fingers were trembling with fatigue, his eyes sagging as each second passed.

The phone rang.

The noise was enough to cause Crandall to jump, his bowels releasing, the bat slipping from his hands and bouncing to the carpet. Buddy jumped, offered a youthful bark, tucked his tail between his legs and made a beeline for the kitchen.

Crandall grabbed for the phone, hoping the noise hadn't woken Angela. "Hello," he growled into the receiver. If this was a telemarketer…

"Mr. Cady?"

"Yes."

"This is Dr. Fernandez from the Clear Haven Nursing Community residence."

Crandall frowned. "Yes."

"We have it in our records that you are the son-in-law to Lucille Akers?"

"That is correct." Crandall sat back down on the couch, the bat at his feet.

"I'm sorry to have to be the one to bring you bad news, but Ms. Akers passed away this evening, it seems, from natural causes."

Crandall closed his eyes. It wasn't Angela after-all. With guilt, he suddenly felt light-hearted, almost gleeful.

"I'm terribly sorry," Fernandez continued, "but I'll need you to come and identify the body and sign off. I'm terribly sorry."

"Can it wait until morning?" Crandall asked. "I can't leave my daughter."

"Of course. Just sometime before noon if it isn't too much trouble."

You're so damn stupid, he told himself, pinching his eyes closed. He had blindly assumed the second casket had been for Angela. He had figured he could save her life and change fate, when things rolled on despite his efforts. The joke was on him, his ignorance his downfall. "I'll be there early," he answered.

"Again, I'm awfully sorry, Mr. Cady. I know what you've been through lately, and I...well, I'm sorry."

"Thanks," he answered as if on cue. He hung up the phone and leaned back with exhaustion.

* * * *

The man pulled back the sheet and revealed the waxy face, as white as the sheet itself, surely painted up to look so ghastly, so dead.

"That's her," Crandall said, filling the formality.

Angela was waiting in the next room, close-by. Crandall wasn't taking any chances.

Fernandez replaced the sheet and nodded. "I thank you, Crandall. I know how difficult these last days have been. With your permission, Clear Haven will make all of the funeral arrangements as indicated from the form Ms. Akers filled out upon admittance to our care. All I need is a signature and everything will be handled."

Crandall nodded and signed, Fernandez smiling. "If there is anything else we can do to be of further assistance, please be in touch."

Walking out, Crandall took his daughter by the hand and made for the exit. If nothing else, Clear Haven was proficient. Emily's arrangements had been tedious, and at least he wouldn't have to go through all that again.

Looking to his side, Crandall saw Benjamin Spoon eyeing him from across the room. His face was stern, leathery and betrayed. Crandall turned away.

The nurse at the door smiled, lowering herself to Angie's level. "Well, if it isn't my favorite visitor. How are you Angela?"

Angela smiled. "My grandma died."

The nurse frowned, caught off guard and immediately flushing with embarrassment. Her eyes darted to Crandall then back to Angela. "I'm so sorry, honey."

"It's okay," Angela answered. "Dad says it was just her time."

Crandall shrugged. It was the best he could do.

The nurse knelt to one knee and brushed the child's hair with the side of her hand. "Would you like to get an ice-cream cone, hon?"

The girl looked to her father.

Crandall nodded. "Sure." He knew this was the last time Angela would see this place, and the nurse was trying to cover her ass for such a stumble.

"Would you like one too?" the nurse asked politely of Crandall.

"You two go ahead," he replied with a smile.

The nurse took Angela by the hand, winked at Crandall and led her toward the cafeteria.

Crandall turned around, meeting Benjamin's stare and approached the old man who sat upon his bed, un-amused by his impending company.

"So," the old man sneered. "Look who showed up one last time? You were going to leave without a word hadn't Nurse Wretched come along, weren't you?"

Crandall sat down, playing the game. "It's not that simple, Spoon. She was watching me, and you know it. If she had seen me approach you, she would have figured you a spy. We'd both be in prison within the hour."

Spoon thought about it a moment then nodded. "You're right, of course. You're learning fast, Cady. Maybe too fast. Just don't get cocky on me. There ain't no points for second place."

Crandall nodded. "I'm all too aware, my friend."

The old man shifted, not sure if he should believe the man opposite him, but his eyes revealed that he had little choice. "So what have you done for me lately, Cady?"

Crandall shrugged. "I got to the President, but he feels it's too risky to speak with you directly."

"Goddammit," Spoon whispered, pondering, his face wrought with concern. "He's right."

Crandall frowned. "He's even leery about sending men. He figured it might be too obvious, so he sent me instead. He wants to know what you know."

Ben shook his head. "You're life is in danger now, Crandall. There's no turning back from this moment forward. I'm giving you an out. Take it and walk now, or accept the possible consequences."

Crandall stared back coldly. "I'm prepared to take my chances. For God, for country. I'm your messenger, Spoon."

The old man nodded his head, a small smile upon his parched lips as his anxious eyes looked each way, seeking out would-be spies. "That's good. Tell the president that the Germans are planning to attack us with chemical and germ warfare."

Crandall frowned. "The Germans?"

"In compliance with Japan that is. They're united to form a unified coalition against the states."

"They're our allies, Ben. Why would they attack?"

Ben waved him off and pretended not to be interested as one of the other patients hobbled by. When the coast was clear, he leaned in. "Because they think we're going to attack them."

Crandall entertained the notion only for the old man's sake. "Okay, Ben. I'll make sure he gets the message."

"Codeword equals Valcohlm. Don't fuck it up 'cause it'll cost you your life."

"Gotcha."

The old man was satisfied. "So what else is on your mind, my young friend? You seem troubled, and I know the relationship you held with Akers. I can't imagine you're that distressed over her passing."

Crandall shifted uncomfortably, carefully choosing his words. "No, you're right, Ben. I'm here for another reason. The Joint Chiefs are frantic for information they believe you hold. I showed them the disk."

Spoon recoiled, closing his eyes. "Damn you, Cady. You have to be more careful. Haven't I taught you anything? I told you, the bastard's are watching. Now, yesterday, tomorrow."

"Not when I showed them the disk. They weren't watching. It was in the bomb-shelter of the Whitehouse. I was escorted by two guards."

"How do you know they aren't in on it?"

"They were screened. I made sure personally. They checked out okay. The information is secure."

The old man relaxed, but only slightly. "I'm not happy about this, Cady, but go on."

"Well," Crandall continued, knowing he had to play Ben's game if he were to get what he needed. "It seems they're extremely interested in its contents."

"How so?"

"They can't explain its existence any more than I can. I mean, the last scene on the disk has a date stamp of August 27th. So far everything prior to today that is captured on the disk is authentic and has occurred. For the life of me I cannot prove it a forgery. The government concludes that the disk is genuine but also stipulates that it cannot explain how the disk with such contents could be made." Crandall stopped. He had exhausted his vocabulary, and he knew he came off sophomoric, but this was his best try. In actuality, he expected more psychobabble from the old man, and he was prepared to sit through it since he was at his wits end.

Spoon smiled. His teeth, yellow and brown, hung in crooked patterns from the roof of his mouth. "You're still wondering about time travel, aren't you, Mr. Cady?"

Crandall shrugged. "I'm still wondering about the origin of my find, Ben."

"I already told you, time travel is impossible. You're asking the wrong questions."

Crandall leaned forward. "If time travel is so impossible, then how did I receive a disk outlining my future, its contents coming true at every frame? Why is the final date several days from today? Tell me, Ben, how is that possible?"

The old man shrugged. "Don't ask me, Cady. I'm just a mental case stranded in a psycho ward for old-fogies, but I'm telling you, time travel is impossible."

Crandall frowned. That was all he needed from the old man. If Spoon would divulge no more, then further interrogation would get him nowhere. This was a waste of time.

He stood up to leave.

"Of course," Spoon continued. "Time travel is only impossible by today's standards."

Crandall stopped and turned. "What is that supposed to mean?"

The old man shrugged. "Well, when you think in terms of the fourth dimension, time travel may exist today because it was invented tomorrow."

"If it was invented tomorrow, then it wouldn't exist today."

Ben grinned, his eyes gleaming. "But of course it would, Crandall. If time travel were invented tomorrow, then its vessel would have the capability of traveling back through time to today. Therefore, speaking from the fourth dimension, time travel is, in fact, possible today. Like I said, you weren't asking the right questions."

Crandall didn't like this, and he shifted uncomfortably, looking around and finding an old woman with white hair and a shriveled face smiling back. He was being played.

"Don't mind her," Ben said softly. "She with us. I converted her."

Crandall turned on Ben. "I don't want to play games, Ben. If you have the answers, your government demands that you relinquish them.

"I cannot read your mind, Crandall," Ben answered coldly. "If you want answers, then be more goddamn specific with your questions. And watch your tone. I still outrank you."

Crandall stopped. The old man was good. He followed protocol to the stripe, always in line, despite his errant logic.

"I apologize, Ben. I beg your forgiveness."

"Cut the crap, Cady. We're adults here. Just remember your place."

Crandall leaned closer, his eyes darts. He remembered his place, and he could be specific if that's what was required of him. "Ben, I need answers. Time travel.

Today, tomorrow, next year or a thousand years from now, tell me something. Is it possible given the right resources?"

Ben licked his gums, and after a moment's consideration, nodded. "Yes it is."

Crandall sat back, pinching the bridge of his nose. "Jesus Christ," he whispered.

Ben snickered. To him it was funny. "But you'd like to know how and when it's possible, isn't that right?"

Crandall nodded. "It just so happens that someone very close to me is in danger, Ben. Her salvation is based on the principles of time travel. The only way to save her is to figure out how it works so that I may discover who's behind it, and I have precious little time to figure it out."

The old man nodded, settling back against the frame of his bed. "I see."

"Yeah, you see, so will you help me out or not?"

The man lifted his brows. "That depends. Sounds to me like a personal issue. I am a private entrepreneur gathering information for the U.S. government, son. Personal issues don't concern me in the least. You told me once before that it involves your family. Am I right?"

Crandall felt his blood pressure rising. He considered attacking the man, ripping his self-righteous eyeballs right from his skull, but he abstained. "Yes."

Ben shrugged. "I dunno. Dollars to beans says it could be risky, Crandall. The information I hold is confidential. I'm sure you've heard that term a million times over the course of your life, but this is probably the first time that it actually applies. Do you understand me?"

"I understand the notion of confidentiality. I'm prepared to take the risk."

"Of course you are. The question begging an answer is whether or not I am prepared to take that risk. The knowledge I hold is more important to your government than the life of your daughter. Can you appreciate that?"

"To me," Crandall answered carefully. "Nothing is more important than the safety of my daughter. However, I respect and appreciate where you're coming from, Spoon. I understand the risks. Please note that I will only use it to protect an innocent girl."

Ben stared forward, his eyes dull, his lips curved downward. Then, unexpectedly, he grinned, his face cracking. "You realize if I had never met the tike I probably would have told you to go to Hell."

But?

"But since I know the darling, I cannot make myself believe that an old, dying man such as myself has more worth to this planet than the life not yet lived by your little Angela."

Crandall smiled. "Thank you." Jesus, it was hard to get answers out of this man…

Ben shook his head. "Today's not right though. Today we are at risk. Come back tomorrow, alone, when visitation starts. Eight a.m. That's the best time. I'll be prepared. Meet me in the movie-room. The other wackos around here are either taking in their morning tea or still asleep at that time."

"Tomorrow's too late," Crandall pleaded. "She's in danger now."

"The child will live through the night if you're careful," Ben answered sternly. "Today is not right for such discussions. Have I made myself clear?"

Crandall considered and finally nodded. "Abundantly."

Ben looked over Crandall's shoulder and saw the nurse approaching, Angela's hand tucked within hers. "Dismissed."

Angela and the nurse were coming toward them, both faces beaming.

Crandall didn't await further instructions. He knew when a conversation was concluded, and while he felt he hadn't picked up much relevant information, there was a sense of hope within him. Crazy or not, old Benjamin Spoon had miles of experience, and he was well educated even if some of his marbles had broken loose. His theories, while somewhat preposterous, had a logical base.

He'd send Angela over to Stacie's tomorrow with explicit instructions not to leave the yard. That same message would be conveyed to Sharon. Under no circumstances should the girls leave her sight. He didn't like the idea of trusting someone else with his daughter's life, but considering the barrier he was about the cross, he had little choice.

"Come back and visit us," the nurse said politely. "You're always welcome here."

Angela waved goodbye, trails of chocolate drying on her lips.

Crandall nearly dragged his daughter through the door, past Mike and to the exit where the lazy afternoon greeted them.

CHAPTER 9

Crandall pressed his driver's license against the window, and the man leaned forward, squinting through his glasses as he adjusted them, his mouth hanging open slightly. "Says there, Crandall Cady. That right?"

Crandall rolled his eyes. "That's right, Mike. We've been over this what, a thousand times before?"

"Yeah, well, I remember the name, but if I ain't mistaken, you were here to visit Lucille Akers. She died, you know."

"Yes, I know. Visitation is this afternoon. Should I expect you there?"

Mike shook his head, rolling down is lower lip. "Nah. Doubt it. I gotta work and all. I just have one question, Mr. Cady."

"What's that?"

"Well, if Ms. Akers is no longer with us, then what's your business here at Clear Haven?"

"I would like to see Benjamin Spoon."

Mike adjusted his glasses again, chewing his gum. "You have no relational ties with Mr. Spoon, Mr. Cady. Why would you want to visit a non-relative?"

As if it was any of the man's business. "He's a friend," Crandall said politely, smiling as best he could despite his disdain for the man behind the window.

"Oh, I see. A friend and all. Well, I'm not sure we can let you in on the basis of friendship, but let me check with my supervisor."

"You do that."

Mike picked up his phone and dialed a three-digit number, all the while keeping his eyes trained on the man opposite him. "Yeah, it's Mike. I got a situation here with a man claiming to be a friend of Mr. Spoon. Last name's Cady, a former relation with patient Akers."

This guy was unreal. Absolutely unreal.

Mike eyed Crandall with suspicion while listening to the voice on the other end. "Uh huh. Sure." He nodded. "You got it." Hanging up the phone, he sat up, folding his hands. "You have permission to enter, Mr. Cady. Let's not make this a habit, shall we?"

Crandall leaned toward the glass, his patience worn down. "I think I'll visit again tonight, Mike. His voice was grainy and from the barrel of his chest. "Maybe twice again tomorrow, the next day and the next. I think I'll visit two times a day for the next six months just so I can specifically make a habit of it. How does that sit with you?"

Mike appeared awkward, suddenly intimidated, his eyes dancing one way or another, never really making eye-contact with Crandall. "Uh, you'll need to fill out a patient-visitor relations task sheet, Mr. Cady."

"I already did," Crandall responded. "Now open the fuckin' door."

The fat man adjusted his glasses, shut his mouth and punched the button, swallowing with fear.

The door opened and a smiling nurse greeted him, her skirt maybe shorter than it should have been. Crandall entered, and the nurse led the way to Ben's bedside where the old man was asleep, snoring loudly.

"Please don't wake the patient," the nurse whispered. "He sleeps little as it is. I imagine he'll awake soon."

Crandall took a seat next to the bed and nodded, wondering how 'soon' it would be until the man awoke.

The nurse walked away, her perfect hips playing with his mind, and Crandall realized suddenly that she was flirting with him intentionally.

Still snoring, Ben opened an eye.

Crandall frowned.

"She gone?" Ben asked.

Crandall nodded without looking obvious. *The sneaky sonuvabitch,* he thought, hiding his smile.

Ben sat up. "Told you, Cady. They're watching us at every second. Stick with me and you'll learn a thing or two."

"It was the only way I could get in."

"You don't think they'll find that suspicious? The fact that you're coming to see me? A known spy? Get your act together, idiot, or they'll be fishing you out of a river."

Crandall countered, insulted. "Somehow I doubt Mike has it in him to think farther than his next meal."

"Maybe that's what he wants you to think." Ben shook his head. "Doesn't matter. Regardless, I told you to meet me at the movie-room, and here you are at my bedside."

"The nurse brought me to you. You should have already been in the movie-room. This is not my fault."

Ben eyed him for a moment then shrugged. "Right you are. Let's get on with it then." Shakily, the old man lifted himself from the bed and hobbled across the room to the door that was locked against his attempts to get through. He pounded. "Hey!" Ben shouted. "Can't a guy get his cartoons anymore?"

A nurse rushed in and, with a key, unlocked the door. "Sorry, Mr. Spoon. It's early yet."

"A feeble excuse from a feebly minded imbecile."

"Yes, sir."

"Now leave me alone."

"Yes, sir."

Ben motioned for Crandall to follow him in. The large screen at the back wall immediately illuminated and the cartoons began. "You gotta talk insane for 'em to believe you're insane, Crandall. Remember that when you get to be my age. As soon as your hair turns white or falls out, have yourself committed. Other than the goddamn roaches-" Ben smacked one flat with his slipper before replacing it on his foot. "You get three squares a day, clean sheets, all the television you want and enough young nurses to keep your hand busy at night—all expenses paid, mind you, by the state, your siblings or some other faction. Not one dime comes out of your own pocket. Free advice on free-livin'. Now, let's get down to business."

The two sat down four rows from the front. They were neither at the front nor at the rear, and they must have appeared as father and son spending an early morning together.

Ben turned to Crandall. "They're watching us, you know, but they can't hear, and as far as I know they can't read lips, but just to be sure, try and guise yourself."

Crandall nodded.

Ben grinned. "So you want to know all about time travel, is it? The incredible semantics surrounding such a theory have been spinning like a top for centuries, my friend, yet here you are, coming to an old man locked up in a retirement joint for all the answers you don't want to hear."

Crandall nodded. "I do want to hear them. Make me believe it's possible, Ben, or convince me isn't because I'm at wits end, yet I got this puzzle in front of me that goes against logic. Make me understand."

"I worked for TEA for five years," Ben said, nudging his friend. "Thanks for coming by, by the way. I always enjoy your company, Cady."

"Tea? Tea's a drink."

"TEA is a acronym for Time Enforcement Agency, Crandall. Pay attention. The name is easily disguised in memos, letters and telephone conversations. We talk about TEA, and naïve individuals such as yourself go on your blissful way thinking we're yuppy bastards riding in off the back nine."

Crandall couldn't argue. "Tea. Creative. I thought you said you were a spy."

"I'm a freelance worker, and I'm repeating myself again. Check out the budget, genius. The president is cutting taxes like a haircut. School funds slashed, road repairs a thing of the past, public health care a cartoon dream out of a Disney film. The economy is down, so my employers are becoming nasty little penny-pinchers. It's only natural that the heavily funded programs are becoming smaller. Therefore, a man finds that he has more opportunities available, but on a lower contract. He might be a spy this month, and an operative of the CIA next month and a member of TEA in the month of October. In all reality," Ben continued, shrugging. "He might be all three at the same time. A forty-hour workweek becomes fifty, tasks divided, family life a 'so-sad, thank me when you're retired and we cut you a decent pension like a game of Monopoly'. You might own Indiana Avenue when you're working, but you land on Boardwalk right before you pass Go. Course, you're likely to die before you retire, but that's the wager we play. Life's a game of poker anyhow."

"We're getting nowhere with this conversation. What does this have to do with my problem? Does such an agency really exist?"

"Officially no. Why would such a useless agency exist? Do you think the public would put up with the knowledge that they're paying taxes for an agency that has no basis for existence?" Ben shook his head. "You're a fool, Crandall. We can't travel today, but we're seeing effects today as though it were possible tomorrow. Tomorrow, of course is a figure of speech meaning 'down-the-road'. Let me ask you a question." Ben shifted, eyeing his neighbor closely. "Have you researched this phenomenon at all?"

Crandall shrugged. "I checked out a couple of books." He shook his head. "What am I supposed to say, I'm an expert? Why do you think I'm here? I'm part of the generation brought up on Star Wars and Flux Capacitors. We accept time travel in the movies only. You can make a time-machine out of good script and better actors."

Ben shook his head. "I guess we should start from the beginning then."

"I don't need to know how it works, old man. I need to know that it can be done and who it can be done by. If it's possible then I have the right to defend my daughter by breaking the constraints of time. If it isn't possible then there's nothing I can do, and my finding is a forgery, though I can't, for the life of me, imagine a mind this devious and attentive to detail. That's why I am here."

"That's precisely why you need to know how it works, Cady. How else can you accuse your finding as a forgery? Details are your only arsenal."

"Fine, then let's get on with it. Convince me that this disk traveled through time and wound up on the road in my path right where I would find it. Convince me that it wasn't coincidence or an elaborate hoax. Convince me I'm not going insane because I sure as hell feel like admitting myself here. The idea of a straight-jacket to prevent myself from cutting my own throat sounds awfully appealing. Three squares a day, clean sheets and good-looking nurses sounds like the way to go." He sighed. "I'm tired, Ben. I need answers."

The old mans gleamed under the light, flickering as the screen changed, the poor coyote falling off a ridge and hitting the ground hard, a plum of smoke following in his wake. "Take off your judgmental glasses, Cady. You must discard everything you've been taught to understand what I am about to tell you."

Crandall nodded.

"No. That's not good enough. You must make yourself believe, not just me. Understand?"

Crandall nodded. "I'm trying, Ben. On the life of my daughter, I swear to God I'm trying."

Ben raised his brows. "That'll do. Well then." He looked up at the clock. "We've got probably an hour before the next patient walks through those doors behind us. Let's use these few minutes to our advantage."

"Make me believe," Crandall pleaded. "I've got nowhere else to turn."

Ben smiled, nodded, his eyes crystal clear. "Science-fiction novels and big-budget scripts would have you believe that a machine made out of a car or trinkets and computers would make time travel possible, but I'm sorry to say that it just ain't so. No, sir. Dollars to beans says that in order to break through the time barrier, you must be able to move faster than light. Imagine, Crandall. Imagine a room as long as a football field, me on one end, you by my side and a light switch by my hand. At the other end, one-hundred yards away, there is a light connected to the switch in my fingers. Tell me, when I say 'go' and throw the switch, how do you get to that light before it illuminates?"

Crandall shrugged. "I don't know."

Ben smiled softly. "But if you did, you could travel through time."

CHAPTER 10

"This is going to take forever, isn't it?" Crandall asked, checking his watch. He rubbed his temples lightly. The headache was there all right, right beside its best friend 'anxiety'. Now that he had asked Ben for his help, he was beginning to regret it. The old man has lost half his marbles, which explained why he needed to be cared for by the state. Anything he had to offer would be suspect simply given the source.

"No one said this stuff is easy," Ben answered. "It might help me to help you if you'd share what's got you all out of rhythm."

Crandall looked up, his eyes red. "It wouldn't make any sense. Sounds ludicrous enough to me when I think of it."

Ben sat back, sighing and yawning at the same time. "Look around, Crandall. Whatever you've got for me is tame by comparison."

The man had a point.

"All right, let's forget about the details. Give me the general premise. If there's a logical explanation around this mess then we'll forget the sermon."

Crandall worked the scenario over and over in his mind. Was it safe to talk about it? In reality, there had been no instructions following his finding of the disk. It wasn't like it was holding him ransom. He'd already tried to go to the police, but they hadn't offered him help. Would it really matter if he told some old conspiracy theorist locked up in a 'retirement community'?

"Get it off your chest, son," Ben said softly. "I can see it weighin' you down."

"The disk I told you about," Crandall blurted with frustration. Calming himself, he shook his head. "It has images on it that I can't explain."

The old man snickered. "Excellent description, Cady. So what are we talking here, CGI graphics? Falsified images? I mean-"

"I told you already," Crandall whispered, "They're images of me."

Ben frowned.

"Before they happen. Images of my new dog before I even adopted him. Images of my daughter and I mourning the loss of Emily before she died." Crandall drew a deep breath. "Images leading up to some kind of murder. The funny thing is I found it on the road with a hundred people and cars around me. How could it be a coincidence?"

Ben shrugged. "Ironically, it probably was a coincidence that you came to find it when you did. Through the course of my work I've discovered that most accidents become coincidences."

"Accidents." Crandall grinned. "If it was an accident that I found it, then it wasn't a coincidence."

Ben shook his head. "You're not looking at this two-dimensionally, Cady. It was a coincidence for you, but it was an accident from the standpoint of whomever it is that's watching you."

Crandall looked either way, but the room remained empty. He suddenly felt nervous and uncomfortable. "Watching?"

"Why else would there be a disk covering the particulars of your life? Haven't you listened to a single word I've said? You always have to be on your toes because chances are you're being watched. When you sleep, when you eat and when you shit, you're being watched. You live on the outer perimeter of a very progressive city, Crandall. This city is going to succeed, and everyone wants to know why."

Crandall grinned, trying to hold it back. "I can't imagine we're all being watched, Ben. There's too many of us. And why me? What makes me so special? I'm a nobody and never has been."

"Specifically, that's probably why you were picked. Now, I have a question for you?"

Crandall nodded.

"You still insist it's genuine?"

"So far as I can tell. I mean, the images on the disk are so specific. Things I said on the disk I caught myself saying as the scene occurred. Crazy stuff, but I'm always one step behind whoever it is. I never see them."

Ben frowned. Deeply. "It seems you're a target, Crandall. There are organizations that run organizations that run organizations, and with technology the way it is today, there doesn't even have to be a man behind the camera. Have you checked your house, car even yard?"

Crandall nodded his head. "Yes, but I also assumed there would be someone..."

"Jesus Crandall, you have to be smarter than them to get ahead of the curve, do you understand me? You cannot assume anything because once you have, you've selectively eliminated every other possibility."

Crandall felt stupid. Even in the midst of a crazy old man, he felt like an amateur. Of course Ben was right, but all he could do was nod.

"Remember who your opponent is."

"I have no idea," Crandall whined, overwhelmed.

"Those details at this point aren't necessary," old Ben said with sympathy, lightly patting his friend on the arm. "Their advantage is that they have many. Combined, they have greater intelligence. They have a head start and a motive. Most importantly, they know people in high places and they have more money than you."

"Sounds like my odds with the lottery."

"Slightly less, I must confess. However, you do have an advantage on them."

"Can't wait to hear this."

"You know about them. They're on skates now, slipping on banana peels as they have to conjure contingency plans should you suspect one of them."

"How do you know there are more than one?"

"There always is," Ben said grinning. "I was skeptical once, just like you, but I remember back in the day, when I first got on their case. I was a lad, like you, maybe a few years younger, and I uncovered a conspiracy that would make you duty in your pants. It involved an insurance agency. They'll go nameless to protect the injured at this point, but a reputable industry giant was working directly with a major car manufacturer to install defects in the new cars rolling off the lots. The deal was worth billions as the manufacturers reputation was on the line, but the results pinched the insurance agency's competition as enough claims were made to jack their rates. In the end, the car manufacturer was able to blame imported parts for a recall. Both came out clean like a mouse."

Crandall regretted ever visiting the old man. "I was an insurance agent, Ben. This idea is ludicrous. I don't remember ever hearing anything about it."

"And I'm sure, of course, that you've investigated every recall in the past thirty years with the same impunity that I have."

Crandall turned on the old man. "No. I didn't. I don't have to. It's a conspiracy, Ben. Who were you working for at the time, huh? Who signed your W-2?"

"I conducted private research, Crandall. My employer is confidential."

Crandall shook his head. "I'm sure he is." He felt so stupid for being there. "I need to hit the road Ben. You know, people in high places to visit and all. I'd hate to monopolize any more of your important time."

Ben gripped Crandall as he stood. "If you want to label me a crazy old man, then by all means do so. Tell everyone you know. It keeps me safe. After all, nobody's concerned about the lunatics locked away. It's those with the knowledge and enough sarcasm to fight the system that pose a real threat."

Crandall yanked his arm free and made for the door.

"Science is knowledge learned through careful observation and the testing of the derived deductions and conditions through experimentation of calculated methods. You go ahead and justify to yourself every image on this disk of yours, Cady, when you know deep in your heart that there was no way in hell it could have wound up on that street without some kind of scientific explanation. It was perhaps a coincidence that you found it, but it was also an accident on the behalf of whomever left it." The old man's eyes were strong. "You are not prepared to deal with what you'll find, and it will consume you."

"You can't explain its existence any more than I can, Ben. Time travel isn't possible. You said so yourself. We can't do it today, and I seriously doubt if we'd be capable of it by the end of this month. That's when the images stop."

"On the sixth day, God created man," Ben countered. "A lot can be done in a small amount of time."

Crandall stalled, meeting the white-haired man's stare from across the room. Shifting, his shoulders sagged. A war with Ben wasn't what he wanted. Truthfully, he didn't know what he wanted aside from a release from the tension bearing down on his mind and soul. "Can you explain it?" he asked softly.

Ben shook his head. "I'm in here, and all your answers are out there."

Crandall turned to leave. "I'll come back…someday."

"I know you, Crandall Cady. I know exactly what you're going to do out there."

Crandall's hand rested on the knob, but he didn't turn it.

"You're going to hug your daughter, tell her things are okay and decide that your fate is in your hands. By this evening you will have successfully convinced yourself that the disk is forgery right up until the next scene comes true, and it'll start all over again. The anxiety, the stomach aches, the headaches—and you'll be back picking up right where we left off. The only difference is, a day or two will have been wasted, and by then it might be too late."

Crandall looked back to see Ben struggling to hold himself up, his old knees quivering as he stood proud.

"I can give you the basics, Cady. I can make you believe it's possible, but I can't explain why you have what you do. It's not within my capacity."

Crandall leaned against the door, his mind telling him to leave, to go check on Angela and make sure everything was right. He didn't have to know science to protect her. He just had to keep her out of harms way. But he didn't leave. "You've got my attention for as long as you can hold it," he said, his voice cool.

Ben nodded, motioned for permission to sit, and did so, his face instantly relaxing. Closing his eyes, he licked his chapped lips and leaned his head back. Drawing a breath, he smiled. It was a small smile; the kind mixed with hesitation yet confidence. "It starts with speed, my friend."

"Speaking of winding up right back where I started," came the sarcastic reply. "You said this a half-hour ago, Ben."

Opening his eyes, Ben chuckled as he looked at Crandall. "See? You've already traveled though time, yet you traveled at a rate of sixty seconds in a minute and thirty minutes in a half-hour. You're a time-traveler and you don't even appreciate it."

Crandall frowned. He had never thought about it that way, but the rate Ben spoke of made sense, no matter how elementary the math seemed. He countered. "We're all traveling at the same rate though."

Ben nodded. "Good observation. This means you understand what I've told you. Happily I can report that time-travel is not much more difficult in principle than the simple equation you just worked out in your mind as I relayed it to you. You need two elements to build your space vessel: speed and gravity. If you can control both, you've got your time machine."

"I don't understand."

"Of course not. This is because you cannot control either any more than I. Nor do you understand either. They're words to you. If I say 'faster than the speed of light', what's the first thing that comes to your mind?"

Crandall shrugged. "Superman."

Ben laughed. "What else?"

"I don't know. Okay, the stars. In school I learned that a star could have burned out hundreds of years ago by the time its light reaches earth. I would say that 'faster than the speed of light' is pretty damn fast."

"Put one hand on that doorknob behind you and the other on the light-switch beside it."

Crandall did.

Ben smiled. "Now, I want you to turn off the light, but before the room gets dark, I want you sitting beside me." He patted the chair lightly.

Crandall grinned with sarcasm. "That's ridiculous. I already told you that I can't."

"Ridiculous?" The old man lifted his brows. "But if you could get from point A to point B before the room darkened, wouldn't you say you arrived at point B by cheating time? You would have traveled at a rate of more than 300,000 kilometers per second, and your aging process would have considerably slowed. Expand our example to, for instance, crossing the country. You could be from New York to San Francisco before the flash of the starting-gun's muzzle was visible to the naked eye. As the 747 flies, you just cheated time out of approximately five hours. You would arrive in the golden state five hours younger than your competition. Now compare our example to, for example, crossing the galaxy. Suddenly, it becomes clearer why science-fiction movies use light speed with their fancy ergonomic spaceships. If Hans Solo had to fly across the galaxy in our NASA space shuttle, he'd be an old man before he arrived. Take a step back and watch Mr. Solo go at light-speed. In reality, when he arrives at the other end of the galaxy, everyone back home would have aged a hundred years. That's very inconvenient for the movies, so they bend the rules just a tad."

Crandall considered the argument. Having never looked at things that way, the old man's crazy thoughts suddenly didn't seem so crazy. He couldn't help but smile. "I guess that makes sense."

"Of course, in your case," old Ben went on. "You have no interest in seeing the other side of the galaxy. You'd want to remain stationary as you travel through time, am I right?"

Crandall nodded. "Makes it a bit more complex, doesn't it?"

"Not really. I mentioned two factors required to build your vessel. You've got speed. Now you need gravity."

"We have gravity on Earth," came the shrugging reply. "There's your mix."

Ben smiled. "Let me explain gravity, my naïve friend. NASA needs to travel at a velocity of 11 kilometers per second to escape the Earth's gravitational pull. Anything slower and she'd slow and eventually fall back to the ocean. We call this Earth's escape velocity. The EV varies depending on the mass and size of the object you're trying to escape from. Jupiter, as an example, requires an escape velocity of over 60 kilometers per second. In mathematical terms, Earth is object E, and the escape velocity is measured by taking 1 over the square of the distance from the center of E, and directly proportional to the amount of matter inside E. The larger and heavier E becomes, so rises the EV."

Crandall frowned. "This doesn't tell me much about time travel, Ben."

"Imagine another object that is so large that the escape velocity is actually faster than the speed of light. These objects could not be viewed because they'd be invisible simply because light could not catch them."

"I don't-"

"A dark star, Crandall, or more commonly known as a black hole. It is said that nothing can escape them. Again, this is convenient for movie-studious, but this time it's not some science-fiction phenomenon; it means that the gravitational pull within its core is so strong that not even light can escape. Hence, a *black* hole."

Crandall hadn't thought of that either. Ben was right. This wasn't terribly complex. "So what's the problem? Why aren't we building time-machines and cruising the universe?"

Spoon grinned. "We can't travel faster than light. Nothing can. At least to our knowledge that is. Nor can we duplicate the mass required to generate an escape velocity of a dark star."

"Then how do we go about publishing facts about things we cannot prove?" Crandall was skeptical. It wasn't his fault, just a part of his nature.

"Because we've come close, Cady. If we can't move faster than light, then by God, we'll learn how to manipulate it, and I'm not talking about light switches and energy fields. I'm saying that we already know how to bend light."

"Bend?"

"Bend it like a curve."

"How?"

The old man sat back, his eyes going to the clock on the wall. "Time is short, my friend. Choose your questions carefully. You won't get everything today."

"How?" Crandall repeated. If they were close…

Ben smiled. "Another quaint yet effective example. Imagine you were standing in a box and holding a flashlight, its beam traveling from where you held the light at one end of the box to the opposite wall. No imagine the box suddenly dropping straight down or propelling upward at a fast rate."

"How fast?"

A shrug. "Doesn't really matter. We'll say at Earth's EV. Think carefully now, Crandall, but what happens to the light? Will it break? I mean, will you literally see the light break as it travels across the box?"

"No. Light is traveling faster than the box."

"So, the beam remains straight, and assuming you never move the flashlight, the beam will remain focused on the same spot of the opposite wall, correct?"

"According to what you've said? Yes."

"Good. However, there's a flaw. An instance in time has passed from the moment the box began to accelerate and the beam left the bulb of the light to when it collides with the opposite wall. Let's assume the box has dropped five feet. The beam has not moved from the opposing wall. How can this be? From the moment the beam left the bulb until the moment it collided with the opposite wall, the light has not shifted, yet the falling box has moved five feet further from its origin. Light has been bent, and we've just manipulated it."

"That's pretty simplistic, Ben. How can this be applied?"

"We bent the light by using gravity."

Crandall shifted from where he stood with unease. He felt the tiny hairs on his neck giving him away. This was an awful lot of information the average citizen did not know.

"It's not new technology, Mr. Cady. Newton made this discovery hundreds of years ago. The corpuscular theory suggests light is bent by the Sun. Given our sun's mass and gravitational pull, this theory is not impossible. Rather it is endorsed. Now throw a dark star into the mix and see how far you can bend light."

"Jesus..." He'd had no idea.

"That's the problem," Ben said. "Science doesn't leave much room for religion. One cancels out the other."

Crandall frowned. "Don't two negatives make a positive?"

Ben smiled. "Yes, they most certainly do. I like the way you're thinking, Crandall. One can co-exist with the other if you're careful."

Crandall's head was hurting again. He'd kill for a Tylenol at this point, but he didn't want to leave.

"We have precious little time," Ben continued, eying the clock. "We won't be able to finish this discussion today."

"No one's going to care," Crandall argued. "We could-"

Ben leapt from his seat and rushed through the row of chairs, his eyes wide. "Don't you second-guess me, boy! I know more than you do, is that clear!?"

Crandall nodded, the stale breath of the old man in his nose, and he cringed, turning slightly away.

"The first hand that knocks on that door behind you seals the fate of this conversation, and it will happen because I will make it so. I'm not risking my life for yours or your family!"

Crandall felt intimidation, and it wasn't welcomed. The old man in his face was scared, actually scared about the consequences of saying too much. Conspiracy theorist or not, this was genuine fear showing itself as sweat on Ben's brow and within his fiery eyes. He nodded, showing his humility through submission.

Ben stood up, his eyes peering through the windows with hesitation. "You don't see it yet, do you, Mr. Cady?"

"See what?"

"The bigger picture. The possibilities. We've already learned how to split an atom, but if we could figure a way to squeeze atoms together so tightly that their nuclei collided, it would be possible to make a dark star without using much more mass than there is in the Sun."

"More mass than the sun? Your time vessel has to have more mass than our sun?"

Ben shrugged. "We have to create a black hole to make it work, Crandall. You can't build one in your garage, I'm afraid. Again, we digress. Think about what I'm saying about the dark star. This is what you wanted to know. Outside the hole, time progresses as usual, but at its core you're free to move about time as you see fit. Your singularity is now like a remote control at your fingertips. You've got play, rewind and pause right there waiting to be used."

"Singularity?"

"A singularity in time is a point in space-time that has infinite density and control. This is where the laws of physics, your mathematical principles provable on paper, no longer apply. A region of mass with an escape velocity greater than the speed of light has a singularity."

"You mentioned reverse, play and pause. Where's the fast-forward button?"

"Traveling into the future is impossible. If you travel faster than light for a year, you can then stop and wait for time to catch up to you, but haven't actually traveled into the future. You've only traveling faster than sixty seconds in a minute and sixty minutes in an hour. In theory, you can't actually travel back in time either. Well, not faster than your vessel anyway. It's impossible to travel to a point in space-time that exists prior to the existence of your time-vessel."

"Why?"

"Because that vessel would no longer exist to travel through time. You've preceded its technology, dumb-ass."

Crandall shook his head. "The disk, Ben. I've already got the disk, but you're telling me that all we need is gravity and speed, yet we possess neither the wisdom nor the workshop to accomplish it."

Ben frowned. "That's true. My God…"

There was a knock on the door, and an old man with wide eyes peered through the glass, turning the knob and pressing to get in.

"This conversation is over," Ben whispered, glaring up at the intruder.

"No it isn't," Crandall returned, standing tall, and blocking the window in. "I need to know."

"Need?" Ben smiled. "Need is the child of greed, Mr. Cady. Greed is come by through carelessness and laziness. You have more to worry about today than inconsequential details. If you want the rest, then you must learn patience. This conversation has concluded."

Crandall knew the old man's temper, and further argument was over. He reached over his head from where he sat upon the floor and twisted the knob, the door opening inward, the staggering old man from the other side wandering in, slapping his toothless gums together.

"Mornin', Spoon," the old man mumbled, ignoring Crandall as he wandered to the front row where he could squint at the screen. "Thought I was gonna miss the Flintstones."

Crandall stood, and without turning back, he walked out, heading for the exit, ready to go home, his mind overrun with questions he wished Ben would have answered. Answers that needed come eventually.

He passed rows of beds, people lying on top, awake and counting their seconds or snoring, wasting their seconds. Life, it seemed, was at a stand still, time, as it happened, passing them by.

He felt sick as he pushed his way past the nurse and out into the waiting room where Mike only laughed, scratching his groin, something wet running from the corner of his lip.

Crandall burst into the new day, fog drifting over the parking lot, the air thick with moisture, the sun a faint, fuzzy yellow ball far away and unable to burn the heavy humidity away.

I'm going home, he thought. Home was where things made sense. Home was where he felt in control of himself. Home was where Angela would be. He could take her to the park, maybe for a picnic lunch. Afterwards, they might go to the movies—whatever she'd like to see.

His Jeep took him home, the trees whipping by overhead, the sky slowly clearing, early morning giving way to the late-risers, slowly emerging from their homes to collect their newspapers.

He pulled into the garage, the door sinking behind him, daylight becoming cut off, and he sat, hunched over his steering wheel, his heart pounding against his chest, his mind whirling, swirling away.

Climbing from the vehicle, he heard the telephone calling to him from through the steel door. Cursing, he fished the correct key from the ring, missed the slot and found it, turning the knob, pushing against the steel barrier, the air-conditioned atmosphere reaching him as he raced across the tiled floor to the phone where he scooped the headset, pressing 'send' and raising it to his ear. "Hello?"

Pause.

"Hello?"

"Mr. Cady?"

"Yes?"

"Good afternoon, Mr. Cady. I'm calling on the behalf of Sprint long-distance. How are you today?"

"Fine."

"We'd like to make your long-distance plan more affordable and convenient. How does that sound to—"

Crandall hung up, replacing the receiver, his face dull.

Gravity, speed, mathematics, equations, possibilities. Too much.

He overloaded, the nearly empty bottle of Jack Daniels in his hand as he slumped in the corner waiting for his daughter to return home. He already had it in his mind that Angela was dead by the time he passed out.

* * * *

It was time.

He dropped Angela off at Stacie's with strict instructions not to leave the yard.

"I'm not a dog, Dad," the girl whined, but Crandall had not backed down. "You'll do as I say or you'll go straight home to your room. Do you understand me, young lady?"

Sluggishly, she had nodded. "Fine."

"We can play on the computer," Stacie piped in, encouraging her friend. She looked up at Crandall. "It's cool, Mr. C. We got enough to do inside."

He nodded, for some reason trusting the girl.

16 August, 14:26:31.

Crandall drove away, pressing his Jeep for speed. He needed to get there early. The pedestrians whipped past, a blur at each side, the cars around him obstacles he dodged as though he were playing a video game.

He ran the red light, horns about him blaring.

The parking lot was nearly crowded as he squeezed into a somewhat-open slot, the cars to either side pinching his space, crowding him.

Locking the door, he hit the asphalt path running, racing past the trees, picnic tables and people, down the hill and up the next, pressing himself against the brick wall of the restrooms. Lifting his watch, he read the time.

14:33:52.

He was still early. Slowly rounding the corner, he became inconspicuous, walking slowly and blending with the people, making sure to stay toward the back and out of line.

The disk had read 14:35:21. The scene had been in the park, him mumbling to himself, unaware of the camera, somewhere on the walk. But this time he was one step, nearly two minutes ahead, and he was wandering along the edge of grass, beside the trees, hunkering down and waiting for the precise moment he was to be filmed. The disk was in his pocket, just so he could be sure its contents could not be swapped.

"Time travel, my ass," he murmured, people crossing before him this way and that. His eyes scanned the trees, bushes, parked cars—even trashcans for an open eye that might be recording, but he saw nothing. Remembering the angle, he knew the shot had been from his left side, straight on, following him as he went.

The camera was close.

Crandall ducked down behind the thick trunk of a tree, his eyes peering around its rim, careful to notice. People were laughing, skipping, talking, walking along and about, the daily exercise of life going on around him. He cast a quick glance at his watch.

14:35:11.

Returning his attention to the main foray, he scanned each face, each set of eyes, each laugh and smile, each mouthful of chewed picnic food, each wag of the chained dog's tails. He watched the trash bouncing across the grass under the pleasant breeze, the American flag at the backdrop loosely waving. Mothers were scolding their children or handing them another plate and shooing them off. Fathers were trying to get back to their games of crochet, their sons anxiously following at their heels, balloons of all colors bouncing back and forth, begging for release.

He cursed as he looked, anxiously scanning one face after another, searching for something out of the order. Dogs yipped with happiness, children laughing and bouncing, mothers saying 'no' and trying to wipe their faces, the common atmosphere a happy one.

And then he saw it.

His vision stopped, trained and locking on the face that didn't seem right. A man dressed in black, eyes hidden behind shades staring directly back, a camcorder in his right hand, its eye peering through the racing bodies. His face was solemn and slim, humorless to say the least.

He knows I'm here, Crandall thought, the eye of the camera pointed directly at him. His mind went to the disk in his pocket, its contents changing as the seconds traveled by.

Lifting his wrist, Crandall observed the time. 14:35:21. It was happening right now. He looked back at the man in black, his own eyes anything but amused. *Gotcha...*

The man in black lowered the camera, stepping backward, trying to blend, looking either way for an escape.

Crandall stood up, stepping forward, fully revealing himself and suddenly unafraid. This man was responsible for his fear. This man was responsible for the threat placed upon his family. As a father, his instincts led him to fight.

A teenager got in his way, but Crandall shoved him aside, the off-guard boy sprawling to the ground and rolling. Crandall never allowed his eyes to drift, the man directly opposed to him backing off, his white face clenched, his eyes hidden behind the dark sunglasses.

"What's yer problem, man?" the boy was yelling as he scrambled to his feet, desperate to save face.

Crandall moved forward, pushing past a woman, causing her to drop her hotdog, the pitiful rubbery thing bouncing on the steaming walk.

"Asshole!" she shouted, looking at her lunch, back at Crandall, back at the wasted food and shaking her hands with frustration. She didn't know how to react.

The man in black backed up faster, hastily looking over his shoulder before turning away and beginning to jog.

Crandall broke through the crowd, spilling two old men, pumping his arms, his pent up frustration carrying him across the baseball field toward the man in black who raced away with speed feeding upon fear.

The man in black was better, faster and stronger. He leapt the ditch in a single, fluid stride, his legs carrying him across the four lanes and carefully between traffic to the school's parking lot on the other side.

Crandall did his best, dodging forward and back, cars screeching to a halt, horns blaring around him. He jumped atop a hood of a slowing Buick, nearly loosing his balance, before jumping off the other side, his momentum slowed but not stopped. Darting forward, he waved off the next offender that screeched to a halt, its passengers whipping back and forth.

Crandall made it to the school parking lot where the man in black was climbing behind the wheel of his Explorer, the engine revving, the tires whirling as they searched for traction they eventually found. The green vehicle raced past Crandall, spinning into traffic, horns again blaring, the Explorer righting itself and racing away leaving a gasping Crandall Cady leaning on his knees, panting for air, his eyes trying to focus, his heart pounding in his ears. For a second he could see the license plate, but he couldn't focus, couldn't read.

"Damn it," he whispered, his eyes slanted, his heart racing, the adrenalin pumping him.

Crandall turned away.

Chapter 11

"It was a green Ford Explorer," he insisted. "I'm telling you, this man has been stalking me for more than a week. He's been in my yard filming me and my daughter, following me. I feel like I'm in prison."

The man smiled softly, quietly folding his hands as he leaned forward on his desk. "Mr. Cady. This is the second report you've filed in a week. Now, while I recognize your concern, you must understand that your fears are unsubstantiated and somewhat unfounded. We've checked your perimeter, secured the neighborhood, done what we need to do to ensure the safety of you and your daughter, but we have seen nothing that would lead us to the conclusion that you or yours are in any immediate danger. Now, I have a doctor that comes highly recommended that might—"

"I don't need doctor," Crandall grunted. "I need your help. Be proactive for once. For Chrissakes, do your job!"

The policeman frowned, his face graying. "Your tone isn't necessary, Mr. Cady."

"Fuck my tone!" Crandall barked. "I filed a report twelve days ago, and you haven't offered my any help"

The cop shrugged, sighing. "Unfortunately, there's nothing I can do for you. You have no solid evidence, and your hysteria seems delusional. I suggest that you check yourself into a hospital as you are, indeed, a very sick man."

Crandall turned away. To Hell with these suburban paper pushers. They were waiting for their stupid little pensions while polishing their worthless little badges. To protect and to serve, right. They were useless.

He stormed the office, slamming his way through the exit, the glass door banging precariously against the perpendicular wall. The situation was now in his hands, and whoever stepped his way was about to get mowed under. Crandall's eyes were fiery as he pounded a path back to his Jeep, slamming its door behind him, the cheery radio coming on and advertising the next best toothpaste as the engine churned to life.

The glove box dropped open, the lid bouncing as the chain caught, and his fingers were exploring for the orange bottle that he pulled out, yanked off the lid and drained the few tablets that remained into his mouth.

He backed up, screamed to a halt and punched forward, ignoring the stop sign and merging into traffic.

* * * *

"Because I said so!" he thundered back.

Angela slunk back, flinching at the rage her father cast her way. She had nothing to offer back except for fear. Her eyes welled, and she turned, fleeing down the hall to her room, the slamming door an indication that she was as upset as Crandall.

Crandall stood alone in the living room, the soft glow of the dining room chandelier casting his shadow, Buddy cowering at the corner, peeing on the carpet, his eyes sulking with fear. He stormed from the room, out the back door and into the back yard where the stars laughed down at him. The veins bulged along his shoulders and arms as he clenched his fear, his mind returning to the teachings of Ben Spoon. He though on how old the light reaching his eyes were and how some of those stars overhead were dead, years ago, their passing not yet tracked by time.

"I'm going to expose you," he whispered, quietly promising his aggressor. "I'm going to expose you, and then I'm going to kill you."

It was a promise he intended to keep no matter how long it took.

* * * *

She was sleeping quietly, and Crandall relaxed somewhat as he pulled the door closed, leaving it open only a crack, his eye still settling on his daughter under her covers across the room. The sheets rose softly with each breath, her face as innocent as an angel, her dreams something sweet.

Crandall walked away and down the hall to the living room where he sat down in the recliner, the television tuned to the news, images of murder and fire and rape and sickness and rebellion making up the headlines.

The microwave beeped behind him, and his cream of wheat was ready.

* * * *

He watched Angela carefully, the wind whipping at his hair, his shirt and shorts tugging at his thin body. Smiling, he watched as Angela jumped off the pier into the water, a white frost bursting around her wake.

Crandall looked each way, the people around him calm, moving about with no concern or any idea that things should be any way than what they were. They chatted, laughed, argued and moved around him the way living things do.

Angela surfaced and giggled, wiping the water out of her eyes, waving, and Crandall waved back.

This part wasn't on the disk. There was no scene where Angela was swimming and he was watching. This was brand new, playing itself out moment by moment the way it should. That alone helped him relax. He didn't have to be suspicious, not just now.

Angela was climbing the stepladder, and he smiled as he watched her go. This was one of the good moments, and lately there seemed to be so few.

The waves were high, breaking over the wall, spraying him, laughing happiness breaking on the pier, people ducking out from under the falling water. Angela jumped again, curling her knees up, assuming the cannonball style as she plunged into the water, Crandall looking each way. His tension ripped apart the youthful boys who had looked and smiled mischievously her way.

"Relax," one of the boys said as they passed. "I only fucked her with my eyes."

Crandall reached out, gripping the boy by the throat and drawing him in. "I'll fuck you with a tire iron, son." His eyes were red with rage, the veins standing out on his forehead and neck. "Sound like fun?"

The boy broke free, and he and his friends raced away, anxiously looking over their shoulders, Crandall glaring back.

Angela wrung out her hair, approaching her father, her eyes chasing after the boys. "Way to go, Dad. The blonde one was cute."

"He was too old for you."

She shrugged. "I like older boys."

Crandall turned back. "Don't you grow up on me too quick, sweetie."

Angie grinned and reached out her arms. "I'm all yours, Daddy."

Crandall returned the smile, but he recognized her tone. It was too late. His little girl was growing apart.

* * * *

He paced back and forth along the pier, his daughter jumping off, swimming back, climbing the ladder, plugging her nose and jumping again.

The waves crashed against the base, the spray dancing over the rim, beads of white water smacking the solid pier and splattering. Looking at his watch, Crandall was glad that his daughter was at least having fun, her laughter and giggles a sign of reassurance.

A sound off to his left, and Crandall jerked his attention to see a teenager hurtling himself off the opposite edge of the pier, his friends whooping and hollering. The boy broke the surface with a raised fist, growling and showing off to the girls who stood shivering at the pier's edge.

The waves intensified, the water breaking higher and higher, falling harder to the deck, smacking with a graceful sound, the plunge somehow serene. Clouds raced overhead, and the sun was doused, shadows falling over him and the water. In the far distance, he heard the sullen rumble of an approaching storm, a bead of lighting freezing the world at his hung suspended, striking the water miles off.

"C'mon, hon," he said, motioning Angie in while keeping his eyes locked on the approaching storm.

Christ, it was so familiar as he paced, his daughter complaining as she swam closer to the ladder.

He plunged his hands into his pockets, his lip curling, unwillingly realizing that he was challenging fate. "Let's go," he ordered as his daughter climbed the ladder and grabbed her towel. Crandall watched the swirling clouds, suddenly recognizing why he was so nervous.

It wasn't new. This scene, this storm, this day was already pre-recorded, and it was safely tucked in his pocket.

Whirling, he saw the man not fifty yards away, his camera pointed straight at him, a stupid grin on his face, his middle finger raised as if he was waiting to be caught, his eyes hidden behind the dark shades before he turned and darted down along the pier, the waves breaking over his head, his form quickly lost among the other onlookers.

"What's the matter, Dad?" Angela asked, her small face wrought with concern.

Crandall turned back, and he smiled. "Storm's coming, hon. We should get out of its way."

The little girl smiled. "Let's go home."

He could think of no other place he'd rather be, and he grinned, his eyes darting back and forth as he led his daughter back to dryer land and the Jeep where Angela helped him raise the top moments before the rain hit.

Inside the small cabin of the Jeep, everything was cozy and dry and happy so far as Angie was concerned as she peered through the window, the rain falling so hard and fast that the world beyond was out of her reach.

Crandall squinted forward, peering between the whipping wiper blades, struggling to see the road and the brake lights of the cars in front of him.

Concentrate, he cautiously told himself. One slip here or there and the prophecy would re-write itself with no regret, compassion or sadness.

He followed the pack and led his daughter home.

* * * *

Crandall knew the man in black was somewhere close, gripping his camera and watching, but he didn't care. This day was his daughter's, and he helped her mourn her grandmother's passing while his eyes lurked around.

He remembered the disk and the images, the gloomy feel of the funeral, his only face sallow, his daughter's even sadder.

The preacher was saying nice words, all of them candy-coated, some kind of inspiration to those around him as he made a cross through the air with is right hand, the Bible carefully tucked by his breast within his left.

Crandall held onto his daughter as she sniffled, her teddy tucked within her arms, tears raining down her cheeks. He glared at the minister and those around him, discrediting their words, realizing that death wasn't a passage to something brighter. Death was only a gateway to darkness.

He was one step ahead, and it was his aim to remain that way.

Barbara approached him, and he unwillingly flinched, knowing what was coming. She was crying, her makeup smeared like in a horror film, her lipstick smeared across her cheeks, her eyeliner jagged streaks rolling downward from her eyes. "I'm so sorry," she whispered, breaking and crying while Crandall stood firm.

Barbara was Emily's sister, and this was the second funeral they had attended together. One for her sister and his wife, the other for her mother and his mother-in-law. She was shivering, looking for someone to hold her and love her the way he had loved her sister.

Crandall didn't budge, his own frame rigid, his eyes dark coals that repelled his sadness. Angela remained safely under the protection of his arms, and he blocked every other emotion.

His eyes darted from one face to another, one gravestone to the next until he locked eyes with the man standing a hundred yards off, his camera raised directly at him. Crandall stared back, not making a move.

"I'm so sorry that things were so ugly for you," Barbara continued, her voice cracking.

Crandall nodded as the small casket was slowly lowered into the earth, the finality of death a reminder to his daughter that happy endings only occurred in Disney World.

"G'bye, Grandma," the little girl whispered even as the rain began to fall.

Perfect.

It should rain at funerals.

The priest was ducking for cover, those dressed in their best cowering beneath their umbrellas as they made for their cars, eager to get to the Carnival Hall where they'd toast the old bitch's death while consuming alcohol and gobbling up the fancy sandwiches and snacks. They'd celebrate death.

Eventually, even Crandall would join them.

"I wanna go home," Angie whispered.

"There's a potluck over at Uncle Owen's, hon. All your favorites. Ham sandwiches, black olives, tortillas. You name it."

"I wanna go home," she repeated. "I just want to cry for a little while. Death makes me sad."

She could have said anything else, and Crandall would have been prepared. He had a response for every comment a nine year-old girl might throw at him except that one.

"Okay, babe," he said back, hugging her tight, her little face buried against his stomach. "We'll go home." His mind worked quickly. What would make her happy? Relax? "What would you like for dinner?"

"My choice?" She brightened, just a little.

"Your choice."

"Pizza. Again. More pepperoni this time though." She lifted her face, her eyes bright. "And root beer."

Crandall nodded, smiling. "Extra, extra pepperoni this time."

The girl looked around herself, the graveyard now nearly bare, the tombstones dull under the bleak sky. She smiled.

"We'll make an evening of it," he continued, but he was mostly talking to himself. Reassuring himself. "Just you and me."

His daughter smiled, and he found himself relaxing, the ugliness around him fading if only slightly and if for only a little while. Crandall led her away from the dripping site of death, the dirt running as mud into the hole that would bury Lucille. They climbed into his Jeep as a dysfunctional family and drove away, not bothering to be a part of the old hag's celebration into death. Instead, they drove cautiously home where they dried off the wet puppy and brought him inside. Crandall ordered pizza, an extra-large with extra, extra pepperoni just like Angela had requested. From there, they barricaded themselves into the coziness of home, away from the ugliness around them, and enjoyed a simply night.

A perfect night.

The only shadow hanging at the back of Crandall's mind was the knowledge that it wouldn't last.

CHAPTER 12

Crandall stretched and rolled out of bed. Beyond his window, he heard the soft pattering of rain against the sill, and judging by the weak light trying to get in, it was going to be a gloomy day.

He buried his face in his hands, poorly trying to block the headache, the clock over his shoulder ticking one second after another away like an annoying peddler that just wouldn't give up. Lifting his head, his crusty eyes went to the digital clock on the nightstand that read sometime after seven a.m. He felt more exhausted than he could remember, but maybe it was because he had slept so long and so hard.

Showering, shaving and popping a few Desipramine, he felt somewhat respectable as he stumbled down the hall into the living room where he sluggishly cleaned up the smelly pizza box and paper plates on the coffee table, tossing them into the garbage can outside the back door and letting the dog out at the same time. Returning to the kitchen, he made himself a small breakfast consisting of stale raisin bran and a glass of orange juice.

Crandall's mind wasn't on the bland food. He was wondering if he should visit Ben again or if it was just a waste of time. The ramblings of the old man held little merit and didn't give him the information he needed. He didn't care about time travel or black holes or gravity. All he wanted to know was how the disk got to where it did and why he found it.

"Morning, Dad."

He looked up from the newspaper to see Angie wandering into the kitchen, her eyes half closed with fatigue, her hair a mess.

"Hey, sweetheart. How did you sleep?"

"Okay."

"Good." By the looks of her, she had slept as soundly as he had, something they both had needed.

Sleepy or not, she found her way around the kitchen, and made herself breakfast, slumping into the chair next to her father and digging in. "Anything good in the papers?"

He looked at her casually. It had always been her custom to ask about the news in the morning, but she hadn't said anything of late. Not since her mother…

Winking, he returned to the front page. "Well, looks like there's going to be a new theater going in over by Veteran's Park."

"What kinda theater? Movies or plays?"

"Movies. Fifteen screens. We won't have to travel very far to see a flick anymore."

"What else? What's that car crash all about?"

"Drunk driver hit a tree."

She looked at him with inquisitive eyes. "Did he die?"

"Would you like to read the article?"

Angie shook her head. "No. It's just that it seems that everyone dies."

The comment struck him funny, but he didn't have a comeback because she was right. The fact that she was only nine years old and already recognized the inevitable saddened him. He put down the paper and looked at his daughter, placing his hand over hers. "Dying is just a part of life, hon. But most people live to be so old that they just know it's their time and they're looking forward to their next step. I don't want you thinking that death is a bad thing, because it's just one more step in God's plan."

"Mom wasn't very old though."

Crandall nodded, hating himself for what he knew he was going to say. "But she knew it was her time, hon. She was very sick and couldn't be cured. She didn't want to feel sick anymore."

Angela nodded and returned to her breakfast. "What else is in the news?"

Crandall was so proud of her, loved her so much that he nearly cried, but instead, he turned the page and began to read aloud, his daughter, seated beside him, silently listening.

* * * *

He decided not to see Ben.

It would do him no good. All his visits with the old man accomplished were the raising of his anxiety and paranoia level. It was time to take care of his daughter and get on with his life. Nobody was going to tell him how to live, and by panicking over the contents of that damned disk, he was making every image on it come true. He was, in effect, playing right into the hands of those making a mockery of his life.

But not anymore.

He took Angela to the beach. Not the river and the small, dirty beach beside the bridge, but Lake Michigan and the dunes that made the mitten state so popular for summer tourism.

It was away from Peyton, away from the disk, and away from Emily's death. The day turned out well, the clouds and rain giving way to patchy clouds and blue skies. The breeze was soft and cool coming off the warm water, and the beaches were alive with life and happiness.

They made their spot in the soft sand, and Crandall settled down with a good book as his daughter played along the water's edge, careful not to go in very deep. The water wasn't exceptionally warm, but there was something else keeping her from going in any further than her waist though she didn't speak of it. It didn't matter. She seemed happy enough, and he felt relaxed to be around so many cheerful voices.

"Crandall?"

He looked up at the sound and saw a shadow hovering over him, silhouetted by the sun over its shoulder.

"Crandall Cady?"

He put on his sunglasses as she kneeled down. While the woman appeared familiar, he couldn't place the face.

"Mary Kellerman," she said with a grin. "Angela and my daughter, Becky, were in the same choir together.

Oh, right. Like he'd remember every parent's face. "That's right. How are you?" His eyes darted to his daughter where she was playing with who he guessed was Becky. The two of them were giggling.

"Good, good," Mary answered. "Look, I'm so terribly sorry about what happened with your wife. I read about it in the papers, and I would have sent a card, but I didn't know if it would be appropriate."

He waved her off. "Thank you for the thought. Angie and I are getting through it."

Mary smiled. "I didn't believe any of that rubbish about foul play. I know you were a good husband."

Crandall frowned. There had never been anything in the papers about foul play. "I appreciate your concern." His words were a bit stiff, but he didn't care. Mary's accusation had been offensive.

"I didn't upset you, did I?" she asked, taken aback. "Oh dear, I'm so sorry, Crandall. That was never my intention."

He offered a plastic smile. "I'm fine."

Angela came rushing over. "Dad, Becky brought a floating mattress. We're gonna blow it up so I can go out deeper. Is that okay with you?"

Crandall wasn't crazy about the idea, but he didn't want to tell her 'no'. "Only a few feet further out, Angie. The waves are getting pretty high."

Mary winked at him. "I've got eagle eyes, Crandall. They won't escape my sight."

He nodded and stood. "I need a walk. Mind watching Angela for a few minutes?"

"Not at all. We'll just set up right next to you." Mary was already unpacking her bag and spreading her towel, the girls unfolding the flat mattress.

Nodding, Crandall began to walk away, Mary watching after him closely as he retreated. Crandall stepped over sandcastles and in-between groups of people along the water's edge, the stink of sunscreen sizzling in the air around him, the chirp of seagulls overhead mixing with the chirp of laughter and talking. He made his way to the entrance of the pier and began to walk along its smooth surface, the water at the pier's sides growing deeper, and the amount of people drifting off.

A low rumble made him raise his head, and in the far distance he saw a black shadow on the horizon.

So much for the perfect day. The storms were coming back.

He continued on his path, wanting to reach the end before turning back, his mind alive with images. Ben, Emily, Lucille, the funerals…everything. He couldn't escape them. One foot over the next, he concentrated on his steps, and tried to focus on his new job that would start in only a couple weeks. What would he have to do to prepare? Maybe he should call the superintendent or the principal and get their advice

The wind was picking up, the dark clouds racing forward, coming closer like in a dream where his fastest sprint away would never be enough. He wouldn't force himself to turn away, and he continued on his path, passing people who were heading back inland, their manner calm, their conversations sometimes fixed on the approaching clouds.

Crandall aimed for the end of the pier, refusing to turn around until he reached it, the wind increasing with each step. He knew Angela would be getting worried and looking for him, but he found himself obligated to reach the pier's edge, reaching the end before starting over again.

The dark clouds were now nearly overhead, the sun continuing to shine behind him, the roll of thunder closer.

I've been here before, he though mildly. *I stood right here and looked on as the clouds rolled in. Just like this.*

The waves were rolling higher and higher, cresting before breaking as they moved inland toward shore, their strength shattering as they crashed against the pier, the spray rising higher and higher with each passing minute.

Crandall stood firm where he stood, his mind rolling through his memories, searching, seeking the moment when he had been here before, the atmosphere the same, the feeling the same, the emotions within him the same.

He'd been here before.

The waves broke against the side of the pier, white diamonds breaking into beads over his head and descending unto him, soaking his clothes.

All so familiar, so redundant. Crandall had been here before. He'd seen this moment in his life. He was on repeat. Whirling, his eyes interrogated the pier, scanning, seeking. He remembered the images on disk that spelled this all out before, his freewill stolen and predicted.

Thunder rolled overhead, the skies swarming. The lighthouse that stood tall above him sent its light across the lake, the light spinning slowly and piercing the falling mist that would quickly turn to rain.

The camera was around somewhere; he just needed to find it. Crandall stormed the pier, climbing the barred walls of the lighthouse, scanning the crevices, creases and cracks, scanning for his salvation.

He rounded the side of the lighthouse and stopped, his attention traveling the length of the pier, his eyes spying a man racing away, something heavy and clumsy in his hand. A camcorder.

Jesus, that was him…

Crandall broke into a sprint, his legs carrying him across the cracked and weathered concrete, his eyes blazing as a flash of lighting broke overhead, splitting the sky and separating one side of the world from the other.

The man in front of him was casting frightened glances over his shoulder, his own legs pumping for speed, the camera in his hands protected safely but slowing him down, one stride at a time. Crandall felt his defenses flare, his anger rising and mounting, building like jest, foaming at his mouth and spilling like spit. The game ended here, the video stopped now, the ending going blank. He was gaining, one enthusiastic stride after the next, his adrenalin driving him, sprinkles suddenly formulating under the weight of the heavy air, the people on the beaches—now growing closer—packing up their things or emerging from the water.

The man raced blindly, his arms pumping, plunging him off the pier and into the sand, into the waves of people, his unique color beginning to blend.

Crandall surged with speed, his face flaming, his eyes wild, his feet carrying him, nearly flying as he gave chase, his body leaping fluently from the deck to the sand where he sank and slowed. He spilled people in his wake, embittered cries of surprise and anger lashing out at him. He ignored his manners, bursting through the crowds, shoving children and women aside, something he'd never do consciously, but he wasn't conscious. He was salivating, his eyes red with rage and depression, his aggression winning him over, his veins pumping acid as he raced, the chase feeling good, the more pain, the better.

Sprinkles turned to rain, and the sand underfoot stopped spraying around him as it thickened like mud. People dodged this way and that, hands over heads as people shrieked and raced for their vehicles—never mind that they were at the beach to swim.

Crandall stopped, his heart threatening to burst, his tongue dry, his face beading with sweat, his lungs too small to accept the gulps of air he was trying to breathe. People everywhere. Kids, mothers, fathers, fat people, thin people, old people, teenagers, foreigners, locals, bathing suits, toys, screams, laughs, giggles and groans. The world was revolving, and Crandall spun, searching for the man with the camera who had been absorbed, his person lost.

"Damn." He continued to search, his brow wrinkling, his age showing. "Damn."

Rain became a downpour, thunder making the world shiver, lightning over the lake making it seem unreal.

Crandall retraced his steps, casting glances over his shoulder every few seconds, looking, searching for things out of place, but people were moving, walking—even running as they moved from the water's edge toward the parking lot, a chaotic scramble turning to a steady stream condensing to groups six deep.

Crandall moved quickly back toward his daughter who stood along at the edge of the water, shivering under the rain.

"Where'd Mary and Becky go?" he asked, reaching her side, pulling her in and wrapping his arms around her body.

"They left me," his little girl said. "They were afraid of the storm."

Thunder cracked overhead.

"C'mon," Crandall said, softly pulling his daughter from the water's edge. "We're going home."

Lightning hung in the sky, suspended like animation, its silent glow followed by a collapse of thunder that shuddered the earth.

"Where were you, Dad?"

"Never mind that now," he answered, dragging his daughter through the sand toward the paved walkway leading to the parking lot.

She was sluggish, or maybe her strides were just somewhat shorter than his. Either way, she struggled to keep up, Crandall's sweating face hidden by the rain that came down in torrents.

The parking lot was clearing out, the weakness of the visitors revealed as they sheltered themselves from the most natural of nature's wrath. Crandall unlocked his daughter's door, and she climbed in, closing herself away from the rain. He found his own lock and ducked into the Jeep, the rain falling on the canvas roof, the laughter insidious. He sat for a moment, catching his breath, water dripping from his face and blending with his soaked shirt before he turned the key and ignited the engine.

"What's the matter, Dad?" Angela asked.

"Nothing, hon," he answered. Had she seen? "Buckle up."

The thunder followed him as he pulled out of the parking lot, following the stream of ants escaping the park and turning for home.

He'd nearly caught the bastard this time. Whoever 'the bastard' was, and the game had nearly ended that quickly. They would have to be just as careful, and maybe that would provide him with his only advantage as they knew he was watching. They had nearly been unmasked, and by God, he was going to find them.

"Dad, you're acting weird."

He nodded, the drying rain slowly drooling along his cheeks. "Yeah," he responded, turning onto the main road, turning home. "I guess I am."

* * * *

He played his good graces and managed to smile as they ordered their dinner. He pushed his tray along the line, Angela in front of him, his own red tray inches from hers. She was smiling politely to the server who piled her tray high with what she ordered. A large burger and a healthy order of fatty fries were laid on her tray and she moved to the drink fountain, Crandall taking her place at the head of the line.

"Bargain Burger Deluxe and a Bargain Fry Guy?" the pimpled kid behind the counter chirped. He slopped the crumpled blobs on Crandall's tray and grinned confidently as he snapped his fingers, pointing at the mashed food. "You have a bargain of a day, mister." With a wink he turned away and went on to the next of the customers in line.

Crandall grabbed his tray and turned to the drink dispenser where he poured a root beer before following his daughter to an empty table by the window.

"Thanks, Dad," she said, curling up and digging into her fries.

He knew how much she loved the Bargain Burger Barn, and he was more than happy to not cook on such an ugly night.

The rain continued to attack Earth, nature foaming at the mouth, the intensity smacking the glass windows, the cars, buildings and people were scampering like rats.

"You're welcome, hon."

She smiled, her mouth full, cheeks bulging and eyes twinkling. So long as she was happy.

Crandall's eyes continued to scan the room. Someone was out there watching him, spying on him, recording him, and he was determined to find out who—no matter the cost.

He ate his own burger, the mayonnaise spilling out the edges of the soggy bun as he pinched it between his teeth, his eyes and ears alert.

"I think I'm gonna be a writer when I grow up," Angela said as she chewed, small bits of burger and bun falling from her lips. "I've decided."

Crandall watched the other patrons of the restaurant. "That so?"

"Mom always wanted to be a writer, but she never made it."

"Your mother was very gifted, Angie."

"That's not what I meant. I mean, Mom was good enough, but she didn't make it. I'm gonna be a writer, like her. Becky said her great grandfather was a writer and was rich. He wrote stories about the Civil War and stuff."

"Are you planning on writing stories about the Civil War?"

Angela shook her head. "No. Just stuff. Things I like to read about."

Crandall smiled. "I think you'll need to work on your grammar a bit."

"I know. I'm young yet. Gimme time."

Crandall smiled.

* * * *

"So how are we going to spend the rest of the afternoon?" she asked as she jumped onto the couch. "It's only five-thirty."

"I haven't got a clue," Crandall answered, slumping into the couch. "Is there anything you'd like to watch?"

Angela grabbed the remote and began to surf through the channels, all the while the volume slightly tainted by the sound of the falling rain outside the window. One commercial to the next, one program to the next. Angela would watch for a few seconds before switching the channel, the ever-flickering screen becoming an annoyance and burden.

Crandall stood and went to the kitchen, pouring a glass of water. He knew what he wanted. A few moments peace to put in the addictive disk and see where he was and what was to come.

Returning to the living room, he slumped in his favorite chair and stared blankly at the screen, a sitcom the main attraction. It was a re-run, but not a bad episode, and Angie was laughing, the remote in her hand.

He stared blankly forward, his eyes darting from the picture to the digital clock on the DVD player, counting the minutes till her bedtime. Crandall felt numb, his hands useless, his legs rubbery. He was living in a state of wait.

The bleak light outside grew even bleaker, giving way to darkness, their inner cave encompassing everything alive, even Buddy beginning to kick in his deep sleep from where he lay at their feet. Angela fell silent, curling on the couch into a ball, the remote drifting from her hand where it bounced on the carpet below her.

Crandall retrieved the remote, muted the volume and scooped his daughter into his arms where he carried her to her bedroom and buried her beneath her soft covers. She shifted lightly to get comfortable and was fast asleep. He kissed her lightly on the cheek and retreated from her room, closing her door to an inch, enough to be able to hear any commotion from within, and he returned down the hall to the living room where he assaulted the closet and produced the disk from the jacket's pocket, plopping it into the player and pressing 'play'.

He zipped through the images he already knew, and slowing it down at the scene from the pier.

It was like déjà vu. He was watching what had happened on a few hours earlier. There he was, standing at the pier's edge, watching the approaching clouds, the waves of water breaking over the rim and exploding in white diamonds over his head, descending with revenge.

The image faded and reawakened, an image of himself within the park, walking along and hiding from reality, his face as white as a ghost's.

Another image of him cutting the grass, the dog barking at his heels.

Another image on the streets, his eyes wild as he searched, the anger within him building and erupting.

—And finally the amusement park, the rides still around him, the grounds absent of people, the protagonist at the center hovering over the fallen body that wore a green T-shirt.

"Who are you?" Crandall asked the television, leaning closer, his eyes blazing. "Tell me who you are."

The figure looked up and turned away.

"*Hello, Crandall,*" the video spat.

Crandall watched with intensity. Who the hell was the pacing man who looked so smug? He pressed pause, the man in the distance at the old man's back, the date clearly displayed in the corner. 21 August, 17:28:36.

Crandall sat in the silent darkness, the manufactured light bleeding from the screen into the room as he thought. Pressing the 'rewind' button, the images reversed themselves, stepping back in time.

Time. He snickered. Time was not what Ben said it was.

Play.

The image stopped and slowly stepped forward.

Pause.

The image froze.

Crandall dropped to his knees and crawled toward the screen, his eyes slits as he memorized the frames.

He had stopped the feed at the earlier scene showing him in the park, unsuspecting, wearing his gray parka and blue jeans, Buddy dragging behind him in the mist.

The date was clear.

18 August. 15:16:43.

Crandall pressed 'stop' and the screen went blue, his shadows defined about the room. He wasn't just pissed; he felt violated and wronged. The idea of not being in control of who he was infuriated him, and he vowed revenge.

"You like to watch, do ya?" he murmured against the blue background, his eyes black pits. "We'll see about that."

He pressed power, and the television died to a tiny dot, his form lost within the darkness.

CHAPTER 13

Crandall mapped it out. He had the time, so he took it, used it and massaged it to his own advantage. Standing back, he determined where he needed to be and at what time he needed to be there, what he had to wear and what he needed to do. Looking at his watch, he made the measurements, calculating pace and stride. His scheme was achievable, his calculations within reach. Grinning, he looked up at the walk of people passing him by. Timing was perfect, precise and mathematically sound.

Smiling, he slowly turned a circle, watching everything around him. "Come and get me," he sneered, his lip curled. "Time's up."

* * * *

18 August; 15:15:41.

He strode through the park, Buddy at his heels, the young puppy tugging at the leash, sniffing every tree, telephone post and barrier in his path, his tail wagging.

"Let's go," he snapped, and the puppy complied, leaping ahead, again tugging at the leash.

Nodding, he added a smile as he passed a jogging couple, slightly turning his head to watch the wiggling rear of the female's rear wrapped in tight spandex. "Not too shabby, huh, pal?" he asked of the dog who only leapt forward, his tongue lolling from his mouth.

He looked at his watch. 15:16:43. It was happening now.

*   *   *   *

Stopping, he turned to look around, Buddy stretching against the constraints of the leash, tail wagging, begging to continue forward. But it wasn't the dog that caused him to pause. Instead, he was seeking something that was trying to appear inconspicuous or perhaps something somewhat out of place. The park was large, and time was ticking by, the moments precious. Then he found was he sought—a man not fifty yards away, partially hiding behind a tall oak, the eye of his camera aimed directly at him.

He smiled. Couldn't help himself. The giddiness he felt was almost orgasmic, and his lips split to reveal toothless gums grinning madly.

The camera lowered, the man behind the eyed frowning, suddenly surprised.

*   *   *   *

A shadow drifted across the grass, silent but furious, a surprised man holding his camera not twenty yards away.

*   *   *   *

The man holding Buddy's leash continued to grin, and he continued to chuckle, slowly lifting his middle finger in a recognizable salute.

The man behind the camera jerked his attention to either side and caught site of the approaching shadow, eyes hidden behind dark sunglasses.

The homeless man knelt down and patted the dog, recognizing the events to follow. "Yer owner was right, friend." He grinned, but even the dog backed away from the putrid breath. "Caught himself a spy he did."

*   *   *   *

Crandall hit him head on, the camera flying from the large man's grip and tumbling to the ground. His balled hand came down with such thrust that the man became immobilized, blood and teeth spraying his fist. With both hands, he gripped the man by the collar and pulled him to within millimeters of his own face, his eyes red with anger.

"Who are you!" he beseeched.

The man lolled around in his grip.

"Who the fuck are you!" Crandall screamed.

The man swallowed his own blood, shaking his head. "lemme go," he pleaded. "I didn't do nothin'."

Crandall slammed his head against the dirt, gripping the man's throat and squeezing his oxygen supply. "Better talk quick. Your time's running short."

The man shook his head. "I was paid to be here," he wheezed. "Fifty bucks to act like I was filming a man wearing a gray parka and walking his dog." His face was turning pink.

Crandall felt his blood freeze. "To *act* like you were filming?"

The man nodded. "Camera's empty, man. They insisted on leaving the camera empty."

Crandall stood, his eyes turning circles around the park, but he saw no one that appeared suspicious. A few faces were pointed his way, eyeing him with disgust, a couple of tough guys trudging past as though they'd bust him up if he tried anything, but their balls were to the wind, and they didn't interfere.

The man underneath him gagged for air.

"Who paid you?" Crandall demanded.

"Hell if I know," the man answered. "Jesus, man, I ain't eaten in four days. You think I give a shit who hands me a fifty-dollar bill? I'd rape the pope at that price."

Crandall continued to scan the park, searching, seeking.

The old man scrambled to a better sitting position. "Why are they after you, man?"

Crandall felt cheated, his own ploy ruined, and now he was exposed. He cursed, clenching his fists and walking away, walking toward the old man that held Buddy's leash, his own eyes wide.

"Well?" the man asked.

A laughter behind him, and Crandall turned to see the homeless man scrambling to his feet, laughing and sticking out his tongue.

"Talk is cheap, fool," he said, backing off. "Buy it fer a dollar? I got bullshit to sell ya." He turned and ran, his legs flailing.

Crandall bit his tongue, grabbed Buddy's leash and sat down. He had been cheated from the truth. His plan so carefully devised had been anticipated. Whoever it was remained one step ahead of him.

Buddy licked his face, but Crandall pushed the puppy away.

They were too good, too smart. He remained strong for a moment before he broke down, the unsolicited tears coming against his will, and he hid his face.

* * * *

The disk had changed. The man walking Buddy through the park was now the homeless man Crandall had paid off.

Other than that, everything else remained exactly the same.

* * * *

Crandall watched, frozen in the darkness, the screen displaying that which he had already memorized. A bloody old man standing over the body of another man, his gun smoldering, his face grim, a sneaky sense of defeat upon his lips.

And the screen drew black.

* * * *

"The University, shall we say, abides by certain standards."

Crandall smiled and nodded.

Principal Rhump continued. "Obviously, Mr. Cady, we have inspected your background with careful scrutiny. After such an investigation, we determined that you were the right man for the job. This decision was reached by a panel of board members. That's how things are done here. There is no singular voice. We believe in democracy. If it is a democratic society we live in, then it is democracy we shall practice."

Crandall fidgeted, but only slightly.

Rhump grinned. "You're not on trial, Crandall. I'm wishing you a 'welcome aboard'. This school needs a fresh perspective. Too many things, these days it seems, are antiquated. Grammar, mathematics, science, you name it. We need something to break the crust. Since this is the technological and business revolution of the twenty-first century, I'm relying upon you to make a difference in the eyes of our students. How do you feel about that?"

Crandall nodded. "I've worked in the industry for nearly thirteen years, Mr. Rhump. I haven't been teaching it, but I have been living it. The real world is cold and callous. It makes no exceptions for the weak. I know the industry's strengths and weaknesses. I feel I can impress this knowledge upon my students. I'm here today to inquire about my boundaries. What are my freedoms and limitations?"

"The Constitution is your guideline," Rhump responded quickly. "We hold these truths to be self-evident, and I'm not just talking in the politically-correct self-interest of the majority public. Peyton University is not interested in breaking through the next evolutionary barrier between justice and progress. We're interested in not being sued, do you understand me? That means we graduate a certain amount of minorities and also start them on our football and basketball teams regardless of talent. It means we grant higher GPA's to the women than they deserve and say nothing that could ever be construed as sexual harassment. PSU currently holds the highest academic average in the nation, Mr. Cady, and I insist that this trend repeats itself."

Crandall nodded.

Rhump smiled. "Good. Of course, this conversation never happened."

"Of course."

"Anyway, outside of those minor barriers, you are free to design your classroom and structure your itinerary as you see fit. NAS is no longer breathing down our necks, so our freedom is somewhat expanded. However, I still expect you to conform to our intrinsic bell-curve. Any questions?"

Crandall shook his head.

Rhump smiled, adjusted his classes, stood and extending his hand across the desk. "Welcome aboard, Mr. Cady. I look forward to the invaluable contribution your experience will, no doubt, play into the shaping of Peyton's future."

Crandall nodded, accepting the handshake.

He left the room with a stale taste in his mouth knowing full well his freedom to teach as he saw fit was limited. But it didn't matter. It was just a job. Do it and get paid. The kids these days didn't listen anyway, so what did he care if he passed a flunking student just to make quota?

He stood within his new classroom, whiteboards all around him, dry markers on their sills, empty desks waiting to be occupied, a stack of textbooks against the far wall by the window. Two weeks. Two weeks until classes started, and he sure as hell better be ready.

Crandall pushed away all of his ill-thoughts regarding the disk. He needed to be in game-mode, prepared to tackle his new position.

Standing behind the teacher's desk, he looked out over the sea of seats pointed at him, and he felt a bit of panic gripping him. Those seats would be filled, eyes and ears trained his way, waiting for the best he had to offer. Crandall swallowed his fear as he stood behind the desk serving as a makeshift podium. In two weeks this was where he'd be, thirty students scribbling down his every word.

In a matter of days it would all be over. The disk, its contents, everything else. It would all be over. For right or wrong, it would be over.

Trying to relax, his attempt was weak, and Crandall left the shaded room, forgetting to close the door and making his way along the quiet hall to the school's exit where he burst into the happy sunshine, his mood sinking even deeper.

A matter of days was all he had. Mere hours to figure out the disk and it's meaning.

Crandall went home.

* * * *

He sat upon his front porch, his eyes glaring out against the sunlight striking him. Crandall watched the things going past him, the world revolving around him, the singularity he called his own compiling its own program and making him a numeral.

"Hey, Crandall!"

He looked up to see his neighbor waving. He nodded just to be polite.

"Haven't seen you in awhile!"

Crandall waved Joe off. He didn't want to be a part of a conversation, but the ignorant worm was coming his way, dropping his rake and peeling off his gloves.

"Helluva summer, isn't it?"

Crandall nodded. "It's been a bitch."

Neighbor Joe chuckled. "Hotter'n Hell this year. My sprinklers don't seem to make much of a difference. Grass is still dyin'." Joe sat down beside Crandall, the smell of alcohol permeating from his body and breath. "You got the same problem by the looks of it. Have you thought of using triple twelve?"

"I'm going for the golden look."

Joe laughed out loud, clapping his neighbor over the shoulder. "You've succeeded, my friend. Gold is definitely your color."

Crandall winced and broke free of Joe's grip. "There's been enough reports of water shortages, I figured I'd do my part."

Joe grinned, winking. "Water shortages. It's a ploy, Crandall. It's the government justifying its presence and authority. What good is a three trillion-dollar budget if you can't spend it?" He waved off the question. "Anyway, my grass is more important than some slacker in the heights who won't work for an honest day's wage. I couldn't care less if they die of dehydration. Know what I mean?"

Crandall nodded, though he was suddenly beginning to understand the motive of his disturbed neighbors, and he felt sickened by it.

"I mean," Joe continued. "We have an over-population as it is. No need to encourage it. Only the strong survive, right?" He nudged his neighbor and chuckled.

Crandall didn't nod, shrug or otherwise agree. He stared forward, offended by the words he was hearing. *Only the strong survive...*

"Anyway," Joe continued. "We're set here. I mean, I'm seeing shit going down all around, and those working the janitorial shifts? They'd better duck. The middle to upper-class is secure. The rich bigots, well, how can we say in politically correct terms that they're about to take it where the sun doesn't shine?" Joe laughed, his sound a geeky, high-pitched one that sounded girlish.

Crandall's fists were clenched, his knuckles white.

Joe slapped him over the shoulder. "Sorry about your wife, man. Must have been tough. You should come over tonight. Me and the missus are hosting a barbecue. Bring that little doll of yours. We don't own anything in the way of toys, but she can bring whatever she'd like to play with. Keep her outta trouble if ya know what I mean." Joe winked. "Hell, half the neighborhood's coming. In case you haven't noticed, half these houses hold divorcees just waiting to spread their legs for their next gladiator."

Crandall looked at Joe with a look of disgust.

"Awful, I know, but they can't help themselves. It's a lousy world, Crandall, and we're all dogs sniffing for the next best catch." He laughed again.

Crandall stood. "I have to take my daughter to ballet," he lied.

"No kidding." Joe nodded, standing as well and extending his hand. "Keep her safe from the little boys, eh, Crandall?" He laughed, his voice sick. "Couldn't blame them. She's a little cutie." He winked. "Well, I'm off. I'm the grill-master." He laughed again. "Stop by if you get the chance."

"Will do," Crandall said, his voice sour.

Joe waved, staggering back to his own yard in a drunken state.

Crandall retreated into his house, closing and locking the door behind him. He peered out the window, watching a woman walking her dog by on the road, her eyes plastered on his house.

The world was watching him, or maybe it wasn't. Maybe it was his own paranoia getting the better of him, or maybe it wasn't. Maybe it was justified, approved by some higher authority. Regardless, his time clock was winding short, the days reducing themselves to hours.

He needed more information...

Crandall moved away from the window and into the depths of his house.

An air-conditioned environment collapsed around him, and he felt safe.

*   *   *   *

He knew they were watching, but he was watching back.

Slowly, methodically, he pushed his Toro across the grass, the shavings cut over and over again, mulched to pieces and recycling. His eyes were trained on the path he was cutting, but he knew eyes were on him. The video told him there were. He was not alone.

Buddy barked at his heels, tail wagging, tongue lolling as he nipped along.

Crandall pushed the mower, the motor humming with confidence, beads of sweat rolling along his face, his eyes careful not to look around. His second pair of eyes were doing the work he didn't have to, so he move forward, the grass becoming a uniform length, golden or not. Triumphantly, he just pushed the goddamn mower forward.

The real eyes lay beyond the glass of his living room where he'd set up the camcorder, one eye recording another.

I'm gonna catch you, he was thinking, desperately trying not smile and give away his lunacy. His hands were trembling even as they gripped the sturdy reverberating bar of the mower he pushed.

He kicked at the dog that had become an annoyance, and he continued to cut grass—cut grass because that's what he was supposed to do as a regular neighbor within this fucked up neighborhood.

Buddy stayed back, sitting down, a curious look on his face.

The moment has passed, he thought. *I've got you on tape…*

Shutting off the motor, Crandall went into the house, leaving the Toro where it stood and the puppy where he cocked his head in confusion.

Yanking the tape from the recorder, Crandall plunged it into the VCR, pressing play, punching the power to his television, sitting back his eyes slits, his face reacting to the elements around him, his nerves getting the better of him.

"Show me what you got."

And there he was, cutting the grass, the dog at his heels, the world around him working the way it was supposed to.

Crandall leaned forward. "Come on…" he whispered.

The seconds rolled past and nothing changed. Just him cutting the grass, just the damn dog yipping and barking, tail whipping back and forth. One lane after another was cut, the grass trimmed and recycled, his expression opposite him focused while thinking he had won.

The mower was left to idle, and he disappeared from the picture, the screen remaining constant for a few moments before the image went black, the recording sharply stopped.

Crandall cussed, spiking the remote on the floor, his face flooding red with rage. Containing his emotions, he bit his tongue lest his daughter hear from where she played in the backyard.

They had won again. One step ahead, they had anticipated this move and recorded him from a distance he couldn't see.

And there was only one more image on the disk.

One with an old man standing over his victim, someone at his back trying to explain it.

Crandall knew he would find out what the last image meant. He knew it in his heart because everything thus far had played to his own reality. He would solve the puzzle—too late or too early. It didn't matter. The truth and the answers were coming.

Still, he wasn't happy. He wanted to win. He wanted to control the feed, ensure himself of his own destiny. The disk played through the final scene, the old man standing over the dark-haired man wearing the green T-shirt.

Over and over he told himself, over and over again, that he was going to win.

Briefly, he even convinced himself.

CHAPTER 14

He could feel her staring at him as he ate his breakfast slowly.

"I thought today was your first day at work," she said slowly.

Lifting his bleary eyes, it was glaringly obvious that he hadn't slept much the night before. "It is."

Angie took mind of her own business and went back to her breakfast.

Crandall knew he should shower and shave, make himself somewhat presentable for his staff meeting. First impressions would be given today, and he looked like a hung-over homeless man who hadn't found a comfortable box to call home.

Whatever. He didn't care much. The clock was still ticking, and he was down to seven days. Seven days, and no more hints to be given from the recording. In a way, it was a disguised blessing that he recognized. Trying to get ahead of the images or trying to anticipate when they would happen and why had been slowly driving him over the edge. He found himself wondering if he could even tell the difference anymore between what was his own natural life compared with what he was subconsciously and unwillingly manufacturing in front of the camera.

Crandall lifted his coffee and noticed that the wet contents within were shivering, not from cold but from under his trembling hand.

Angie was eyeing him again suspiciously. She noticed the quake, and her concern was written in her eyes.

"I didn't sleep well last night," he muttered, trying stiffly to smile.

She wasn't satisfied with his answer, and her eyes accused him of lying. "You've been acting weird ever since Mom died."

He set his coffee down without sipping. "I miss your mother, hon, that's all."

Angela's eyes didn't let go, and she shook her head. "That's not it. I saw you on the pier the other day when we went to the beach. You were chasing some guy. Yesterday you were taping yourself mowing the lawn. I know you went back to Clear Haven, but I don't know why."

"How did you know that?"

"They called when you were out and said you were welcome to come back whenever you wanna see Mr. Spoon. Grandma didn't like Mr. Spoon, Dad. She said he was a nutcase."

He didn't know how to respond. Her interrogation caught him off guard, and placed him in an awkward position. He didn't have time to argue with her, and he stood up, dumping the coffee in the sink. "We'll talk about this later." It was easier with his back turned.

"So, are you gonna tell me, or just lie to me like usual?" Angela snapped from her place at the table.

"I don't appreciate you calling me a liar. I am not lying to you."

There was a commotion behind him, and he turned to see her abandoning her seat and storming out of the room. His eyes went to her breakfast bowl that remained over half-full with cereal growing soggy as it sat.

At least the conversation was over.

Crandall washed his mug, dumped Angela's cereal down the disposal and washed the bowl, setting it to dry. Habit took him down the hall and into the bathroom where he did the best he could with a razor and a comb. Satisfied only slightly, he shrugged and clicked out the light.

Angela was already in the car, but she had on her 'pouty' expression that he knew too well. There was going to be little or no conversation as he drove her to Stacie's. That was just fine with him.

The radio offered little help. One dumb morning talk show after another

"Did you do something wrong?" she asked timidly yet suddenly from beside him.

The question struck him funny, but he suddenly began wondering if he had. After all, what else could explain this mess? "No, honey."

He pulled the Jeep into the driveway of his daughter's friend.

"Then what is it? And don't lie to me."

Crandall put the Jeep into park and turned to her. "I don't know," he said honestly. His eyes were as sincere as his tone. Suddenly, he felt guilty because he knew he'd shown his weakness. Dads were supposed to know everything. They were there to protect their children and make the monsters under the bed go away and the owie's feel better. He was ashamed to have to admit he didn't know what was going on, but he would have felt more ashamed to lie again.

He found that his eyes were welling, but he didn't turn away. Forcing a smile, he touched the side of her little face. "I don't know what's going on, honey, and I swear that's the truth." Crandall fought himself and searched for inner-strength. "But I promise you that I'm going to find out."

Her eyes showed him both relief and fear. Relief that he had confided in her, and fear that he wasn't all-powerful as she had grown up to believe.

He was smiling, parting the hair from her eyes. "When did Daddy's little girl grow up so fast?"

She was having a hard time hiding her fear. "Can't we just run away from it?" she pleaded. "I don't mind changing schools."

Crandall shook his head softly. "I'm sorry, babe, but it doesn't work that way. Our problems will only follow us."

Angela didn't like the answer, but it was apparent that her trust in him had been returned.

"I'm going to take care of things, so I don't want you to worry, okay?"

She nodded.

The door opened, and Stacie was coming out, her mother standing in the doorway with her arms crossed. She offered a little wave.

Crandall turned back to his daughter. "I've got to go to work, Angie. This is our little secret."

She nodded, grateful for such a responsible burden.

He grinned. "How about a good-luck kiss for your old man?"

Angela giggled. "You're not old, Dad. You're not officially old until you're fifty."

"Well, thank you very much, but that's only a few years away."

"Yeah, like seventeen. I'll be twenty-six and married by then."

He smiled, kissing her on the cheek. "You'll always be my little girl though."

She pecked him quickly on the cheek. "Good luck at work today." Opening her door, she hopped the ground and waved as she darted around the front of the Jeep toward her friend. "Bye, Dad!" she called over her shoulder without turning back.

Crandall beeped the horn lightly as he pulled away and headed for the school. His job was the last thing he wanted to deal with, but he was still a father, and he was responsible for feeding, clothing and sheltering his daughter. She came first.

Not that the disk was far from his mind.

Even as the school administrator spoke out over the large faculty, a hot, Styrofoam cup of coffee in Crandall's hands, unfamiliar faces all around him, crowding him, he was ignoring the words. Even as he was introduced to a fever of polite applause as he stood up and waved lightly, he mind was elsewhere, somewhere else. The lights struck his eyes, and he shrank back to his seat, just praying that it would soon be over.

In between breaths, he managed to swallow some Prozac that he had hidden in an ordinary Tylenol bottle. He took three, and smiled as best he could at a woman eyeing him suspiciously.

* * * *

He didn't eat lunch with them. 'Them' being his new co-workers and superiors. They were granted a few minutes away from the pamphlets being passed around, stating the new year's agenda and schedule of events. Most of the faculty took their place in line at the buffet set up in the cafeteria and retreated back to their seat where they mingled with their clique of friends. Others were summoned to a standing circle at various points around the room. Laughter exploded here and there, around him, encapsulating him within a bubble begging to burst.

Crandall found a seat beside the far window at a table unoccupied, and he used his plastic fork to spear the fruit he'd accepted from the buffet. Nobody wanted to talk to him, and on the flipside, he wasn't all that interested in talking anyway.

It was like the first day of school back as a child when his parents dragged him from one school to the next. Each time, things were going to get better, this was the last stop. On and on and on. No more moving, no more changing schools etcetera. Six months later they moved anyway. This feeling was the same. Being an adult didn't make things any easier. He was still the odd man out.

Crandall could only watch the clock, in effect, waiting for the bell to signal his 'release'. But when he was finally released, he didn't pick up his daughter the way he had planned to. She wouldn't be ready to come home anyway. There would be a fuss, him arguing with her, coaxing and bargaining with her until she glumly obliged. Instead, he went home, popped in the disk, zipped through what was no longer relevant and pressed 'resume' on instinct as though he had watched the recording a million times if not a hundred.

Crandall needed clues. Something to look for. Crazy or not, he wanted to be one-step ahead. He wasn't going into the final scene with his back turned. He needed to know who the two men were and who the third voice belonged to.

He was obsessed.

The video played, the filmed scenery jagged, recorded by either an amateur or someone playing an amateur.

...and there it was. An old man hovering over a younger one. The old man, grayed and wrinkled, barely clutching a smoking gun, his face drawn and lost, sad to the epitome of regret.

"You've finally made it," the third man, hidden behind the lens said.

The old man looked up, but only slightly.

Crandall pressed pause, the screen freezing. He stood up, rounded the coffee table, and sat down, his face inches from the television's face. His fingers reached up and traced the outline of the objects behind the man.

It was definitely an amusement park or carnival of some kind, but one he didn't recognize. The surroundings were sad, the rides old and empty, the bright colors dull from age. The noticeable difference that separated this park from the next was the atmosphere over the old man's shoulder. The rides were frozen. Not so much frozen as they were simply not in use. They appeared dilapidated and weathered. The weeds stood tall and un-manicured about the bases of light posts and concession stands, the paint flaking, the brilliant whites and oranges and yellows somewhat dull and uneventful under the overcast sky.

Crandall studied harder, wiping the questions from his mind. The questions could come later. Right now he needed details. He pressed play.

"What just happened?" the old man in front of the camera demanded, his voice distant and breaking against the wind that attacked the cameras microphone. *"Everything's different."*

Pause.

Crandall studied the old man's clothing. It was a bland blue T-shirt with no print. Un-tucked and wrinkled, it was the same color as his jeans, his wiry arms protruding from the sleeves, his knuckled hand gripping the gun, the gray hair just patches on his scalp.

Frowning, Crandall looked closer, his eyes dropping to the fallen man and what he wore. White Nike's, jeans and a green T-Shirt, tan print on the back. From where he sat, he couldn't read the lettering, so he backed off, the large pixels on the screen cramming together and formulating to make words.

Hannison Auto
Since 2010

An employee maybe? A customer? Crandall had never heard of Hannison Auto, but he could definitely do the research. He scrambled for a pad of paper and a pen where he hurriedly scribbled the name.

It was still a game. A wild-goose chase. Just like everything else, this was a challenge, but he didn't understand where he fit into the equation.

He pressed play.

"This was your doing. Enjoy it."

What was who's doing? Crandall, frustrated, his eyes bleary, spiked the remote that bounded away as if alive upon the carpet.

Laughter.

"It's not my fault," the old man on the recording was saying, his shriveled hands quaking.

"Who are you!?" Crandall demanded of the television. His body tingled with sweat as he curled up, his fists clenching, his eyes pinched, the stress closing his lungs. *Who are you…*

He rolled over, a million questions circulating through his mind, every one of which went unanswered.

The video stream continued on. *"Turn that fuckin' thing off."*

Crandall couldn't have agreed more.

* * * *

He pulled the Jeep to a rest and cranked on the emergency brake before killing the engine. Climbing down, he took note of how quiet the neighborhood was, and how uncommon that seemed.

Shaking off the thought, he approached the front door and rang the doorbell, the chime sounding deep within the home. Shifting uneasily he waited, and finally, after what seemed like minutes, footsteps were heard from inside the house.

The door opened, Stacie's mother smiling softly. "Hello, Crandall."

He nodded. The thought of small talk made his stomach squirm, so he offered a pleasant smile, his arms tucked behind his back, his stance worth a thousand words.

Mrs. Graham opened the door, extending an invitation inside that Crandall accepted out of courtesy. "The girls had a big day today," she said, her eyes gleaming. "We went to the zoo, McDonalds, and on the way home, we stopped at the ribbon-cutting ceremony of a new car lot over on James. They were handing out prizes and stickers. You're daughter, she..." A soft smile. "Well, I suppose she can tell it better than me."

Mrs. Graham whisked away down the hall, calling for Stacie and Angela.

Crandall waited, his eyes going to an elderly gentleman sitting in a chair at the opposite end of the living room. His eyes were fixated with Crandall, his expression sour, the magazine in his hands 'Time', a current edition. Slowly, the old man returned his attention to the text within the magazine, his jaws working overtime as he chewed on something, one crunch after another.

"Hey, Dad!"

Crandall turned to see Angela smiling as she crossed the room towards him. She offered a firm hug before standing off, her eyes becoming serious. "You're late."

"They kept me late. First day and all," he lied. "Paperwork that needed to be done for taxes. Major 'yawn' stuff if you know what I mean."

Angela smiled. "It's okay. We got back late anyways. We went to the zoo."

Mrs. Graham smiled from where she stood a few feet away.

"So I hear," Crandall answered. "Did you visit the bears?"

"They were asleep and kept farting. Buncha flies all around the cage. Smelled terrible." She wrinkled her nose. "The elephants were the best."

Crandall smiled. "Ready to go home?"

Angie smiled. "I won you a prize."

"You did? What's that?"

Angela looked over at Mrs. Crandall with a grin, but he woman only nodded.

"I'll tell ya when we get home."

"How do hamburgers sound?"

"Can I grill 'em?" she asked.

"You're the master-cook of the house. You know that."

Angela laughed. "Let's go then."

"Don't forget your bag, dear," Mrs. Graham said, holding up a paper sack.

"Oh, yeah." Angela chirped, breaking away and dashing across the room to where she grabbed the bag, Graham's eyes never leaving Crandall's—a hidden silence therein unsatisfied.

Crandall handed over a fifty-dollar bill, and the housewife accepted it. "She was a darling, Crandall. As usual."

Nodding, he turned for the door and followed his daughter out.

* * * *

"First I hafta explain what was going on," she said with enthusiasm.

Crandall nodded. "By all means."

Angela had a hard time sitting still. "Well, me and Stacie first went to the zoo. Stacie's mom said she needed to get out of the house anyway. So anyway, we went to the zoo. They got it all set up like a tropical jungle."

Crandall remembered. He had visited the new facility last summer. Apparently she had forgotten.

"They had these new trees, like, hanging over the pathways, and there were all these jungle sounds. It might have been a recording for the kids, you know, but I'm not sure, 'cuz I didn't see anything."

Crandall couldn't help but silently grin. Angie was so cute when she tried to act grown-up.

"We saw the monkeys and the alligators. One of the alligators was eating a fish. Blood everywhere. Ick!" She made a face. "But it was cool though. Alligators gotta eat too."

Crandall nodded. "Yes they do." He began rummaging through the cupboards for the proper plates and seasonings for the burgers he was about to prepare.

"Then we saw the bears, and they were sleeping, but the elephants were playing with each other. They kept squirting each other with water. It was funny."

"Sounds fun."

"Then Mrs. Graham took us to McDonalds, and I had some nuggets. The nine-piece deal thing. And fries too."

"Sounds good."

"On the way home we saw a new business opening up. Not really a new business, but a new one of them things. A chain store. It was ribbon-cutting ceremony. They had these big 'ol scissors to cut a yellow ribbon. We pulled over, and they were giving out stuff."

Crandall worked the balls of beef in his hands, squeezing out the blood and squishing them into patties suitable for the grill. He finished them off with a sprinkle of Lawry's.

"I won a T-shirt!" Angie exclaimed, leaping from her chair. "I shot a basketball through a hoop, and I gotta T-shirt!"

"Good for you, hon. Why aren't you wearing it?"

"Dad, you're not even turning around."

Distracted, he washed his hands of the blood under cold water, the sticky liquid disagreeing with him before he turned.

"It's too big for me, so I got it for you," she was saying, her face beaming as it unfolded in her hands, gravity rolling it downward.

A green T-shirt, tan lettering. He didn't even have to read the lettering to know what it said, but he was drawn to it like a magnet, his stomach suddenly sick, his hunger gone.

Hannison Auto
Since 2010

He turned away, his face to the window, his breath coming in short heaves. "Thanks, sweetheart."

"It's an extra-large so it might be kinda big," Angela went on. "I figured you might wear it as a work-shirt of something."

Crandall felt his hands shaking, his stomach feeling rubbery as though he was about to purge a stomach-full of acid.

Jesus Christ. They were winning. The dead man in the video, the man wearing the T-shirt in the video, the dead man laying still underneath the white-haired man in the video was him.

It was *him* all along.

Jesus.

He was supposed to wear the T-shirt in seven days to an amusement park. He was supposed to be shot dead in seven days. Fate was knocking on his fucking door, and it was pissing him off.

"Don'tcha like it, Dad?" Angie was asking.

He turned to her, his mind doing funny things to him. He should be all smiles, grateful for his gift that had been earned through his daughter's talents. She took after her mother after all. They both had what he lacked, and he felt so suddenly proud that he found his chest caving as he remembered Emily in her better days, a blushing girl full of laughs, a full life ahead of her. He was cornered, boxed in, his oxygen supply cut off, and he gagged.

"I love it, Angie. You always were the athlete in the family."

"Well go ahead and try it on." She came forward, holding the shirt up, but Crandall backed away as if being challenged by a snake. He awkwardly tried to mask the tension in his eyes by laughing.

"Not now. Maybe later. I've got dirty hands, and the burgers are about ready to go on. Why don't you go out and start the grill?"

Angela shrugged, tossed the shirt onto the table and made for the door. "Okay."

He was suddenly left alone with the shirt, a terrible urge deep down telling him to burn it while Angela was out of sight, but he held back, realizing that his future wasn't bent upon the clothes he wore. The shirt wasn't the culprit. Whoever was holding the camera was the culprit. Whoever owed the mysterious voice on the recording was at blame. At that end lay the enemy mind behind the game being played.

He returned to the counter, cutting his finger badly as he sliced through a tomato. The blood began to mix with the vegetable, and he only stood, watching it mesh, watching it run, seeping along the cutting board before drooling along its edge and spilling to the countertop.

Jesus.

It was *him* all along.

According to the disk, he was going to die in a little under seven days.

His hands were trembling as he switched on the water and ran his wound under the piercing cold rush.

*   *   *   *

Crandall waited up long after the shadows fell across the lawn. His weary eyes were dull against the night sky as he sat, his mind dull.

They wanted him. All along, they wanted him.

Whoever *they* were.

It was enough to drive him mad.

He wanted to win, and he vowed to himself, swearing on his daughter's life, that he would do everything to do just that.

CHAPTER 15

"I'll just need to see your ID," Mike said with a timid, pleasant smile. "For the paperwork and such. You know."

"Mike," Crandall said cheerfully as he slammed his license against the glass window, a shudder passing through the clear wall. "You're an idiot."

Mike frowned and leaned closer. "I'm sorry, but I can't read the identification. Would you mind passing your ID under the widow?"

Crandall glowered as he pulled out the plastic card and slipped it through the small hole.

Mile leaned forward, adjusting his glasses and examining the license closely. Using his thumbnail, he scratched off a smudge, squinted and took his time with reading the card. "This could be a forgery. I'll have to speak with my superior, sir. One moment please."

Crandall closed his eyes, pinching off his urge to retaliate. "Fine."

Mike drummed his fingers, staring Crandall down as he waited. Finally, the door opened, and a nurse entered, listened to the fat man's complaint, took one look at Crandall, shook her head with disgust and apologized through the glass. "Sorry, Mr. Cady. I'll let you in." She retreated and was gone for a moment while Mike sneered, his upper lip quivering.

"I got my eye on you, mister."

Crandall nodded as the door to his side opened, the nurse smiling with embarrassment. "Mr. Spoon is right this way."

Crandall followed, lifting an obscene gesture at Mike as he passed. Mike returned the greeting, his eyes blazing, his teeth clicking, his large frame shifting back and forth. Clenching his fists, Mike pounded the glass once, his chest heaving from the energy spent, his eyes locking with hatred upon Crandall. He stood and fogged the glass with his breath, lifting both middle fingers, curling his lips downward.

"Don't pay any attention to him," the nurse said pleasantly, but she hadn't seen the violent reaction, and she continued walking while using her hips to accentuate her femininity. Clear Haven definitely had its own rolodex of issues.

They passed through the main living quarters. Living. Or so it seemed.

Everyone was the same. Individuality had been stolen to make cardboard cut-outs of what patients were supposed to look like. White hair, white faces, parched lips. Half of them looked dead and might as well be considering their environment. Crandall paced through the rows upon rows of beds, one blank face after another staring out or sleeping, tucked under the covers.

Spoon was sitting on the edge of his bed, his legs dangling over the edge, his eyes tired.

"How are you, Benjamin?" the nurse asked.

Ben lifted his weary eyes, his face grim. Suddenly, he jumped up, opened his robe and exposed himself to the nurse with a hideous laugh. "Things are fine," he snarled.

The nurse turned her head. "Spoon, I'm warning you once again not to do that anymore."

"Or what? You're going to kick me out of this joint?" He wrapped himself up again and sat down. "Naw. I don't think so. There's nowhere to send me, so what are you gonna do, Nurse Stanford? Cut off my nightly dessert? Restrict me from playing Bingo? You have no power here. I'm paying your salary, so kiss my ass, and leave me alone with my friend."

Stanford glared at him through slits. "Don't push me, Spoon. I can make your life a little less fun should you encourage me to do so."

Spoon looked at Crandall. "Can you believe that? An old fart like me being threatened by a young hussy like her. It's no wonder this place is only nine hundred bucks a month. What a shit-hole." He brightened. "Have a seat, Cady. By the look on yer face, we got lots to talk about."

Stanford snorted with disdain.

Ben turned on her. "I believe that means leave us the hell alone, nurse."

Stanford eyed Crandall who only offered a weak shrug. "Enjoy," she said with a smirking smile.

Crandall grinned. "I'm sure I will. Thank you."

She turned and walked away, her hips flirting with him.

"She's got the hots for you," Ben said with a hoarse giggle.

"Funny," Crandall answered, taking a seat beside the old man. "I don't see her thinking much of you at all."

Ben chuckled. "That's a blessing in disguise, my friend. That wench has teeth that bite deep. Be warned."

"I'll keep that in mind."

"Yeah. Sure you will. Laugh it up. I'm just an old kook looking out from the inside."

Crandall wasn't amused by the old man's tone. "Frankly, Ben, I couldn't possibly care less." He lowered his voice to a whisper. "But I do have something that will interest you." He lifted an eyebrow. "Is there somewhere we can talk?"

Ben looked around, shocked by the question, alarmed that it had been raised within hearing distance of his neighbors. "Jesus, Crandall. Why don't you just announce it via PA to the entire lot of wackos here?"

"Is 'wacko' a technical term?"

"Fuck you, Larry," Ben sneered.

"My name isn't Larry, Ben."

"It's whatever I want it to be, smart ass. Pay attention. You're at my mercy. It's not the other way around." He looked both ways, his eyes darts. "Follow me."

The old man crawled off his bed and crept along the rows of beds, tiptoeing like a child around his parents on Christmas morning. He turned and urgently motioned for Crandall to follow.

He was led into the restroom, Ben shooing out the only occupant, some old man who was pulling up his pants, eyes white with fear as he shuffled out of the room. They were surrounded within silence.

Ben turned, his eyes concerned and sincere. "What do you got, Cady?"

Crandall pulled out a copy of the disk. "This."

Ben took the disk and examined both sides as if he'd see something suspicious. "This is it, eh?"

"It's a copy. Close enough to the original. Everything leading up to the last scene has come true."

Ben smiled. "You seem somewhat shaken. What's the matter? Afraid of the boogeyman?"

"Yes," Crandall answered definitively. "I am. The last scene shows an old man hovering over a corpse. That corpse is mine. Needless to say, I have an intrinsic need to figure out when, where and why this image takes place. I don't want your psycho-babble bullshit on time travel. I want to know if it's genuine and who has the means to make it."

Ben stared back, his lip slowly curving upward. "They've already got you, Cady. You're their pawn now."

"Who's 'they', Ben?"

The old man shrugged. "The maker of this disk. The puppeteers. Who else? What you don't realize is you're playing right into their hands. You're afraid, aren't you?" He didn't wait. "No need to answer. It's written like ink upon your brow." Ben yawned. "Anyway. I'll take a look at your disk; give a look-see. The problem is, Cady, understanding whether or not it's genuine isn't relative."

"The hell it isn't," Crandall snapped back. "If that disk is genuine, then my life ends on August twenty-seventh. How isn't that relevant?"

"You're not thinking straight, my naïve friend. If it's, indeed, genuine, then your troubles are already over. There's nothing you can do to stop it. If it's a forgery, then your troubles never started. Do you understand? You're all upset over a scenario you cannot control. One way or another, this little piece of plastic is without value."

"I don't believe that, Ben. I've altered the contents of that goddamn disk just by knowing when and where things happen. I'm in control of my life, not the man behind the camera."

"Then why hasn't the ending changed?" Ben shrugged. "We can argue about this all day, Mr. Cady, and I won't profess to speak about it intelligently without having previewed it firsthand, but you must understand that if this disk is genuine, and judging by your stink it most definitely is, it doesn't matter how hard you fight or how far you run. In six days the prophesized conclusion of this disk will come true, and if it's bogus, you'll laugh yourself into a bunk beside me in this loony bin. There are two possible conclusions, and I am unhappy to report to you that neither are acceptable by your standards."

"You're damn right that's not acceptable by my standards. Watch the feed, Ben. I'm coming back tomorrow. You tell me what you see."

The old man nodded. "Won't be easy. The retarded old bastards of this place seem to have a craving for the big screen. They drool over the commercials. You know how is. Advertisements with women shaving their legs, beer commercials with women playing tackle football in the mud, car commercials with women donning shades cruising the strip. The men jerk off while they watch the commercials, Cady, and they do it proudly."

Crandall pulled his wallet and produced five twenty-dollar bills. "I'm giving you my trust, Spoon. This is your incentive to do a good job."

Ben pushed the money aside. "In here that's only smelly paper. I'm a goddamn prisoner. If you want my trust, then you get me out of here. Take me to the beach. Let me feel the sand under my toes and smell the water breaking against the pier. That's gold to an inmate such as myself."

Crandall returned the money to his pocket. "You got it. I'm coming back here tomorrow, and I'm taking you on a field trip, and I swear to God you better talk or you're not coming back, understand."

Ben frowned a half-smile. "Sounds like a threat to me."

"If you're holding out on me, then I would suspect that it is."

The white-haired man leaned forward and grinned toothlessly, his stale breath an offense to Crandall. "I like the chase, Cady. Don't push it." He licked his lips. "Consequently, if this disk is a fake, I'll know by morning." He looked around, his expression bland. "And consequently, if you talk to anyone between now and then, you'll be dead by morning."

"Yeah, like you have connections with the outside world, right?"

Ben eyed him starkly. "This joint is a cover. Be careful. You're treading in deep waters now."

The resident's sincerity was what intimidated Crandall, and he sat back. "We're on the same team, old man. I'll be back tomorrow."

"You're taking me to the beach, Crandall. Remember that."

Crandall nodded, stood and walked away. "And you're going to spill your beans."

Ben snickered as he eyed the disk. "Yeah." His eyes traveled to the man walking away, already at the opposite side of the room. "I suppose I will."

After all, there was nothing left to hide.

Crandall shoved his way past the nurse and into the waiting room where Mike attacked the glass window, splattering himself against the resistance before fighting back, his chubby fists clubbing the glass, his eyes wiry red.

"Traitor!" he screamed. "I'll kill you!"

Crandall chuckled as he turned his obtuse grin on the fat man imprisoned within his glass tomb.

Nurses rushed in, needles spraying as they plunged the pointed tip into Mike's arm. He shrunk back, his lip remained curled. "Traitor…"

* * * *

She was watching him from across the table, her mouth moving as she chewed through her spagetti, a bit of sauce drooling along her lip that she lapped up with her tongue. Her eyes interrogated him, and she was none too pleasant about it.

Crandall just went back to his meal, his face flushing with embarrassment.

"You can't just be a temporary dad when you feel like it," Angela said. "You can't just push me off."

"I'm not," he tried, but recognized after the fact that he had failed to look his daughter in the eye, a telltale sign of his lie.

"Don't you have to go to work tomorrow?"

"Yes, I do, and that's where I'm going."

"Then why are you dumping me off at grandma's and grandpa's? I hate the way their house smells. It's all stuffy like an old-people's house."

"Grandma just keeps her place cleaner than ours, and it's old-person's not old-people's." He grinned lightly.

"Funny, Dad. Why won't you just tell me what's going on? It would make things a lot easier for us both."

Crandall sat back, chewing what he had left in his mouth and forcing a swallow. "You know what, Angie? You're right, it would."

His daughter stopped eating, confronted with the sudden weight that he had openly agreed with her statement.

"Unfortunately, easiness is not a luxury I can afford right now. There are a few things that I have to deal with that I don't want you to be a part of. Now, I can't be any more honest with you than that, so you're just going to have to accept it. Understood?"

Her eyes were wide, a deer in headlights. "Does this have something to do with Mom?"

Crandall considered his answer carefully and realized that his little girl had Emily's instincts and keen ability to detect the truth. "Yes," he said after a lengthy pause. "In a way it does."

Angela went back to her meal, dropping her eyes. "Did someone kill her?"

"I don't know," he answered honestly. "That's what I'm trying to figure out."

"Why don't the police help?"

"It doesn't work that way."

"Why not?"

"Because this isn't that kind of a mystery." Crandall tried to take an interest in his spagetti, but his appetite was gone. Part of him felt relief washing over his body, his ability to tell the truth surprising even him.

Angela dropped her fork into the mush left on her plate, sitting back, her eyes soft and sad. "So when can I come back home?"

"When it's over."

She sighed with frustration.

"The twenty-eighth," Crandall said with a small smile. "It'll be over then."

"How do you know?" she demanded.

"I..." He bit his tongue. "I can't tell you that, honey. Sometimes it's better if you don't know."

Angie conceded and tried to eat, though it was obvious that her appetite had slipped as well. The two sat at the empty dinner table, the light from the overhead chandelier a pathetic reminder that this was no longer a family meal, the corners of the room shadowed in fear, a distant hum coming from the stereo. Things were trying to look normal, mimicking brighter times, but the scene came off as a mock-up.

Crandall sat down his fork, forced a gulp of water and sat back, his mind furrowed with frustration. "I'm sorry," he whispered. He didn't know why he was apologizing, but he felt like he needed to. Maybe it was because he was pulling his daughter out of her normal routine and sending her away for a week to live with his parents in another city. Maybe it was because he didn't trust himself or how he was going to behave when the truth finally presented itself to him, or maybe he was apologizing for reasons no more complicated than he didn't know how it was going to end.

Angie looked at him, her lips pouting. She didn't say anything and Crandall could tell that she was sorting things out in her mind, never really coming to a satisfactory conclusion to satisfy herself.

The grandfather clock began to toll from the corner, and Angie looked longingly toward the television set in the living room. Her favorite program was ready to start.

"Go ahead," Crandall said softly. "I'll clean up."

She dared a smile before tearing away from the dinner table.

There was so much leftover food on the table, he had no idea where to begin. Maybe he'd just throw it all away.

It's not like it mattered anymore...

CHAPTER 16

22, August

Mike pounded the glass, saliva dripping along his chin, his eyes paranoid. Little, puffy white digits curled into fists, his stomach poking out from under his un-tucked T-shirt. "Traitor!" he screamed from behind the glass. "You shall not pass!"

The nurse opened the door, smiling. Dark rings circled her eyes, but she was pleasant enough, her uniform straight and ironed. "Don't mind him," she said. "We had to lock him in there until the doctor shows."

"Doctor?" Crandall asked.

"It seems Mike hasn't been taking his medications. Don't worry though, Doc Wallace will be here shortly."

Crandall frowned. "He's been behaving this way since yesterday."

"I know." She sighed. "The doctor has been delayed."

He offered no reply, no resistance. He became a follower even as his eyes locked with Ben's, and then he panicked.

The old man sat on the edge of his bed, legs dangling over the side, his head cocked to one side, his eyes crossed, a string of drool clinging from his lower lip.

"He went berserk yesterday," the nurse explained. "Cussing and spitting, talking about the end of the world. Blasphemy. That sort of thing. We had to dope him up."

"Dope him up?"

The nurse giggled. "It's just an expression, Mr. Cady."

"I'll bet."

"Mr. Spoon," she said with a disgustingly sweet voice. "You have a visitor. Mr. Cady is here to see you."

The old man shifted his eyes, but his lip hung low, the expression his face remaining dull. The nurse turned and smiled at Crandall with reassuring confidence. "He's all yours, sir."

"Um," Crandall interjected. "Actually, I had promised Mr. Spoon that I'd take him to the beach today."

The nurse frowned, stopping where she stood. "Was this cleared?"

"Of course it was. Yesterday. Your superior." Crandall accentuated his impatience with the nurse. "The guy with the glasses." In truth, he'd only seen the man pass through on one or two occasions, and he'd never exchanged anything more than a head nod or a smile, but that would have to do.

"Smith?"

He shrugged. "I didn't catch his name because he never offered it, but he said that some fresh air would do Ben some good."

The nurse frowned. "Doesn't sound like Smith."

"Whatever. I'm taking my friend out for a couple of hours. If you want to hold me back then get the old man on the horn and make it happen."

She shook her head. "If you're cleared, you're cleared. By all means, Mr. Cady, though I doubt you'll get much out of Mr. Spoon."

Crandall grinned. "He seems to warm up to me." With that, he took the old man by the arm and led him toward the exit, past the beds, past the nurse and through the door where big Mike was pressed against the glass, his breath fogging the window in front of him, four doctors behind him, handcuffing his hands.

Crandall winked, but Mike only scowled, limply mouthing the word 'traitors' as they passed.

* * * *

The doors split, and Crandall led Ben from the retirement community home, down the steps and into the bright sunshine. "So what did you find out?"

The old man didn't answer, but wandered feebly down the stairs toward the parking lot, his mouth continued to hand open, his eyes dazed.

"They're out of hearing range, Ben," Crandall said. "What did you find out about the goddamn disk?"

The old man just stumbled along following as he was led, his mind astray, the thin hairs on his head wisps in the wind.

Crandall bit his lip, suddenly panicking, afraid that the drugs had stolen Ben's mind.

"Lookit the purty flowers," Ben mumbled, pointed as he stumbled along. "Echinacea, Daisy's, roses. How splendid this time of year…"

"Wake up, Ben," Crandall hissed. "I swear to Poseidon that I'll dump your ass on the beach if you don't snap out of it."

The old man just stumbled, and Crandall found himself shaking with dread. What had they done to him? Electro-shock therapy? Drugs? What did they know? Had they found the disk?

Ben knelt down and watched.

"What's this?" Crandall demanded. "Now you're protesting?"

"The ants have found the way…" the old man whispered, tracing a line through the sand along the crack in the sidewalk, a line that disrupted the ants rhythm. "They found the way home. Home."

Crandall scooped the old man up and dragged him in between the rows upon rows of cars, multi-colored, all sporting a unique sign that reflected not only its owner's personality but also the bleeding sun of the weary late August afternoon. "We're going to the beach," he scoffed. "Get in the car."

Disarmed, the Jeep grinned under the sun, open for entry. Crandall pulled open the passenger-side door and nearly tossed the feeble old man into the seat. "Buckle your belt," he sneered. Jesus Christ, what a waste of time this was. Ben was off his rocker.

He slammed the door shut and rounded the rear of the vehicle.

Taking his seat, he ignited the engine. "I said we'd go to the beach; we're going to the beach. Hang on, old man."

"The crossroads in life meet but once," the old man mumbled. "An intersection by rights of your God."

Crandall sped from the parking lot. "Yeah. You and your filth, Spoon. You're a crazy old man wasting my time. I'm driving blindly into the abyss."

Spoon turned, his eyes blazing. "Crossroads in life meet but once, Cady. Don't fuck with me because I am not in the mood."

Crandall hit the brakes, the tires locking and skidding over the sand on the road as he pulled to the side, his heart pounding in his chest. "What did you find out?"

Spoon lifted his eyes, a glint reflecting underneath the afternoon sun. "The disk is authentic."

Crandall felt his bowels release, his jeans went wet, and his hands began to shake.

Almost like a miracle.

*   *   *   *

The door slammed shut and old man Spoon walked with a smirk into the sunshine toward the beach. He spread his arms, closing his eyes, relishing the stiff breeze that attacked him from the shoreline, pushing his hair back, a crisp, clean smell, tainted only slightly by the memory of dead fish.

"Life thrives upon the beach, Cady. Life is here. If you can feel it, you are among the few. If you cannot, you are nothing more than an observer. Life revolves around you in circles. One circle within another, making a complete ring. Is this making sense?"

"I dunno. Are you still drugged up?"

Old Spoon chuckled. "I developed a resistance to their drugs long ago, Cady. There's nothing they can do to me now."

"Their? Who's They?"

"The Presidents, of course."

Crandall frowned. "I don't understand. We have one president. President Starchild."

The waves lapped against the edge of the beach, attacking and retreating, pulling the sand back, exposing the carcasses of dead fish, white eyes staring at the sun, becoming bleak.

Ben grinned, smirked and laughed. "You are a member of the mushy masses, Crandall. Dollars to beans says you'd believe something just because you read it in the press. Open your eyes, man. Congress equals the Senate and the House of Representatives plus one. That's your leader, dipshit. It's not one man. It's a legion out for themselves, and where do you think they're going? Where are we being led? Like sheep, we are on the edge of the cliff staring down into the breakwater below. It's not one man, Crandall. This country is being led by a legion of presidents, and they are the wave of the future."

Crandall snickered.

Ben grinned toothlessly. "It makes it easy to laugh, doesn't it? A preposterous idea is merely a joke, but the elected politic hides within the shadows and preys off of your sarcasm. Remember that once you discover you've been bitten upon the ass."

"This country is run by one man," Crandall responded as they wove their way toward the water.

"Is it, then?" Spoon shook his head, grinning, chuckling. "Well, you would know of course."

"I want to know about the disk, not some crazy conspiracy theory," Crandall answered with. "I brought you to the beach. That means you owe me, old man. I want answers. Now."

Spoon nodded as he trudged against the grain of the rolling waters.

"What about the disk?" Crandall demanded.

"Ah," the man answered, nodding, his face wrinkled with joy against the sun over the afternoon waters. "The disk. That which has imprisoned you."

A frustrated snicker. "I'm out of patience, Spoon."

"Patience is always there waiting for you, my friend. The problem is, you are too hasty to receive it. You are much too consumed with details to see the overall picture. You're stuck back here when life is somewhere in front of you, blazing the trail ahead. You are a sad man."

Crandall stopped, the waves lapping around his shoes. "You know, I could leave you here to rot, and rot you would. Don't hide behind your own philosophy."

Ben grinned. "Welcome aboard. You've just taken the first step toward understanding this mess."

"I'm not sure I understand."

"Look around, Crandall. You're treading water in a world that surrounds itself about Sunday afternoon football games, Friday night happy hours, Monday night grocery shopping sprees, Wednesday night Bingo and the Thursday night comedy lineup. Everything here is predictable and controllable. The masses believe themselves unconquerable, invincible and in all probability, invulnerable. Someone stronger, mind you, *one* individual who is stronger, could take over this entire city, maybe the country. Who's there to stop it?"

"The President?" Crandall offered.

"President*s*," Ben snapped, emphasizing the 's' like the hiss of snake. "And the answer is no. They follow the masses like an overrun bank of the Mississippi in the spring."

"I hate clichés."

"Me too." Ben winked. "Good observation." He continued along his path, his feet digging into the wet sand, patiently leaving his mark. "Problem is, clichés are what defined us, and they are what will break us."

"I am not defined by your rules, Spoon."

"I don't have any rules, Cady, but you do."

"Whatever."

"Tough guy, huh? What about your daughter? What about little Angela? Do you—"

"Leave her out of this," Crandall snapped.

"It's not me who's including her. It's you, and you know it. Don't even attempt to pass the buck."

"Ben, leave her out of this. I sent her away."

"I watched the feed, Crandall. I saw you die. Don't think it's that easy. Now focus."

The waves broke against the beach, laughing, mocking or maybe just playing along, the white foam breaking against Crandall's feet. The feeling was cold, like early autumn, the hint of winter making its announcement. "So your opinion is that the disk is authentic?"

"Dollars to bean says you found the original."

"I don't follow."

"The copy you gave me was distorted. Even though it was a digital copy, there were mistakes made by the computer that duped it. I imagine the feed that was recorded to disk you've got was the original, Crandall. If there are other copies, they are duplicates of your original."

"Why would you suspect that?"

"Like I said, I've already examined the pixels of my copy, and the time-stamp reflects when the copy was duplicated, meaning that the copy you duped for me yesterday had yesterday's time stamp. The original, however, would record the original timestamp, a stamp more accurate and older than a duplicate. If you were meant to be shot on the twenty-seventh, it would make sense that the feed was recorded exactly as you observed it. Exactly at the time you observed it."

"That's not a lot of comfort, Ben."

"Cut me some slack. I'm fighting the system. They've pumped me up with so much shit that I don't know if I'm coming or going."

"Why?"

"Why? Because they suspect I'm up to no good which is exactly where I am. Don't think for a second that they ain't watching us. Right now we're in the spotlight. Like it or not."

Crandall shook his head. "We're on a beach, Ben. The people here aren't looking for us. Everyone you see is living out their lives without the slightest concern as to who we are. We're as alone as a couple of Eskimos in the North Pole. Nobody's listening." He shrugged. "Nobody cares."

"No? You feel that confident then?"

"Of course."

Ben chuckled, smirked and looked off with a confident sense of dissidence. "Sure. You're a rock."

Crandall nodded, the waves stopping, freezing, becoming blocks of ice that stalled and corroded around his feet. He turned to Ben. "You promised me an answer."

Ben nodded and continued forward. "Yes, I did. The problem is, you're not ready."

"Fuck ready. I want answers."

"You're not prepared."

"Fuck prepared, Ben. What did you find out?"

The old man stopped, his ankles hidden beneath the late August water, his face stern against the setting sun. "You're a child, and you're reacting." He shook his head. "Makes you sloppy."

"I want to know where the game ends."

Ben began to laugh. "That's your decision, not mine. Pay attention."

Crandall straightened and looked around. Ben looked back, staring out from under heavy lids, his eyes bloodshot and sickly. "It ain't a game, Cady. It ain't a game."

Crandall nodded, looking around.

Spoon snickered, giggled, laughed and spit into the oncoming trail of the man beside him. "After everything we've been through, and you still don't get it, do you?"

Crandall shrugged.

"Time travel is not an anomaly. But you're so damn concerned with how the shit works that you completely forget that it already works."

"Just a few days ago you said it was impossible."

"It came to me yesterday that if this disk is real, then I was wrong. It can't be impossible, because you hold the argument against my charge in your hand. Like I said, you cannot travel to a point in time prior to when the vessel was built. Therefore, the vessel must already exist. Now, I gave it some thought, and this is how it would work." He took a breath. "Imagine two objects moving at the same rate, equally opposed to one another. One force, yours, eliminates your opponents, which, for the sake of argument, is the wind. Acceleration ceases and becomes null. You have, in effect, controlled gravity. That's not a difficult machine to construct."

"This has nothing to do with moving faster than light. I thought that was your argument."

Ben was frustrated, held back to explain. "Imagine you're a black hole that is created by man."

"That would be hard to imagine."

"Try. This is not a game."

"Very well. I am a black hole. Why does the nurse hate you, Ben?"

The old man grinned. "Because I know what she does not understand. Now focus. The actual hole, abiding by the laws of physics, would be so small that it would be nearly impossible to swallow anything at all. A proton or neutron would be similar to you trying to swallow a pumpkin. Yet, the stored energy of something capable of time travel would be radiating away energy that of a rate of 6,000 megawatts, somewhere in the vicinity of six large power stations."

"This means nothing to me. What's your point?" Crandall was frustrated.

"It goes back to my whole argument that light can be manipulated by gravity. If we can control light through the use of gravity, then we are one step away from controlling time." He frowned. "At least in theory that is."

Crandall shook his head. "I'm taking you back to the Looney bin, Ben."

The old man grinned, nodded, the waves washing around his ankles. "Makes you feel better, don't it? In control?" His face hardened. "If a black hole has a gravity of mass that can move faster than light, then light must be absorbed or slightly bent. Black holes do not have angular momentum. They rotate, and the more compact they are, the faster we would expect them to rotate. This rotation is measured by gravity times mass. Mass is the key to the creation of a black hole, and once we can create such a hole is the moment we can control time travel."

"I don't care about black holes or bending light, Ben. I don't care about theories or mathematical equations. The truth is, you're talking about a black hole way out in space that has the capacity of enough gravity to hold time captive. That disk did not come from outer space, and it was not delivered to my street by little green men in a flying saucer."

"What if we could build one?" Ben asked. "I'm not saying like in a basement, but in a controlled environment? The necessary ingredient is a rotating massive cylinder spinning fast enough so that a naked singularity will form at its center. The greater the mass, the lower the density you need to close off, squeeze, if you will, the space-time collected around that matter."

Clouds raced over the sky.

The old man grinned. "If you can control that matter, you can control a singularity in time. You control a few micro-seconds of space-time and what happens within it. You can move faster than it would take for you to cross the room once the light is shut off and sit down beside me before the room grows dark.

You could control time because the density within your manmade black hole requires more speed to escape than the velocity of light." He grinned. "You've won."

Crandall frowned. "So who could do it?"

Spoon shook his head. "I don't know. Hell, man. We haven't even figured a way to get John Doe from Earth to the moon without aging. Doe takes off at age fifty and returns x times one plus the number of days since he departed. Aging continues because we're too slow. We're eight steps behind the eight ball."

Crandall didn't quite follow. "So what are we talking about? You don't have a clue as to who has the technology, and you've said before that actually traveling into the future is impossible as is directly traveling into the past."

The old man shook his head. "The theory behind time travel is being able to stand still and allow the past to catch up. That's it. I cannot explain how you got that disk. It's authentic. The images are real, not a staged act, but it's impossible. Defies everything I know."

Crandall shook his head, reached into his pocket and pulled out an orange bottle. He read the label to see what the day's treat would be.

Paxil. Great.

"Does that make it all go away?" Ben asked.

"Enough of it."

"Good for you."

"Don't push it, Ben. You know nothing about me."

"I'm sure I don't," the old man answered, shaking his head. "None of my business anyway."

Crandall shook his head, eyes lowered. He downed three, thought better of it, and took a fourth. "I don't know what to do, Ben."

The old man shrugged. "You can't change it."

"I already did. Some of the images changed. I know."

"You're certain about that?" Ben shook his head. "Truth is, you're not certain because you don't have proof. All you have is your memory, and a person's memory is flawed, especially when under strain." He sighed, all the while offering a soft smile, his eyes filled with knowledge. "You want answers to the 'who done it' question, but my answer is simply I don't know." He grinned. "We've got a jigsaw puzzle here, Mr. Cady, but we don't have all the pieces."

"And why me?" Crandall asked, sulking. "I didn't do anything. Why me? Why my family?"

"Maybe it has nothing to do with you specifically, Crandall. Dollars to beans says there's thousands of disks just like that one floating around. You just happened to find yours."

"Mine?" Crandall laughed at the preposterous idea. "How would I? Me, little ol' me, find my specific disk, yet there's thousands others out there that I didn't find and nobody else found?"

The old man shrugged. "You're not looking at this from every angle, Crandall. Maybe others haven been found, just not by their subject. What would you have done had you found a home video of someone you'd never met before? Would you have studied it so carefully to determine the date in which is was filmed? Would you have tracked down that person and returned it to the rightful owner? Or would you have watched it, anxiously hoping for some amateur porn before throwing it away?" Ben shook his head. "There's a million different reasons why nobody has seen this before, and there's a million more to explain the how's and why's you wound up with your particular copy. But before you go crying conspiracy, you better round up your facts the way I do, and make sure it's more than just gospel before you freak out and jeopardize your name." He snorted. "Or you'll wind up at Clear Haven beside me."

Crandall sat down, the soft sand forming around him. "Right," he said. "Like you do."

Ben paced a few steps before facing the lake. "My theories are too preposterous for you or anyone else to believe, aren't they?"

"What do you think?"

"Then imagine how your story must have sounded to me?" Ben turned with a slick wink. "I'm not crazy, Crandall Cady. I just living in a crazy world—like you."

Crandall lay back, the soft sand catching his fall. Overhead, the world looked so large, so unbelievably large, that he didn't feel like he was a part of it. "I have no leads, Ben. You're sure this isn't the work of our government?"

Ben sat down. "Could be, though unlikely. I'm not a guessing man, but if I were, and I were to guess, then I would agree that there probably ain't thousands of them floating out there. My hunch, though the odds weigh heavily against it, would be that you stumbled upon a one-of-a-kind that you weren't supposed to stumble upon. I'd guess that you are the center of an experiment headed by a group of private investors funded independently by bored millionaires who, for some reason, chose you." He shrugged. "Among others."

"There's nothing unique about me."

"More than likely, that's why. Results are being weighed upon a man who is your average John Doe, living in Average USA, with an address and telephone number beginning with 555."

Crandall sat up. "So what do I do?"

"I would suggest that you use your remaining five days to figure out who has the most money in this world, and who likes playing mad-scientist."

"What if I just locked myself into the house? The ending on that disk wouldn't come true."

Ben chuckled. "Fate doesn't work that way, I'm afraid. The ending would have already changed." He shook his head. "No. You'll wind up where that feed was shot, one way or another."

"That's very comforting. Thanks."

Ben smiled at the sun that hung limply over the water, his face golden beneath its color. "There is nothing more I can tell you, Crandall."

Crandall nodded.

"My lunch is getting cold," the old man continued. "I would like you to take me home, please."

Crandall looked at Ben curiously and saw there was no joking in either Ben's expression or tone. "Home? To that penitentiary?"

Ben nodded. "That's where they'll never catch me. Out here? It's anybody's game…"

Crandall thought about the statement for a moment for nodding and standing. "Well then, we better get going."

Together, they started up the beach toward the parking lot and Crandall's silent Jeep.

* * * *

Mike was sitting in his chair, his eyes rolled back into his skull, a string of saliva stretching from his chin to his chest as he punched them in. He didn't ask for ID or even budge from his heavy position for that matter. He only muttered something that might have been: "Have a nice day, folks."

And that was all.

CHAPTER 17

23, August

The house was empty without Angela and Emily. The counters were clean, the bathrooms available, the magazines stacked on the coffee table exactly as they had been stacked the night before.

He hated the silence.

Slowly padding from one room to the next, Crandall looked for signs of life but found none. Everything was tidy—the way he liked them and demanded them to be when the females of the family made a point to mess them up. Now that everything remained in order, he was irritated, and the cleanliness disturbed him.

As did the quiet…

But he shaved and showered and pulled out the Cheerios, pouring a bowl and floating them with what was left of the fat-free milk. He ate in silence, his eyes drifting over the newspaper spread out in front of him, but he couldn't focus, and the words ran like ink until he gave up.

Crandall went to work and smiled in front of his peers, cracked some jokes, accepted his syllabus for the year and watched the clock. Next week it would start for real. Students, lockers, bells and books. Part of him was excited, but part of him knew he'd never see it.

The house felt no better at night when it seemed twice as quiet as it had that morning. He tried fixing a frozen dinner, but when the microwave told him that his meal was ready, he left it to sit and cool, his stomach telling him to leave it alone.

Instead of eating, he switched on the computer and checked his email hoping for a message from Angela only to find eighteen spam messages that he promptly deleted. Sitting back, he stared at the screen for a long moment and the animated advertisement dancing at the top of his screen. He thought about Emily, his daughter and everything that had gone wrong over the past weeks all leading up to August 27th. Either that, or he had been driven mad, and nothing was going to happen on the 27th at all except for a normal routine and a few laughs at his expense.

Sitting up, he moved his mouse to the 'Start' button, brought up the menu and hovered over 'Shut Down…' before backing out.

*…figure out who has the most money in this world, and who likes playing mad-scientist…*came Ben's voice from the back of his mind.

Crandall went to his search engine and typed in 'billionaire'. The keyword returned eight pages of hits. He snickered with righteous disgust, cursed the computer, and shut down the PC, slamming the chair under the desk and retreating to the living room where he sank into the couch, grabbing the remote and switching on the television.

The screen illuminated the room as did the comforting laughter of a sitcom. He recognized the faces, but he couldn't place the show. In all honesty, he doubted he had ever watched the show before.

He changed the channel. Commercials. It was either Chevy is better than Ford or Ford is better than Chevy. Either way, both trucks looked the same and boasted the best numbers.

Crandall began to surf. The image changed and he was watching a cop running across a road, gun in hand, dramatic music filling the sequence as he pursued some guy who looked the stereotypical thug.

He changed channels.

Another sitcom, but this time one he recognized. The remote was laid to rest upon the couch, and he settled down, folding his hands across his chest and trying to relax along with the sound of laughter and the familiarity of faces and characters. He tried to imagine that things were the way they had been before…

Dinner's almost ready, hon.

"Give me a minute," he answered, smiling.

The sound of silverware gently nicking glass plates drifted from the dining room along with Angela's hum as she set the table, the familiarity craved.

Use the nice silverware, dear.

Okay, Mom.

The television was laughing at him, intimidating him, the cheery voices an insult.

Dinner is served, Crandall. Get it while it's hot.

C'mon, Dad. It's your favorite!

"Coming," he answered as he fumbled for the remote, the sitcom cutting to commercial, the screen fading to black before returning to white, a smiling face of a woman grinning at the camera.

"For years we've reacted to symptoms," the woman on the screen said, her smile soft yet firm. *"For years we've fought to catch up only to find that we were too late. We sat and watched as our loved ones went through the agony and humiliation of chemotherapy."*

His finger touched the 'power' button, but he did not push it.

The dining room was as dark as the kitchen, the voices in his head silenced.

"But now you *don't have to."*

The woman's face faded and drifted to children playing in the grass, a dog barking at their heels, the woman pacing toward the camera, her hands carefully folded. *"With today's technology, the fears and anxiety's of yesterday are a thing of the past."*

Another face; a smiling man. *"ZayRhran saved my life by catching the cancer before I did."* A football settled into his hands. *"And ZayRhran gave me a second chance that I might not have had."*

The woman returned, her face sincere. *"Thousands will testify to the drug-free, pain-free procedure we call ZayScan that can detect and diagnose the smallest inflammation that may result in a serious ailment. With the latest in technology, can you risk not being scanned?"* She smiled—perfectly.

Crandall frowned.

"Call us today for your free, no obligation ZayScan. We have experienced medical staff on-hand to assist you with questions, concerns and treatments that will allow you to continue living your life the way you currently enjoy it without interruption and without risk."

Crandall sat up, his face furrowed in a frown.

"Catch it before it catches you," the woman said with sincerity. *"Take back your life and live with us."*

'ZayRhran' flashed across the screen, a toll-free number at the bottom.

Ben was grinning at Crandall from the television, his yellow teeth marking his cynicism. *I'd guess that you are the center of an experiment headed by a group of private investors funded independently by bored millionaires who, for some reason, chose you.*

He sat up; sat forward, Ben's words somehow sounding true to him.

They're not scanning for cancers; they're learning about you.

This was ridiculous. The old man was off his rocker…

Spies, my friend. Spies.

Crandall looked over at the dining room but neither Emily nor Angela were in there waiting for him. The table was dark due to the lack of lighting, and the placemats were collecting dust as they had been for the past week.

He looked back at the television, the telephone number fading. His thumb pressed the 'power' button, and the screen went black.

It's a stupid idea, he thought with a smirking grin on his face, yet he was thinking about what Ben had said, and he was considering the possibilities. At the end of the day, he had never been scanned by ZayRhran; nor had anyone else that he knew, so this had nothing to do with him directly.

…they're learning about you.

Crandall didn't go for the dining room or the kitchen or his dinner that had grown cold in the microwave. He returned to the computer, switching it on, not bothering with the lights, the reflection of the monitor flashing in his eyes and coating his face under a blue hue.

Crandall dialed into the internet, the hideous scratch of the modem singing to him like a hot-match against his skin. He directed his browser to the search engine and typed in ZayRhran, punching the 'enter' key with a vengeance.

The screen flooded with links that loaded up the pages one after another. He found ZayRhran's home-site and clicked it, the screen changing and paying homage to flash and fancy script. Text filled the left side, images changing along the right.

Apply for your free ZayScan now!

Crandall clicked the link and a form popped up asking for his information as detailed as his social-security number. Frustrated, he moved his mouse over the *Contact us* list and clicked. The mailing address came up along with the telephone number and email address. He scribbled down the information and moved on.

One link after another, researching procedures and information that cautiously covered the ZayScan procedure without giving away the recipe. He clicked on a few links, reading the text that loaded on his screen and noting that most of the verbiage was fluff and said little about the company. All he could find was more and more positive feedback on how the scan saved the life of such-and-such or spotted cancer before it was too late in who's-it. There were no intricate details. Just more and more smiling faces, quotations, and fancy-sounding script that sounded hollow to Crandall. In fact, the only consistency that he found was every procedure ZayRhran offered had something to do with a full-body scan. The machines pictured on the various sites looked enough like conventional CT scanners, and Crandall could find nothing to lead him to believe anything was out of the ordinary.

Still, Ben's conspiracy that ZayRhran was not what it was advertising hung in his mind, refusing to let go, though Crandall would need more if he planned on accusing this company of so much.

Frustrated, he returned to the search engine and scrolled to the bottom of the screen where a string of numbers were lined up indicating how many pages of links were available for viewing. He moved his mouse over page 22 and clicked it, hoping that the further away from ZayRhran's homepage he got, the more he might find out about the company that he shouldn't.

The list of links came up, and they were as off the wall as he had feared. One was an off-reference comment made in a web-forum to the success of ZayRhran while another was a site devoted to the 'most ridiculous company names around'. Crandall scrolled through the list of links, chuckling at some of the links, frowning at others where the text was in a foreign language with only the word ZayRhran highlighted. His eyes darted over the two or three lines of text that described each link, reading as fast as he could, absorbing whatever might be relevant.

> ....and ZayRhran CEO Jeff Chessman met Thursday...

—was the headline that Crandall stopped on. The text below was nothing special:

> Associated Press:
>
> Cancer survivor Gwyneth Blair and and ZayRhran CEO Jeff Chessman met Thursday for the first time since her life saving surgery last month. Blair, 32, was diagnosed with a rare case of liver cancer that went undetected for over a year until the newly-patented ZayScan revealed the life-threatening ailment. Governor Whittaker has supported ZayRhran since its conception with...

Crandall didn't like the last sentence. Whittaker had been the mayor of Michigan for eight years until he retired at the end of his term two years earlier. The link was obviously old, but he was curious as to how ZayRhran had been supported, so he clicked the link and was taken to a dated news-link.

> Governor Whittaker has supported ZayRhran since its conception with personal funds and funds raised on the behalf of his fifteen year-old daughter, Allison following her premature death related to an undetected brain tumor.
>
> "The relationship between this government and ZayRhran will only continue to grow so long as I am in office," Whittaker claimed this afternoon before a sparse gathering of sun-burned reporters.
>
> Chessman was all smiles as he held up a check presented to him by Mr. Whittaker "I am excited by the support I have received in Michigan and especially the Detroit Metropolitan Police Department. We at ZayRhran will continue to work closely with all public and private factions to grow and improve upon the direction ZayRhran published in its first annual mission statement. Such generous contributions are accepted with humble gratitude."
>
> ZayRhran's practices have been approved by the Michigan Department of Health and are awaiting approval from the FDA.

Crandall frowned, sitting back as he considered the donated check on the behalf of the Michigan PD. Such a contribution could not go unreturned, and the mere fact that the police department had made a contribution was a warning flag.

*They're not scanning for cancers; they're learning about you...*Ben's words came home, and the connection seemed more than just a coincidence.

Crandall's eyes remained locked with the screen, but he wasn't seeing; he was thinking. After Whittaker retired from the governor position, he promptly disappeared from the limelight, never seeking the next rung up the ladder to the top. He was just gone. Whittaker had disappeared and taken with him all of the influence and power he had acquired while in office.

Crandall returned to his search engine and typed in 'Governor Joseph Whittaker'.

The list of links was smaller than he expected. Only four pages, and everything he found was mostly dated back before his term as governor expired. The only recent link was a tiny blurb on the third page of links stating that Whittaker had recently sold his share of the stock market at a value of nearly one million dollars immediately following the sale of his house.

> When asked where he was moving, Whittaker answered: "Somewhere over the rainbow."

Crandall didn't like the answer, and while the odds were heavily stacked against him, something about this name, this company sounded right to him. Maybe it was because Ben was filling his mind with useless mumbo-jumbo and he was beginning to believe in it, or maybe he was buying into the idea of conspiracies. After all, whoever was responsible for the disk had to be something of a risk-taker, something of an eccentric.

He felt frustrated and tired. If he was off-target, he was way off, but there was only way to find out, and his answers were in Detroit and ZayRhran headquarters.

Crandall shut down the PC, grateful to stop his search, his mind spinning with ideas and arguments. It was a perfect black beyond the window, the stars hidden behind clouds, the world hidden behind shadows. Within only two hours, it would be a new day and only three days from the final sequence captured on the disk.

He had to concentrate, remain focused, stay alert. He had one chance at this, and only one. If he messed it up, he would wind up on the down side of a gunshot wound, his daughter orphaned, his goals ruined.

ZayRhran.

Though the screen was blank in front of him, the room dark, he still imagined his angered frown being visible to the invisible ghosts that haunted him.

Angela was on his mind, and he swore that with every breath he took, he would not let her down. He'd already failed his wife, and that was enough to make him feel a lifetime's worth of regret. His mistakes would not be repeated. Not now. Not ever.

Ever.

CHAPTER 18

24, August

"Mr. Cady, it is very important that you attend all meetings this week. I would not recommend that you take a personal day so early in your association with PSU."

"I understand that, but this is family emergency. I'm sorry, but there is nothing I can do about it."

The voice on the other end of the line was not pleased. "The rest of the week though?"

The tone pissed Crandall off, and he was suddenly insulted that his personal life was being called into question as though he were an elementary student. "I'll tell you what, Smith," he said, a sneer in his voice. "If you don't like it, then fire me. My family comes first. My daughter is more important to me that you are. The kids aren't in school yet, the books haven't been passed out. All you've got are seminars and pep-talks. Don't treat me like a child. I don't work that way."

"Settle down, Cady. I wasn't implying that your position was in jeopardy. All I was saying was—"

"Then I'll see you on Monday," Crandall barked. He hung up before the conversation could go any further by pressing 'end' on the digital phone. He tossed the tiny little thing into the seat beside him and punched the gas, his Jeep responding with energy as it tore along the interstate. He was heading East as fast as he could, the blazing August air scorching his skin and drying his eyes that he blinked from behind the shades that hid his real emotions.

Absent mindedly, he fumbled with his right hand through the Jeep's glove box until his fingers closed around the familiar shape of the bottle. He popped the lid with his thumb and down the few-five or six—tablets that remained at the bottom. He was comforted as the pills began to dissolve and he realized that for better or worse, the chase was drawing to a close.

* * * *

The building was tall, but not as tall as he figured it would be. In his mind, he figured he'd be approaching a building that dwarfed God, but instead, he found a man-made structure that stood maybe thirty-stories high, its appearance modern and exceptionally clean, a marble patio a hundred yards squared leading to the entrance.

There were no armed guards standing outside, no guns pointed at his skull as he approached the entrance and very a few cameras. ZayRhran was as open as a Burger King, the tall glass doors inviting him in.

There were guards beyond the glass doors, but they were more of an aesthetic addition than a threat as they stood at pre-ordained positions, their posture almost wax-like. The floor beneath his feet was clear glass that went down several feet and covered what looked like real water rolling under his shoes giving the impression that he was walking on water as he timidly approached the front desk.

Welcome to ZayRhran, the world's leader in personal health care. The electronic voice repeated every few minutes or so—Crandall wasn't keeping track.

"May I help you?" The woman behind the desk was young. Maybe twenty. Her eyes and lips were as glossy as the lights overhead, her skin as soft as the water underfoot. She seemed out of place—too innocent to be in a building like this, and Crandall felt guilty because maybe ZayRhran wasn't what he thought it was.

"I'm not sure," he answered.

"ZayScan is a free service offered by ZayRhran," the girl replied as if on cue. "You're never too young or too old to take the necessary precautions to ensure a long, carefree lifestyle. Here at ZayRhran, we promise to give you the independent attention you deserve in ensuring your health to be at an optimal level. If you're unclear about the procedures we offer, I can recommend a one-on-one meeting with one of our top specialists. Would you like to wait?"

Something was wrong. The girl was grinning and saying all the right things, but most of her information was unsolicited.

"I'm not sure," Crandall answered.

"Very well," the girl answered. "Perhaps you would like to browse one of our brochures while you wait." She extended her hand to a display in front of her desk. "Please feel free, sir."

He frowned, stepping closer to the counter and waving his hand in front of the pretty girl's face.

"Is there something else I can assist you with?" she asked politely, not disturbed by his gesture at all.

"Yes, there is," he answered.

"And what might that be?"

"Who's leading the American League Central in the pennant race this year?" he asked, studying her reaction closely.

"I am sorry, but that question is not relevant to the services offered by ZayRhran," she offered with a pleasant smile. "My opinion is neutral. Is there something else I may assist you with?"

Crandall looked over his shoulder and across the empty lobby. There were a few chairs by the window, but other than that, the enormous room was empty. He returned to the pretty girl and her pleasant smile. "Doesn't your phone ever ring?" he questioned.

"Our telephone service is available twenty-four hours a day, seven days a week, sir. Would you like a business card?" She held one up.

Something was definitely wrong.

He figured he'd test the waters. "No thank you, honey."

"All right then. Would you prefer to wait for a doctor?"

"Yes, but in the meantime, I would really like to have sex with you. What do you say? You and me, right now?"

"I'm sorry, but that question is not relevant to the services offered by ZayRhran," she answered with a pleasant smile. "My opinion is neutral. Is there something else I may assist you with?"

He stepped back. The girl was a fake. A plastic mannequin that looked real, sounded real and even smelled real. Her (it's) perfume was alluring, bringing him to an uncomfortable state.

"I'll just wait," he answered, taking a step back.

"Very well, sir. A doctor will be with you shortly." The girl smiled pleasantly.

Crandall backed off, making for the chairs at the opposite end of the room. He took a seat by the window, sunlight spilling over his shoulders as he picked up a magazine and absent-mindedly began to thumb through the ads.

The girl at the desk offered nothing more.

He became dimly aware that the sound of a repetitious tick was coming from an enormous clock overhead and several stories up. The hands must have been ten feet long apiece, the face of the clock larger than any other he had ever seen.

Dropping his eyes to the front desk again, he watched the girl as she stood perfectly motionless, her eyes staring forward but not really seeing anything.

The door opened, and a woman entered, her knee-length skirt swishing about her legs as she made her way across the glass floor toward the receptionist, her heels clicking as she went.

"May I help you?" he heard the receptionist ask.

An exchange was passed between the two women, their voices carrying but not clearly enough for Crandall to hear what was being said. Shrugging, he went back to his magazine, the moments ticking away.

The woman came clicking back and vacated the building, the receptionist returning to her statuesque stance, the enormous clock overhead continuing to call out the seconds and the slow minutes.

He shifted uncomfortably. The chairs in the lobby were like bricks, and he felt himself becoming anxious if not irritated. The magazines were boring. Not one of them had articles on sports or entertainment. Glancing over the titles on the table beside him, every magazine had the exciting flavor of the Wall Street Journal. No articles on anything but medicine and the stock market. Glancing at his watch, Crandall realized he'd already been waiting twenty minutes. Looking across the room, the receptionist was still frozen where she stood, her eyes unblinking.

"Is this going to take much longer?" he called, his voice echoing more than he thought it would, and he was somewhat embarrassed.

"A doctor will be with you shortly," the receptionist answered.

Crandall shook his head and went back to his magazine, flipping through the pages, looking for something, anything of interest. The best he could come up with was a cigarette ad featuring a cute blonde in a bikini. He sighed.

The clock continued to count one agonizing second after another away.

Looking up again, the receptionist was frozen in time. Frustrated, he tossed the magazine back to the table, leaned forward and rubbed his weary eyes. The small hand on his watch rhymed with the larger clock overhead, and he felt his impatience mounting. Standing, Crandall paced back and forth, his hands locked behind his back, one step after another, back and forth over and over again, his footsteps in sequence with the maddening tick of the clock that called out the heartbeat of ZayRhran.

He checked his watch again. Forty minutes. *Jesus Christ, who were these people fooling?*

Crandall approached the front desk, his face flushed with frustration.

"May I help you?" the reception asked pleasantly.

Biting his tongue, he contained himself and responded with sarcasm. "You most certainly can, hon."

"How may I help you?" she answered, her perfect face beaming.

"You said that the doctor would be with me shortly," he sneered. "It's been nearly forty-five minutes."

"I said *a* doctor would be with you shortly. We have many doctors on hand here today. You will be treated in the order you were received. Have a seat, Mr. Cady."

Crandall felt his blood freeze. "What did you just say to me?"

"A doctor will be with you shortly, sir. Is there something else I may assist you with?"

He looked around, turning a full circle, his eyes searching for cameras, secret eyes that were watching him, but he found none. Turning back to the receptionist, he was stern. "What did you call me?"

The mannequin shivered as her processor calculated a response, her eyes blinking as if on cue. "I'm sorry, but that question is not relevant to the services offered by ZayRhran," she answered with a pleasant smile. "My opinion is neutral. Is there something else I may assist you with?"

A door opened at the far end of the room, a man dressed in suit and tie stepping out and approaching, his hands plunged into the deep pockets of the overcoat, his stride confident but not intimidating.

Crandall stepped away from the counter and eyed the approaching man, his heart pounding.

Extending his hand, the man offered a smile. "My name is Dr. Pope. How may I be of assistance, Mr…?" The man dragged out the sentence opening the way for Crandall to fill in the blank.

"Don't play with me," Crandall snapped. "Your puppet already slipped up, Pope. You know who I am, so cut the foreplay."

The smile vanished from the doctor's face, and his eyes darted to the receptionist.

"Don't look at her," Crandall ordered. "I'm right here. You'll deal with me."

The doctor returned his gaze, and slowly he smiled. "Let's step into my office, Mr. Cady."

To hear his name being called without having ever been asked sent shivers up Crandall's back, but he hid his emotion behind his over-protective sense of fatherhood for his daughter, and he took the game being played at his expense as a direct attack against Angela and Emily. "Lead the way, Doc." His voice was anything but pleasant.

CHAPTER 19

Pope led him into a tiny office with no windows and a large desk dwarfed by the amount of papers that covered it. The doctor rounded the desk and sat down, his aged chair squeaking as the springs rocked back. He crossed his hands over his lap, a smug grin on his face. "Have a seat."

"I'd rather stand."

"Sit." It was an order, but the tone remained friendly. Crandall looked around and saw only a small chair against the wall. He wiped the papers from its surface and sat down.

Pope looked at his watch. "Well, your timing is good."

"Why don't you tell me why I'm here," Crandall said, making sure he sounded as angry as he felt, making sure his anxiety was hidden.

Pope shifted slightly. "My guess is you already know why. That would explain why you are sitting where you are. I would expect that you have better questions for me, Mr. Cady. After all, I am a busy man."

"I'm sure you are. So how am I a part of your busy schedule?"

"Who says you are?"

Crandall leaned forward. "I've got the disk, genius. You know, the one that got away? The one showing me that my wife and my dog were going to die before it actually happened? The one that concludes in three days with me dead on the ground and some old guy standing over me? Ring a bell?"

"I thought you were here on an appointment to ask about the ZayScan." Pope smiled. "Sounds like you might need one."

Crandall grinned, but his grin got away from him, and he smiled broadly even as he leaned forward, his eyes flashing with hatred, the venom more than obvious.

"I know you think this is a game, doctor," Crandall hissed. "But I can assure you that it is not. No one will hear you scream."

Pope raised his hands in submission. "Let's not get ahead of ourselves, Cady."

"If I kill you right here and now, I'll go to prison. My little girl will be placed in the custody of my mother and father where she will receive insurance and remain in the best school district around. All in all, she'd probably be better off than if I don't kill you, so give me a reason why I should not get ahead of myself, and maybe we'll talk."

The doctor shifted uncomfortably. It was obvious that the man across from him was not joking. It wasn't so much his words as much as it was the sincerity behind those words. "What do you want?"

Crandall smiled. "Everything. Why did I find the disk?"

"Disk? You're talking in-"

Crandall shook his head, laughing lightly with frustration before standing, his fists coiling into balls, white at the knuckle.

Pope sighed, lowering his eyes, fidgeting with unease. "You're here because we committed an error. Not a major error, but one that, as it turns out, was necessary. It was an accident, but its outcome was generally predictable."

"Go on."

"Well, to be quite frank, Mr. Cady, you were supposed to figure enough of the puzzle to find yourself at that fairground three days from now because the events we filmed on that disk you found had to come true in order for our experiment to be complete."

"Your experiment? I'm your experiment?"

"Don't flatter yourself." Pope stood and paced. "You mean no more to me or anybody else here at ZayRhran than you do in your tiny little tight-knit, slow-motion community that's about as exciting as watching grass grow. Don't go thinking you're special or that you were selected for some kind of purpose."

Crandall allowed his lip to drop. "Oh, I guarantee you I'm special, Dr. Pope."

The doctor turned, smiling. "How's that?"

"Because I'm the only who penetrated your fortress and stands opposed to you willing to trade my life for yours, and I know you can hear me because you've given yourself away by that hairline wrinkle of concern residing directly between your beady little eyes."

The doctor didn't like the answer and he stopped pacing. He leaned forward on the desk. "If you were going to assault me, you would have already. I'm not an imbecile."

"And what makes you so certain?"

Pope reached for a remote that lay on the edge of his desk, raised it toward a small screen at Crandall's right, and pressed play. The video feed Crandall had all but memorized appeared. All over again. The new puppy, the funerals, the walk along the pier. All of it.

"Because," Pope whispered. "We already know the outcome."

Crandall dropped his eyes to his hands, noting the tremble, and felt sick to his stomach. Was he really prepared to hurt a man? What if he failed, or worse yet, what if he succeeded? The repercussions would be severe. He'd be hauled off to jail, and despite the pep-talk he'd quietly held with himself, he didn't fancy the thought of never seeing his daughter again. He didn't like the idea of incarceration in a square box, barred off, the air as stale as the food. But how did Pope know this?

"Don't worry yourself over it," the doctor said, relaxing. "I'm not going to call the police and tell them you were threatening me. You're free to walk out of here unmolested if you choose to. At any time. I don't want you to ever feel that you're in danger here."

Crandall lifted his eyes to the doctor.

"I'm sorry, Crandall. It wasn't in the plan to have you beating on my door today, so I'm a bit off-balance. You must understand that it wasn't my decision to break the news to you in this manner, but fate plays a role that we sometimes cannot overrule, and here we are."

"Who's 'we?"

The doctor shrugged. "The board members of ZayRhran."

"So what's the mission statement?"

Pope sat forward. "It isn't clear, Mr. Cady. We have goals, but we argue and argue and argue. You know how it is. Life at this office isn't much different than it would be in, say, a school room."

Crandall held his posture, his face glazed.

"In all honesty, you weren't supposed to find that disk. A former employee of ZayRhran misplaced it and was let go as a result. In retrospect, however, these were the events that were supposed to happen in order for you to find your way here today, at this time, at this moment." He chuckled. "Irony is not without a sense of humor."

Crandall shook his head. "I'm not predictable, doc. I could snap at any second and have your eyeballs ripped from your head before the guards were able to break down the door and pull me off thereby ruining your little experiment. I'd never see that fairground, wherever it is. I'd never be shot, and all of your studies and theories would be wasted. The only thing holding me back is my curiosity to hear how you plan on explaining this."

Pope pressed pause, and the screen froze with the old man hovering over Crandall, his gun still smoldering, a small wisp of gray smoke hanging suspended like a painting. "I disagree. Not that I'm any better, because I've learned that the road of man is predetermined. I try like hell to break the pattern, but you know what? I still drive home by taking the same shortcut I do every night. I get home at the same time, give or take five minutes. The little woman is there with dinner ready to go on the table, and I eat the same meals, watch the same television programs, laugh at the same dumb jokes, take the same shower and read the same kinds of books before turning out the light at virtually the same time. We are creatures of predictability, Cady. I could see you coming from a mile away because I studied the way you think and break down the problems you're presented with. You're not a difficult subject to understand."

"I'm here today aren't I? Didn't you say that surprised you? Put you, 'off guard'?"

"Maybe. Maybe not. Maybe I've told you what you wanted to hear."

"I changed that disk," Crandall countered. "The images changed, so don't preach to me."

"Did they?" Pope asked. "Did they change? I mean, you would know, of course, but are you sure they changed?"

"Yes, I am. Dialogue I had with my daughter out on the front lawn. It was on the disk when I first watched it, but I never said those words, and the disk changed."

"You sound awfully confident. Are you sure you're remembering the exact order of events? Are you sure you're not remembering things the way you want them to be?"

"I see what you're trying to do here, Pope. I'm not a pawn in your chess game. I remember."

Pope grinned. "I don't think you do. Why don't you tell me what's in those orange bottles you keep in your pockets, your glove box, your kitchen cupboards and your medicine cabinets? Alone, an anti-depressant will tickle those endorphins and make you feel somewhat giddy, but when you start to mix them, can you confidently say that you are in full control?"

Crandall shrunk back. "The medication I take is none of your business."

"No? Five doctors, five different prescriptions, and you're mixing them all. Let me guess." Pope relaxed. "Zoloft, certainly Prozac, probably some Tricyclics like

Effexor or Desipramine. Stop me if I'm cold, Crandall, but I think I'm heading right on course."

Crandall softened, his confidence giving way.

"What you've been telling yourself is that you remember exactly how the events on that disk played out, but what you're forgetting is that the mind works in mysterious ways when under the influence of drugs."

"So, which parts did I imagine?"

The doctor laughed. "Your guess is as good as mine, my friend. Would you like a complimentary ZayScan?"

Crandall's face hardened, the insult testing his resolve.

"Sorry," Pope said. "I was out of line with that one. My mistake. I apologize."

Crandall thought things through, focused, his mind trying to concentrate. "Fine. I can't incriminate you or your company for what I saw, but you know how it ends. You know the old man who shoots me dead. Who is he?"

"Are you so certain that the old man is the one who pulls the trigger? You never actually saw the gun fire, Crandall. You see what you're doing? You're jumping to conclusions with nothing to back up your suppositions. What's the difference between green and blue when you're blindfolded?"

"The fucking disk changed!" Crandall snapped. "Don't play psychologist with me, Pope. I am not in the mood."

Pope leaned forward, his eyes glinting as he charged Crandall. "The truth of the matter, Cady, is that you don't remember any events the way they really happened. You're so delusional that you've told yourself how things were supposed to work out when you dismissed your actions leading up to the very moment when you passed through the doors of ZayRhran."

"What the hell are you talking about?"

Pope smiled, rocking back, the chair squeaking with him. "How did Charlie die, Crandall?"

"My dog?"

"Yes, your dog. How did he die?"

"Old age." Crandall shook his head. "What are you getting at?"

"Old age, was it? The dog had arthritis, Crandall. It wasn't terminal."

Crandall shrugged. "What's that supposed to mean?"

"Well, I don't mean to be so blunt, but I did find it curious when you mixed rat poisoning in with his Gravy Train."

Crandall stopped. He wasn't sure he had accurately heard the man across from him the way it sounded. The accusation was too preposterous to even entertain. He had just been accused of killing his dog. His pal of twelve years.

"Don't look so surprised, Crandall. You did it, and you know you did it. The problem is, you don't want to admit to yourself that you did it."

"You're suggesting that I-" He composed himself, biting his tongue. "Why would I kill my dog, Pope? What's my incentive?"

The doctor's face went gray. "What was your incentive to create that terrible accident when you were a child?"

God saw you do it, you little shit.

"I was..."

"You were looking for attention. You hated being the odd boy out, the last one picked for a game of dodge-ball. Name your cliché, but you were not happy with who you were then any more than you are today, and those memories still haunt you, don't they?"

Crandall's demeanor went cold. "How did you know about that?" he demanded.

"It's all public record, my friend. These days, if you want to know where someone is masturbating, all you have to do is ask the computer. Nothing is sacred or private anymore. But it was that moment in your life that makes you such an exciting subject. It is one reason why you were chosen."

"Subject..."

"Yes. Subject. Combine your adolescent tragedy with your current state of guilt and dependence on prescription medications, and we've got a very exciting subject to study and manipulate."

"Manipulate?"

"Well, some of the events on that disk, no doubt, were enhanced by your reaction. Now, they're all genuine lest you think we tried to deceive you, so be warned that the feed you watched was the original product filmed from the end of a camera in real time."

Crandall felt cold, his fingers greasy with sweat. "I didn't kill my dog."

Pope chuckled. "It doesn't end there. I wouldn't bring it up, but you threatened me, so it's my turn. All's fair in love and war, but I digress."

"Bring what up?"

Pope sobered, his eyes fortuitous and incriminating. "Emily wasn't suicidal."

The words hung on the air for a long moment, Crandall staring at the man opposed for him, a million thoughts racing through his head, the ramifications of Pope's words sinking in, his own soul scarred, humiliated, attacked and insulted before he lurched just as the doors at either side swung inward, men rushing forward as Crandall leapt from his chair, jumping the table and bearing down on the doctor who sat calmly, hands folded as Crandall closed to within inches before being yanked back, the crook of a large arm around his neck and squeezing the air from his lungs, huge hands immobilizing his as he was slung backward into his chair. His face turned purple with rage, his eyes bulging from the lack of oxygen.

"Predictable," Pope said with a calm smile, never having moved.

The guards released Crandall who sat shivering with rage, and he was poised to strike again when four cold barrels were lowered to his face level.

Pope shook his head. "Saw that one coming too. We recorded it actually. You probably wouldn't believe it, but your reaction was anticipated based on studies we've generated over the past twenty years. Believe it or not, seventy-nine percent of all homicides are knee-jerk reactions to an accusation that is absolutely true. Those guilty merely react violently when confronted with it."

"I didn't kill my wife," Crandall growled from where he sat. "Don't even fuckin' try it, or I swear to God I'll-"

"You'll what?" The doctor smiled before shaking his head. "You already had your chance. See, the problem is, Cady, is that you don't understand the future. You were there to make every image on the disk come true, and the final scene is no exception. The future is already the past. You cannot control it."

Crandall shifted uncomfortably.

"Lower your guns, guys," Pope ordered of the guards. "He's not a threat. Not anymore."

The guards relaxed their weapons, but they cast uncertain eyes toward Pope.

"Leave one of your weapons," Pope instructed. "Place it on the desk in front of him, and please leave."

"Uh, is that wise, sir?"

"Relax, gentlemen," Pope responded. "I've already seen the future."

A heavy handgun was placed on the desk in front of Crandall, and the guards looked at one another before unhappily making their exit, uncertain that it was the right thing to do.

Pope smiled. "If you want to kill me, now is your chance," he said lightly.

Crandall looked at his gun, himself and over at the doctor across from him. "You already know I won't."

Pope raised his brows. "That's true, but where's the drama in that?"

He shook his head. "No more games. I concede."

"Of course you do. I already knew that. *We* already knew that."

Crandall felt numb, his fingers tingling, his legs rubbery. He felt that if he tried to stand that his bowels would release, and he'd leave a mess on the floor, so he sat, staring at the gun on the table, an object that looked so deadly, so powerful. There were more questions than he could possibly ask. "I loved Emily. I love her still. I'd never do her harm."

"But then there's all that pent up rage. All that, 'why me? How come I can't have a normal life like the Johnson's across the street?' She was a crutch to you, Crandall. In the back of your mind, in that tiny little crook that you kept hidden away, you hated her for that. You wanted back the girl you married, but you knew it would never happen so long as Emily lived. She was gone, already dead. The happiness you dreamed of was lost to doctor bills and nights of restless sleep."

"Fuck you. You hear me? You don't know anything about me."

"Of course not."

"I changed that goddamn disk. I know I did. My daughter was supposed to die, but she didn't. That small casket became a larger one. You can't tell me that everything I do from now until my death has already been predetermined."

"Angela would have been your next victim had you lost your composure. I am so very glad to report that your love for her is genuine and cannot be broken even by psychosis. Instead, you killed her grandmother. There's always a victim. It just depends on who that victim is supposed to be. We figured your mental state was on the edge and you'd go for the daughter, but you countered. We underestimated you more than once, Cady. A mistake we won't make again."

Crandall closed his eyes. "So you tried? You tried to destroy her? You tried to make me destroy my own daughter? What do you people want from me?"

"From you? What is this? You think you're so important? You're one face in a million. You're one disk in a million. I deal with these same accusations each and every day. You are not unique any more than you are special. You're a name on a wall and nothing more. So you tracked me down. Kudos. That's a bronze star, pal. A bronze star from someone with a messed up sense of direction. A misguided, over-eager child who thinks he has solved the mystery behind 'why'." Pope shook his head. "You're nothing, Cady. Not even a front-page headline. You're a man who manufactured his hard-knocks so he could retreat to the erotic guilt he felt as a child when that car slammed into the old oak and killed a young woman you would have wanted to fuck."

"You know nothing about me."

"No? As it turns out, it seems I know everything about you."

Crandall didn't respond, his mind twirling, whirling with questions, confusion, rage. How had they done this? Why him? How could it be real? Be true? Fate was a myth. If someone wanted to change the direction of their life, they could through will alone. What he would do forty years from now was not written. Couldn't be written. No way. "Why me?"

Pope grinned. "The answers to all your questions will be made available to you in three days, Mr. Cady." The doctor reached into his pocket and pulled out a piece of folded and crinkled white paper. He leaned forward and dropped the piece of paper directly in front of Crandall.

"What's this?"

Pope smiled. "For days now you've been pining over that disk. Hours upon hours you watched, re-watched, played and replayed the events recorded on it. Everything now makes sense because you've lived it. Every moment, every emotion, every second captured on that disk is real in your mind except for the last ones. Those you cannot account for, and they seem bogus to you." A wink. "I mean, you're in control of your own destiny, right? So what does it matter that the last scene played out there is your own death. You can prevent it, can you not? No one tells you how to live."

Crandall's stomach was rubbery, sick, whatever he had eaten for lunch sloshing around and trying to retreat.

"On that piece of paper," Pope continued, nodding toward the crumpled sheet, "you'll find explicit directions to where you need to be on August 27th at five twenty-nine p.m. Nothing more. This is not a hoax or a scam. I'm simply pointing the way to alleviate the stress of trying to solve the riddle yourself."

Crandall looked at the paper and back at Pope. "Bullshit."

"I'm not the bad guy here. I'm just a player in the mix. The conclusion to your story was already filmed, so I have nothing to gain by giving you this. You would have discovered it anyway, without my help."

Crandall reached for the paper, his hands tingling with adrenalin, but he held himself back. Slowly, his eyes went to the man across from him. "If I don't look at this piece of paper, I won't know where to go on August 27th. If I lock myself in my house on August 27th, lock the doors and the windows, bury the keys to my Jeep and unplug the telephone, I cannot be killed at the location that the disk shows. If I'm to be murdered, it would have to happen in my own home. The disk would be wrong and I'll win, Mr. Pope. You'd lose."

Pope grinned. "That's true." The man grinned with sedition. "But remember that fate is stronger than you are. It's stronger than me, and it's stronger than the foundation that supports this building. The ending of your story was filmed because that's the way it is supposed to end. Period."

Crandall flicked the piece of paper back at Pope. "No. I'm not going there. If I don't know where it is, then I can't find it. You lose. End of story. Game over. In your own words, name your cliché."

Pope smiled, lifting his eyes from the crumpled wad of paper to Crandall who sat directly opposed.

"What's so funny?" Crandall demanded.

"I'll make these directions available to you."

"I don't want to hear it."

"I think you do." His confidence was sickening. "The park. East side. There's a tall oak with a cavity that's rotted out. You can reach all the way in."

"I'm not listening."

"Young boys think it's fun to pee in the hole so it most often stinks of urine, but I'll protect the instructions in a zipped baggie. I'll even shelter it in a plastic container so it's completely isolated from any elements."

"I won't go there," Crandall argued.

"Of course you won't. You'd be sealing your own fate if you did, and why would anyone consciously do that?"

Crandall felt his blood boiling. "I don't have to let you live, doc. Fate or no fate, your life right now is mine to control."

Pope smiled. "Control? I swear on my life that the directions will be where I promise. I'm not the bad guy, Cady. If you want to control the outcome of your story, then the power is now in your hands. Don't make me a pawn to your weakness."

It was all so confusing, all so wrong yet it all felt so true. This ugly man and his ugly calm demeanor. His ugly words and ugly honestly. Crandall felt betrayed by the power of ugly pestilence.

Pope was grinning. "You'll go there because you want to. Your need to know is stronger than your resolve, but it's not your fault. After all, you're only human."

Crandall stood and shook his head at Pope. "My future is not pre-determined, Doctor. You'll discover that soon enough." His lungs expanded with each breath of hatred. "I won't go there. All your work, research and money was wasted on someone who's strong enough to stay away if only to spite you."

Pope grinned. "I'll see you Saturday."

Crandall shook his head. "I don't think you heard me right. I win. Period." He turned his back and stormed out of the room, breaking into the open foyer of the mammoth building, the mannequin doll behind the front desk turning his way. She even smiled a perfect smile.

"Have a nice day, Mr. Cady."

"Whatever." He pushed his way through the glass doors and into the sunshine that bled so innocently unto his shoulders that for a moment he was hypnotized with the world and wondered why he felt so much vengeance. Crandall paced the sidewalk, steady eyes around him, watching him, forgetting him, ignoring him as they blocked his forward progress, bumped him, made his path a trying one. He pushed back.

He wanted to go home. Back to his soft couch and the unbiased television. He wanted the soothing smells of pasta and bubbling sauce floating in from the kitchen, making him jealous of what he'd once had. He wanted something more than he had. Something equivalent to what he'd lost.

Crandall's Jeep rolled over the potholes of the uncared for road as he pushed the needle beyond the legal limit. He wasn't going to go to the park. Not now. Not ever. He'd win. They'd lose.

Pulling into the driveway, the garage door opened slowly, the light drifting out, and he pulled in, the Jeep settling in its familiar, predictable position. Killing the motor, Crandall listened to the hot ticks of the engine before climbing out and slipping his key into the lock.

The house was empty. More empty than he'd ever known it to be, and never before had he wanted to hear his daughter racing across the kitchen floor to give him a hug or see the happy smile of his wife as he came home.

Welcome home, dear...

Instead, the kitchen was lit only by a nightlight, the shadows hanging heavy like ghosts and anticipating his movement.

"It's not over yet," he whispered, his glower hidden in the darkness. Crandall slumped against the wall, his eyes attacking the darkness even as his body fell, and he sat there, consumed beneath the leeches of Hell while the moments ticked by, and seconds challenged his strength.

CHAPTER 20

25, August

The house was unnervingly quiet, and he hated the gnawing sense of emptiness that tickled at him where he sat in the corner listening to the grandfather clock ceremoniously call out the noon hour, the bells ringing throughout the entire house only to silence and return him to the quiet, heavy enough to make him shiver. Crandall's mind was winding itself into a knot, going over the same questions, the same conclusions and the same consequences. The pressure was pinching his sanity and driving him mad.

Buddy whined from where he lay at the edge of the kitchen tile, as close to his master as he could get without lying on the forbidden carpet he'd been trained to avoid. Crandall looked as his hands and saw that they were still shaking. "I'm not going there," he whispered.

Buddy lifted his head, his tail thumping the kitchen floor clumsily.

The park. East side.

Crandall wished he could just push the images on the disc from his mind and concentrate on something else. He had tried watching television, but to no avail. He had tried the radio, but the songs just became annoying to the point of driving him to rage. The silence was no better, the seconds ticking by slowly, one after another, the day dragging on and on. Understanding his personal mission, Crandall knew that all he had to do was wait it out until after five-thirty p.m. on the twenty-seventh of August. If he could wait that long—only another fifty-three and a half hours—everything Pope had said would be a lie. If he failed and made the ending come true, then it was all true, every blasphemous word, every grotesque scene.

"I won't go there," he repeated.

Buddy lifted his head again and whined, the thump-thump of his tail a friendly sign of understanding.

There's a tall oak with a cavity that's rotted out. You can reach all the way in.

He shook his head, a sudden pain behind the front of his skull so severe that his eyes began to water. Cursing, he stumbled to his feet and bumped the walls, applying pressure to the pain with the palms of his hand as he clumsily wove along the hall to the bathroom where he yanked open the medicine cabinet, the mirrored face smacking the wall. He fumbled amidst the bottles, knocking a slew of them into the bathroom sink, and he popped the lid to an aspirin bottle, dumping five or six dusty tablets onto his tongue. Pouring water into the glass beside the sink, he drank them away, burping lightly as he fumbled again through the cabinet, finding an orange bottle, his eyes seeing the name Effexor across the front before he dumped another three or four into his mouth, rinsing them down.

Crandall held his breath, afraid he'd vomit if he didn't, and he sat down on the edge of the bathtub, his hands and knees trembling, the pain in his skull enough to reduce him to tears. Gasping, he sat where he was, listening to the breeze beyond the window, no other sounds audible.

The silent world remained.

I have to get out of here, he thought, forcing himself to stand. It would be ten minutes or more before the pills took effect, but he couldn't wait that long. Having no idea where he would go, Crandall locked the doors, opened the garage and backed the Jeep out into the sunshine where the soft rays soothed him.

I won't go there…

He slipped on his shades and used the remote to close the garage door, his face as steady as he could hold it, his neighbor waving from next door, a gesture Crandall ignored as he reversed into the road, dropped into first and pulled away.

Where could he go? What would distract him?

His head was pounding, every beat of his heart making his eyes swell and his face flush. His Jeep swerved all over the road even though he concentrated as best he could on holding the wheel straight. Switching on the radio, he rolled through the dial, stopping on something unfamiliar but as intense as he'd ever before heard, the rhythmic grunge of the guitars and drums as angry as the voice growling hateful lyrics. Crandall pushed up the volume until the speakers began to distort, and he left it, grinding the transmission into fourth gear and accelerating, moving in the opposite direction of the east side park.

I won't go there, he thought, forcing his mind to accept the decision.

He didn't know where he was going, but it was all he could do to keep from causing an accident, so he didn't worry about it too much. Wherever he was heading would be completely unrelated to the disk, ZayRhran or his recent history. After all, he was in charge. He knew exactly how the day was going to end.

Exactly.

* * * *

"May I help you?"

Crandall frowned. "I'm here to see Benjamin Spoon," he stammered, wondering who the new face behind the glass was.

"What is your relationship with Mr. Spoon?"

"He's a friend."

"I'll just need to see your Id."

Crandall held out his driver's license, looking around the room. Something didn't feel right. "Mike knows me. Where's Mike?"

The man behind the glass lifted his eyes, a daring glint accusing Crandall of any number of crimes. "Mike who?"

Crandall shrank. "Mike. The guy who used to work where you sit. You know, short…chubby…"

The man's face remained rigid. "Mike is a patient here now, Mr…" He checked the Id. "Cady. Mind if I run this?" he asked in reference to the license.

"Go ahead."

The large man stood, hitched his pants and lumbered out of his little room where he shut the door behind him, leaving Crandall alone in another silent room.

Of all places, why had he chosen this place? Jesus, it was enough to drive him mad. He had no further business with Ben. This was a waste of time, and it would only confuse him further. In the back of his mind he knew he had arrived at Clear Haven because he needed to talk to someone who would understand—even under the duress of a delusional mind, Ben Spoon could relate, and he knew Crandall's dilemma. He would enjoy the company and lend an ear and any advice he might have to help Crandall overcome.

The new man returned and passed the license back under the safety glass. "You've been visiting for some time now, Mr. Cady."

Crandall controlled himself. It seemed that no matter how much things seemed to change, the more consistent they became—the more predictable. "Yes, I have."

The security guard grinned as he punched the button to summon a nurse while sliding the license back under the glass window. "Seems strange, that's all. We get fewer visitors around here than you might expect."

The door opened and a nurse greeted him with a smile, recognition in her eyes. "Hello Crandall. Welcome back."

Crandall nodded his appreciation to the guard and followed the nurse into the main room. His mood barely brightened as he passed the beds lined against the walls like a hospital, the residents groaning from where they lay, their skin sagging and as white as the sheets.

Ben was no exception. He lay with eyes open, his mouth dribbling spittle along his face.

"We had to give him a sedative," the nurse explained cheerfully. "He was causing a stir with the other residents."

"How much did you give him?" Crandall asked, horrified.

"Just enough to settle him." She was defensive. "He was talking about the end of the world and scaring the be Jesus out of everyone here." She giggled. "Myself included, I must admit. You know Benjamin. He can be quite convincing."

Crandall was scornful. "Well, I guess you solved the problem then."

The nurse was not apologetic, her face souring. "I'll just leave you two alone. Take as long as you like." She quietly walked away, the rubber soles of her white sneakers silent on the shiny floor.

Crandall sat down on the edge of the bed and looked over at Ben. "How ya doing, bud?" he asked, knowing there wouldn't be a response. He patted his friend on the shoulder and took a deep breath as he listened to the old people talking to themselves or their friend in tired whispers around the room. "I met a man by the name of Pope yesterday," he said, chuckling at the ironic name. "Some doctor over at ZayRhran, that place you told me to be wary of. Well, you were right, old man, ZayRhran isn't what they advertise. I wanted to thank you for the heads up." He smiled with pride. "They were surprised to see me to say the least."

Ben just stared at the ceiling, his eyes wide, his mouth hanging open as though he were dead. The only indication that he was, in fact, alive was the fact that his chest rose every few seconds to draw in a breath before slowly settling as he exhaled.

"I was hoping you might be awake because I need your advice, Ben." Crandall looked up at the ceiling and the network of tiny cracks in the ceiling. "Pope told me where I can find directions allegedly leading to where the final scene on that disk is supposed to occur." He shook his head. "Messes with the mind. I mean,

I'm curious as hell, but it messes with me to know where I can find directions to the exact location I am supposed to die."

Ben continued to breathe and stare. He was a living man trapped in a coma, hearing nothing, seeing nothing.

Crandall felt like an idiot talking to the vegetable beside him, but he talked anyway. "I don't know how to keep away. In my mind's eye I can already visualize myself tracking down those instructions just so I can see for myself how the video ends. I don't know. The doctor was going on about fate. Maybe he's right. Maybe we have no control over what is or isn't supposed to happen. Maybe I'm just a weak-minded fool too ignorant to stay away."

He felt the pressure digging at his brain again, and he winced, his hand going instinctively for his pocket where the orange bottle lay, but another hand, one cold and clammy wrapped around his wrist and held him back.

Crandall jerked, his heart leaping into his throat as he turned to the old man who continued to lay with his eyes and mouth open. "Christ, are you awake in there?" he hissed quietly.

Ben didn't answer.

Looking around, Crandall saw that nobody was paying attention so he leaned over to Ben's ear. "Can you hear me?"

"Pray," the old man whispered without moving his lips.

Crandall frowned. "Excuse me?"

"Get on your goddamn knees and pray, ya idiot," Ben said with stale breath.

Confused, Crandall eyed the room, looking for the catch, but finding none. Finally, he did as he had been told and kneeled on the floor, crossing his hands over Ben's chest and bowing his head so his ears were close to the old man's lips.

"ZayRhran, huh?" Ben whispered. "I knew it. I called that one."

Crandall was stunned. "I don't get it. They tranquilized you."

"Fed me a damn pill, Cady. Held it under my tongue till they left me alone then spit it out. They're part of it, you know, the evil sonsabitch's."

"You're crafty, my friend," Crandall said with a timid grin. "They'll never get the better of you, will they?"

"Not if you keep your voice down," came the dry reply.

"Sorry."

"So, they left you with instructions to your maker, did they? But you haven't followed up?"

"If I can hold out another couple of days, it'll be too late. I'll win. The ending on that disk won't come true. It can't come true."

"Maybe that's their plan. Did you ever figure that?"

"I don't follow."

"Maybe by ignoring their so-called instructions you'll wind up concentrating on something so drastically opposite of that fairground that you'll wind up there accidentally, which wouldn't be an accident in the grand scheme of things. At that point, that became your grandiose plan."

Crandall closed his eyes with dread. "What if I just don't leave the house? How could I wind up there then?"

"You already left the house. What the hell are you doing here?"

"I needed advice."

"From an old kook like me? Dollars to beans say they figured this little visit into their game. You're playing right into their hands just like the amateur you are."

"I'm sorry." Crandall stuttered. "I'm new to this whole...conspiracy thing, Ben."

The old man shifted his eyes to meet the younger man's attention over him. "You think this is just a conspiracy? That's all this is? A conspiracy?"

Crandall shrugged.

Ben lightly shook his head. "This is the first step at the fringes of war, Cady. The first war that goes beyond bombs and guns and the adolescent technology of guided missiles or nuclear weapons. War will be waged using time, and you are among the first of its victims."

An old woman at the next bed began laughing hysterically, rocking back and forth, smacking her head against the wall, tears rolling along her wrinkled cheeks.

Ben lifted his eyes to the ceiling again, resuming his trance-like, glazed stare. "Avoiding those instructions won't solve your problems," he whispered. "ZayRhran will just come back for you. You've been marked."

The old woman was weeping, her laughing subsiding as she rolled over, falling face first into the mattress, her sounds muffled.

"What can I do?" Crandall pleaded.

Ben rolled his eyes back into his head. "You must go. The doctors are coming. They'll hear."

"They're not here yet," Crandall said, his hands still folded as though he were praying. "Help me, Ben. What can I do?"

Ben waited a moment, sinking back into his pillow, a thin line of clear saliva running from the edge of his mouth. "Don't let them see you," he whispered. "They're coming."

"Mr. Cady?"

Crandall jerked at the sound of the voice looming over his shoulder, and he stood, poorly hiding his emotions. His heart raced as he tried to compose himself, his demeanor disheveled by his disrupted state of mind.

"Your friend appears to be very sick," the nurse said with a sympathetic yet weakly effusive grin. "It is in his best interest that we allow him to rest now."

"Of course," Crandall managed. "I've never seen him like this."

"It's the sedative, I'm sure."

Crandall didn't dare a look over his shoulder as he followed the nurse from the large, open room.

"Traitor!" came a scream from the other side of the room, and Crandall jerked his attention to see a man writhing at his constraints, the long white sleeves holding him back, his eyes digging deep into his opponent's soul. "Fucking traitor!"

Crandall waved lightly toward Mike before passing through the door and out of sight.

The cries over his shoulder died down.

* * * *

Taking the wheel of the Jeep, the engine humming calmly, Crandall didn't touch the gas, instead allowing the engine to idle while he sat and pondered the words Ben had muttered.

Don't let them see you.

If only it was that simple. Wherever he went, whatever he did, they were watching it seemed. They knew his every move because it had already been recorded.

That's ridiculous, he thought with disgust. Even Pope hadn't been so bold to explain the contents of the disk. Ben was wrong. He had to be. If Crandall could hold out in his house for another two days...

His hands were still trembling.

Don't let them see you...

"I'm going home," he whispered, and threw the Jeep into reverse, peeling the tires, laying rubber on the cement. Go home, make a nice dinner, put on some relaxing music, take the edge off with a drink or two. Do whatever was necessary to pass the time. Kill one hour after another. Murder them one by one, and he could win. It simply wouldn't matter what happened after 17:29:59 on 27, August. The road was open, and he'd have the advantage.

He hit every red light on the way home and wound up screaming at the car in front of him, punching his steering wheel, gunning the engine, tears squeezing through the slits of his pinched eyes, his nostrils flaring, his face flushing with confused rage, faces from the vehicles around him turning in his direction and watching with amused grins. All at his expense.

The engine had cooled in the garage before he undid his seatbelt and slumped from the jeep, his legs too weak to carry him to the door.

Crandall sat down on the step and cried.

CHAPTER 21

26, August

"Everything's fine, Crandall. Angie's fine, we're fine, the weather outside is fine. Everything is fine except for the fact that I don't know why I'm watching your daughter while you're at home. That is still a mystery."

Crandall leaned against the wall, his eyes closed. "I promise that I'll explain everything to you on Sunday when I pick her up," he answered.

"That's the best you can do?"

"For now? Yes. It is. Now may I please speak to my daughter, mother?"

There was a sigh on the other end of the phone and a pause. "Sure."

Crandall looked over at the dog who sat, his mouth open, tongue hanging out, his ears slightly perked as if he were anticipating a walk.

"Hello?"

He felt himself relax at the sound of his daughter's voice. "Hey, hon. How are you?"

"Hi, Dad. I'm okay. Grandma cooked homemade pizza last night and lasagna the night before. She cooks it just like mom."

Crandall smiled sadly. Emily had borrowed his mother's recipes years ago, so of course they tasted alike. "I wish I could be there."

"Why don'tcha come up tonight? Grandpa is grilling steak out on the grill. That's your favorite. I 'member."

The thought of a normal dinner around a normal dinner table with his family sounded like just about the best idea he'd ever heard, but he couldn't go, and he knew it, his eyes welling at his own internal disappointment. "There's things I need to take care of at the school," he lied. "The students start on Monday."

"No kidding, Dad. It's my first day too, you know."

"Hey now, kiddo, I didn't forget. I'm going to be calling Ms. Johnson to make sure you remember all your homework," he said with a smile. "You know, now that both she and I are teacher's, I'm sure she'd be willing to keep an extra eye on you."

"You better not," his daughter quipped. "What would Jim White think of me when you're checking up on me every day? He'd never ask me to the dance."

He chuckled. "Well, Jim White will have to get in line behind the other number one guy in your life."

"Dad…"

"You just make sure you eat all of Grandma's ice-cream while you're there, stay up late and watch all the movies I won't let you watch here."

She giggled. "I did that last night. I think Grandma and Grandpa will be happy to see me leave."

He smiled. "I doubt that. Listen, dear, I have to go."

"Okay. Thanks for calling, Dad."

He loved the sound of her voice, and he didn't want to let go. He could have talked with her all morning, but she would sense the urgency, his fear. Drawing a confident breath, he forced himself to sound calm and in control. "I'll see you in a couple of days, Angie."

"Okay, bye."

"I love you, honey."

"Love you too."

There was a click on the other end, and the transmission was terminated leaving Crandall holding a useless phone. Replacing up the receiver, Crandall stood where the conversation ended, his head heavy with sadness. The image of his daughter's smiling face was replaced with the repeating images he had memorized from the disk. Over and over they came to him, his resolve slipping, his strength waning.

*I miss Mom…*came the soft voice from the recording.

Crandall felt the heat attack his forehead, and he broke from his stance, walking into the living room, hands on hips. He couldn't let them win. It was game time, and he had to step it up a notch.

Won't come true.

How do you know that?

Crandall began to pace, wearing a track into the carpet, his lungs trying to seize up as he consciously sucked in the oxygen, filling his lungs, cooling the adrenalin trying to take over.

Cause she's already dead.

His mind saw the red sheets again and her lifeless, pale skin. He saw the knife, and he remembered the pain, the loneliness.

Emily wasn't suicidal, came the dull drone of Pope's voice.

Crandall felt sick to his stomach, another knot pulling his intestines together, squeezing them, cutting off his air, leaving him with only anger to defend.

"I won't go there," he whispered. His eyes darted to the clock. It had been one day. One day since the last time he'd lost it, his mind fearing his weakness. Holding on wasn't an option.

How does it feel?

"I'm going to win, Pope," he muttered, sinking to a crouched position.

Buddy whined from the kitchen.

"I can wait this out. You'll see."

Pope was grinning in his mind, his confidence the most disgusting feature about him. *There's always a victim. It just depends on who that victim is supposed to be…*

"There's no victim," Crandall whispered. "Not this time. I won't let it happen."

Irony is not without a sense of humor…

Crandall was shaking, his body trembling, sweat breaking out all over his body, a stink rising from beneath his clothes, a sense of defeat upon his tongue. "I'm not going there," he repeated. "Not going."

The clock mocked him, ticking and ticking and ticking. Nothing slowed its rhythm, and nothing sped it up. The sound just lumbered along as if nothing bothered it, as if nothing could stop it. Time was invincible, and it came and went no matter what.

Pope was grinning in his mind, the smug bastard. *There's always a victim. It just depends on who that victim is supposed to be…*

Crandall jerked, standing and lurching at the doctor's face that stared at him only a few feet away, his fist connecting, a spider web of cracks trickling through the mirror that hung over the fireplace, Pope's face becoming Crandall's and changing as the image distorted behind the broken glass.

Ben was somewhere at the fringes of Crandall's failing mind, chuckling the way only he could. There was no fear or anticipation, just knowledge. *Don't let them see you.*

He ran for the door, relief spreading through his body as he gave in, succumbing to his weakness and taking the wheel of the Jeep, igniting the engine and backing out, the tires encouraging him on.

He needed little encouragement.

*   *   *   *

There were people everywhere staring at him with beady eyes, accusing him—he just knew it. They were all spies, all watching and waiting for him to make a mistake, all watching and waiting for him to make his move.

Crandall fished the orange bottle from his pocket and swallowed a few of something. He didn't even know what they were, and he didn't care.

Pick me up, little buddies, he begged. *Pick me up.*

His eyes darted either way, watching the children on the swings and slides, the adults on the benches or walking by—some jogging. They all *seemed* innocent, but none of them were innocent. None of them. They all had to know, because why else would he be in the park? Why would he be standing fifty yards from a talk oak tree with an open notch that was surely used to hide things for others to find. It was obvious why he was there, and they were there to watch him, mock him and point him out.

He didn't belong there, and it must have showed because a woman smiled at him as she walked by, her little rat-on-a-rope trailing her, barking and hopping around like one of those battery-operated dogs in a toy-store that would do somersaults before returning to its yipping nature.

Pick me up.

Crandall stepped forward, onto the path, trying to look inconspicuous, standing out so awfully he might have had a target on his chest.

I'm insane, he thought mildly, his mind returning momentarily. "I have gone insane."

A man frowned, eyeing him suspiciously as he passed by.

Funny. The whole thing was funny in a way. Crandall suspected that this was the end-result ZayRhran had sought all along. Their experiment was to study the mind and figure a way to crack it. His had been cracked. They were inside, digging through the wormy entrails of his brain like termites, taking a bite here and there, tasting the flavor and moving on, laughing at him. It was so funny that he chuckled as he walked along, one footfall after another, his balance shaken.

Little children were laughing at either side, chasing balls, building castles or making ominous sounds as they played G.I. Joe. Laughter on the swings, the merry-go-round, the slides, the rocking horsies...Parents sat in the shade, talking grown-up talk, murmuring, pointing Crandall's way.

They were spies. All of them. They were watching him, knowing where he was going, and at the precise moment he'd reach for the plastic baggie hidden in the trunk of the tree, they'd attack, and the police would come running. The kids would spit on him, the parents would curse.

Crandall wiped away the sweat on his forehead as he cautiously moved forward, the dancing pavement difficult to hold under control. Someone was standing at the edge of the fence, a camcorder directed toward him, the red eye flashing.

ZayRhran…

Another man with a camera a few yards off, pretending to take pictures of the kids.

One footfall after another.

The tree was close enough to where he could hear the individual leaves rustling among one another, pointing him out and laughing. They were all traitors. Even the damn trees…

Don't let them see you.

Crandall took a seat on the nearest bench and pretended to relax, stretching back and sucking in the soft breeze sifting through the park. The scene was manufactured, as perfect as it was, it was just that. Nothing could be this serene. Nothing. Not with so many spies.

The man with the camcorder continued to roll tape, a little girl playing in the grass not ten yards in front of him, but the camera wasn't on her. Crandall was sure the camera was watching him. The girl was merely posing. She was likely a spy.

An old woman sat down next to Crandall and smiled politely.

Crandall glared back. "I won't let you get her," he whispered. "I'm two steps ahead. Remember that."

The old woman recoiled, shrunk and stood, quickly making her retreat.

"I'm not fooled!" he called after her. *I'm not fooled…*

But maybe he *was* fooled. Maybe the joke was on him, and he could no longer tell the difference between black and white. Maybe the game had already caught up, and he had missed the move.

Crandall stood. He *had* to make it to the tree. He *had* to find out if Pope had kept his word. After all, if he hadn't, the whole thing was a scam, and Crandall could relax. There were so many people, and Crandall knew he should wait for the sun to set, wait for them to go home where they would be safe from the dark, where they could cram themselves around the television and numb their minds with crap the government seduced them with. Shampoo commercials, car commercials, insurance commercials, skin-care commercials and silly laughs paid for by the common consumer unaware that their pockets were being stripped clean.

But he couldn't stop. Crandall felt his weakness, and he was repulsed by it, but the tree was so close he could almost reach out and touch it.

"Beautiful day, isn't it?" came a voice to his side, and Crandall jerked, his eyes scanning, seeing a blur of faces, smiles, and good humor.

Sounded like a woman, but his eyes wouldn't work. She was just a spy anyway. "Beautiful," he answered. "In a tragic way."

Children all around him burst out laughing, pointing and giggling, mouths open wide, bodies wracked with laughter.

One little boy ran streaking through. "Monster! Monster!"

The woman looked at him with a confused, horrified look on her face as if an alarm had gone off, some warning that he wasn't a normal visitor to the park.

Crandall cringed, moving along the path, noting every moving thing to either side, intimidated by each and every one as he passed. People stopped what they were doing and looked up, a sea of faces looking up, all in chorus, pairs of eyes locked on him, judging him, accusing him, spying on him.

—Or maybe they weren't.

Crandall couldn't be for sure. Everything seemed out of place, or maybe just too conveniently placed. He felt his feet hitting the asphalt with every step, but there was a part of him that felt like he was floating.

They were standing, rows deep, beside him, arms overhead, rocking back and forth, eyes white and glazed over, the children the same, moving as if to music that he couldn't hear, the scent smelling something like dog-manure, enough to make him cringe.

His hands went for the orange bottle, and he popped three more, praying that they'd—

Pick me up.

—settle into his system quickly.

His head hurt—bad. The people were standing still, the swings slowly rocking to a still, the children standing where they had played, the adults standing where they had sat, the leaves overhead slowly calming.

I won't let them anywhere near you, Angie, he promised, one foot after another.

The tree was so close, but he couldn't touch it, no matter how he reached.

A jogger raced by, her eyes fixated with his, a look of morbid confusion in her eyes, maybe a hint of disgust. What the hell was her problem?

Crandall sat down.

Suddenly sat down.

He had to wait until the timing was right. A bike-rider squealed his tires, jerked off the path and went head over heels into a bush, his bike smacking the trunk of a tree before collapsing, the rear tire still spinning.

Crandall concentrated on his breathing, the dirty evils of his anti-depressants fucking with him, toying with him. The oak was only a few yards away, the open cavity yawning to him and laughing, belching its regurgitated age, a stream of sap at its rim. There was nobody around to disagree.

The tire continued to spin from the idle bike, but its rider had not emerged, and there was no one around to call him out. It was as if the rider had never existed and the accident had never happened. The park was perfectly silent.

His hands shaking, Crandall slowly stood and made his way to the open mouth of the old oak, the smell of stale urine pouring out, moss all around the base and inside the hole. Timidly, he reached his hand into the mouth, expecting at any second for the trap to close, severing his wrist from his forearm, but it didn't happen, and his fingers were exploring in a moist region beyond the shadows, the smell overwhelming and causing his stomach to churn.

There was laughter at his back, and maybe they were laughing at him, or maybe they hadn't noticed.

His fingers found something solid, something manmade, something cold, wet and metal. It felt like a tin box, but he couldn't be sure, his mind concentrating on not regurgitating his lunch. Retracting, he found that he was holding a rectangular tin with a laughing clown on the top, its hand offering an offensive gesture at the forefront, the face complete with a round, red nose, high eyebrows, and crooked lipstick.

Crandall popped the lid, the face falling away and clattering to the ground. Inside he found a zipped baggie, just like Pope had described, a familiar piece of paper protected beneath the plastic.

He grabbed the bag, dropping the tin, which clattered and danced on the ground about his feet. Shoving the bag into his pocket, Crandall retreated, going the other way, the eyes of those accusing him emerging all from every angle.

Leaving the scene, he was paranoid, his eyes wide with trepidation, his fears becoming real as he felt himself being pursued even as he scrambled over the fence and drifted into the traffic, cars squealing their tires around him, vehicles shivering to a rapid halt mere inches from his knees, the furious drivers cursing out their open windows.

They couldn't hurt him. Not here. Not this way. His future had already been written, and on this day, he was invincible.

The thought caused him to laugh, and Crandall played in the street, his mind blurred by the drugs invading his system. He rocked back and forth, dodging the skidding cars, backing to the opposite side of the street where he tripped over the curb and spattered on the sidewalk, his head knocking the concrete.

Bustle all around, but nobody cared though a few laughed and pointed, making jest at Crandall's expense, enjoying themselves. Righting himself, he managed to get to his feet, his glare making contact with those who mocked him, their humor fading at the sight of his crazed eyes as if he meant to attack them. Crandall wandered the street, wandering further from his Jeep, further from home, looking for a place to hide, a place to find security.

A man sold hotdogs to his left, another man sold newspapers to his right. Taxis along the curb, horns blaring under the late August sunshine. The smell of exhaust was overwhelming, the stale stench of the city stalling the minds of those wandering about.

Crandall found his shadows down an alley where the trash bags were stacked against the wall along with the homeless, an empty or half-empty bottle of liquor clenched between dirty fingers. Here he was safe for those who would persecute him were too weak to follow him into the bowels of the city's darkest corners. Crandall stumbled into an open doorway, burnt out by an ancient fire, the interior still smelling of soot, the support beams around him black and cracked. The floor was a haven for puddles that formed at uneven regions, the wall charred and moldy. He sat down in a shaft of light, pulling the baggie from his pocket, fingers trembling.

Don't let them see you.

He was breathing heavily with anticipation as he pulled the crumpled sheet of paper from the baggie and unfolded it, its crispness an insult to the effort he'd had to give to retrieve it. The paper should have been like an old treasure map, damp with mildew, yellowed with age, valuable by the standards of any antique shop. But this was an ordinary piece of modern-day stationary, the header reading: *ZayRhran: Your Modern Day Solution to Modern Day Health. 1-888-ZayRhran.*

The scroll beneath it wasn't anything special either. Instead of the fancy scripture he might expect from an antique scroll, he found the modern day scribble of a doctor, the letters barely legible. But there was enough, and enough was all he needed.

Route I-94 North to exit 126.
Right on Cavalier, 2 miles East

Left on Lincoln. Five miles north to JNCT 44.
Right on Main to Heaven's Gate.
Heaven's Gate to main entrance.
Wake up Crandall. This is where the dream becomes reality…
—Pope

Crandall looked at his watch.

14:22:48.

He was twenty-seven hours away from knowing how the puzzle pieces fit. Twenty-seven hours away from solving that which he had failed to figure. Twenty-seven hours away from the future that decided his fate.

"Focus…" he whispered, the smell of a damp cellar around him. "Don't give up now."

Cramming the piece of paper into his pocket, Crandall reemerged from the burnt out building and into the sunshine where the world went on about him as if nothing had changed and nothing would change

If only he could be so naïve. If only the future would allow him to go back to the boring days of cutting the grass, setting the dinner table, tying his tie, watching Monday Night Football and taking his little girl to school, he wouldn't take those moments for granted. He'd take a step back, maybe even smile as he went about his routine, performing his duties as a loyal husband and devoted father. Those stupid little moments where he'd ask about how Angie's day had been wouldn't be so stupid, and those tiresome talks as Emily turned out the light and rolled over, trying for sleep wouldn't be so redundant. The small things in life would mean so much more. They'd be precious like gold, irreplaceable memories stored at the back of his mind.

But that wouldn't happen, couldn't happen because that was then, and now was now.

Now was the time to fight back.

Now it was his turn.

CHAPTER 22

27, August

Crandall got up like always and went about his business while pretending that it was a normal day. He fed the dog and grabbed the morning paper before sitting down to cold cereal and hot coffee. The food tasted fine, but his stomach threatened to return it where it came from, so he gave up and just drank his coffee, his eyes darting to his watch every few seconds. At the back of his mind he could still hear the voice of reason telling him to lock himself in the house—tie himself up if need be—and wait it out until five thirty. Then there was a second voice that told him that if he wished to fight back as he'd planned, then taking control of his life did not include overdosing on Prozac and caging himself into his house. ZayRhran's game had to be exposed, and Crandall felt that he had enough inside information to take the necessary precautions in protecting himself.

Shaking his head in disgust and giving up, he dumped the rest of his coffee in the sink before plodding along the hall, his eyes unable to avoid the living room clock.

10:29 a.m. Seven hours.

Entering the bedroom, he slid open the closet door and reached to the top shelf where he pulled down the metal box. Its lid was coated with years of dust causing him to wonder how long it had been since he'd last opened it. The combination was easy enough to remember—the day he'd asked Emily to be his wife—and with a few rotations, back and forth, the lock clicked. Crandall lifted the lid, and he felt a giddy sense of excitement at the sight of the handgun. So much power in such a small tool.

The Glock 17 had been a gift from his father on his twenty-first birthday, and the two of them had shot it the same day. That was the only time the gun had ever been fired due mostly to Emily's morbid fear of weapons of any sort. She had pleaded and cried for him to put it away, and he had obliged although insisting they keep it for home protection. He never spoke of the combination so only he would ever be able to get to it in case of an emergency, and now, with Emily gone and Angie away, he could think of no better emergency to bring it as a precaution to the day's fight.

So he was going.

Deep down, he always knew that he would. He could tell himself that he was going for no other reason than to expose ZayRhran, or he could tell himself that maybe Pope was right, there is no controlling fate, but when it came right down to it, Crandall knew that the decision to go had been reached out of curiosity, and being a weak-minded individual, he was powerless to stay away. However, there was no instruction booklet that came with the disk, so there was no reason why he couldn't carry a weapon as protection. If he was supposed to get shot, maybe it would serve in his best interests to shoot first and ask questions later.

The thought of killing terrified him, but his plan didn't involve the gun. If things went according to the plan he'd devised in his head, no one would even know he was there. He'd only be a spectator to whatever was supposed to happen at the Heaven's Gate Amusement Park. For his daughter's sake he had to stay out of sight. He couldn't allow his curiosity to be the death of him.

Crandall loaded the clip with ten bullets and slid the magazine into the handgrip, hearing the internal click to indicate that it was ready for use. He pulled back on the slide, and another click loaded the cartridge into place. Checking the safety, he made sure it was on just so he didn't wind up shooting his foot before he tucked the gun, barrel first, into the front of his pants the way he saw cops do it in undercover movies before allowing his loose, green T-shirt—Angie's gift—to hide it from view.

Crandall left the box open and on the bed, reassuring himself that he'd be closing the box again later that night. Returning to the living room, he rummaged through the closet until he found the camcorder under blankets, coats and several pairs of Emily's and Angel's shoes. He replaced the batteries and made sure a disk was loaded, even testing the recording feature to make sure the thing still worked. It did.

"Gotcha," he whispered, Pope's face burned on his mind.

He had no intention of letting ZayRhran get away with this whole scheme without repercussions. They'd be made to pay, and he'd laugh out loud in court as the judge handed down the sentence. He just had to play his cards right, be calm and not too ambitious.

His hands were sweaty and cold as he headed for the garage. He wanted to get there early—in plenty of time to hide and be on alert when the ZayRhran party showed up. He knew he needed to get some lunch first, not necessarily to satisfy hunger but because he knew he it was necessary. Besides, the thought of spending one more moment in the empty house was enough to make him cringe.

The Jeep swung out of the driveway, the garage door slowly settling down, and Crandall dropped into first, moving forward, the sun just beginning to hide behind the dark clouds that were lazily drifting across the sky.

* * * *

Crandall parked his Jeep a mile away, off the road and behind some pines while making sure that it wasn't plainly visible from either direction along the road. From there he hoofed it, taking to the animal trails that led through the trees, keeping himself hidden as best he could from passers by. He didn't want ZayRhran knowing he was already there, and he was taking every precaution to ensure his little secret, despite the scratches he received from the small branches that whipped him as he passed. He took his time, going slow to remain quiet, watching his every footfall, trying hard not to disrupt the wildlife.

Reaching a tall fence, Crandall knew he had come to the outer boundary of the amusement park, and he searched along the fence until he found a hole in the rusty wire large enough to fit through. Thinking back, he didn't remember the amusement park ever being open, so he figured it must have closed before he was old enough to understand what they were. That meant the old facilities had been abandoned more than twenty-five years earlier, and they showed their age what with the collapsed roofs and rusty rides. The carnival wheel appeared on the verge of tipping, the wooden roller coaster already having done so in some places.

Crandall had to think back to how the scene appeared to him on the playback of the disk. He tried to remember what the background had been made up of because he wanted to find a place to hide while he still had time.

His watch read 2:56 p.m.

It was close. Two and half hours, and the nightmare would end, for better or for worse it would be over no matter what.

He popped two more Zoloft pills, and swallowed them dry, hoping the effects would settle his nerves, afraid they wouldn't. Concentrating, he remembered an old concession stand to the left of the screen on the video, painted orange, gray wood poking through, and a pine tree standing tall in the background. Staying out of the open, Crandall made his way through the park's playground, searching for what he surely remembered, and he found the small stand just as he knew he would, the tall pine where it was supposed to be, the gray clouds swarming overhead and recreating the same atmosphere.

Feeling fear spread through him, it all became too real. All along he'd been hoping the park didn't exist, or the sun would be out, or there would be some indication that the disk was a forgery, because if it wasn't, then what Ben had told him was possible. Everything Ben had said was technologically impossible was actually conceivable. It only made him further wonder how many other secrets were being held from the common man? What was science capable of?

Didn't matter.

What mattered was stopping them, and for the moment, 'them' was ZayRhran. Crandall crept into the small orange stand and set up his camera, under a shelf, the recording eye pointing through an open hole in the rotting wood. The disk could record for eight hours, so there was no reason not to start it now.

There was another stand a few yards away, and he figured he'd hide there. This way, regardless of what happened, the camera would film everything, and someone, someday would eventually discover it. The feel of death collided with his obligation to do the right thing, and he satisfied himself that it wasn't fate for him to be there. It was for Angela. Someday she would understand.

Settling into the darker shadows, he made himself comfortable, his impatient eyes once again going to his watch.

3:36.

Less than two hours, but it seemed an eternity.

* * * *

Crandall heard the approaching footsteps, and he felt like reacting, standing and running or at least shifting for a better view, but to hide properly was to hide intelligently. His eyes could see only so much of the open ground before his little stand, though it was unmistakable that the footsteps were somewhere behind him and drawing closer. The approaching man came swiftly and was suddenly beside him, only the thin, rotting plywood wall separating Crandall from the man who emerged quickly as he made his way into the center of the circle and into Crandall's forward vision.

Pope.

The short man looked around, his face wearing a badge of discouragement as he scanned the area, checking his watch.

Crandall quietly checked his own.

Christ, it was already 5:06.

"Where is that guy?" Pope murmured to himself, his voice barely audible as he continued to turn circles, searching in vain.

Crandall smiled, the playing cards suddenly settling in his lap. The game was his to win, and all he had to do was wait another twenty-four minutes.

"Crandall Cady!" Pope yelled, his voice carrying over the open ground. "I know you're here, you son of a bitch! I saw where you hid your Jeep, so I know you can hear me!"

Crandall's fingers traced the outline of his gun through the cloth that covered it. Part of him wanted to jump up, fire enough rounds to make the sick little man in front of him Swiss cheese like John Wayne and Clint Eastwood had done in their heyday, and part of him just wanted to stay quiet, enjoying the man's discouragement. So they had found his Jeep? So they knew he was here? So what? It didn't change anything because the clock was ticking.

"You can't stop us!" Pope shouted, the echo calling Crandall's bluff.

You can't stop us...

Can't stop us...

Stop us...

Pope stopped turning circles, his beady eyes carefully passing over the small stands and hiding areas around the circle, his face intent on victory. Crandall was grinning in silence until Pope's attention stopped on the little orange concession stand he'd hid his camera in. The little man's eyes squinted, his head moving for better position until he took a timid step forward and closer to Crandall's secret.

Crandall panicked. What had the doctor seen? The camera was hidden, so maybe he was just taking a closer look, but a closer look would ruin everything. Once the camera was found, any evidence he could have used against ZayRhran would be lost. He looked at his watch and saw that it was only nine after. There was still time.

Pope was walking toward the orange stand, his pace increasing.

Cursing under his breath, Crandall stood. "I'm over here, Pope."

The doctor turned, his concern turning to relief and even happiness. He stopped and stood, his arms behind his back. "Thought you could hide from me?"

Crandall nodded.

"The problem is, my friend, you cannot hide from your destiny. Time found you, didn't it?"

Crandall emerged from the stand and stood in the open, his shirt still concealing his last resort, and it was this knowledge that kept him from panicking. He had ten bullets, and it would only take one effective shot to kill a man.

Drawing a breath, Crandall was confident and demanding. "You promised me answers. I want them. Now."

Pope shrugged. "Feel free to repeat your questions. The next twenty minutes are all yours. The rest belong to me."

Crandall told himself over and over to keep his control. So long as Pope didn't know about the gun or the camera, he was reasonably safe. He matched the doctor's expression of calm, and frowned, his dislike of the man showing.

Twenty-minutes wasn't a lot of time to ask all of the questions he had, so he had to choose the right ones. "How was it possible?" he started, blurting the question. "I spoke with a reliable source who said time travel is impossible. He spelled out all theories and concluded that with today's technology, we cannot make the process work."

Pope chuckled. "Benjamin Spoon isn't a stupid man, Mr. Cady, but is a crazy one. We considered hiring him for his experience and knowledge at one time…until his mind started going." He cocked his head. "Don't look so surprised. You know that we know everything about you. It's not like your visits to Clear Haven went unnoticed. Rather, they stuck out like a sore thumb once your mother-in-law passed on. There was no reason for you to be there."

Crandall stiffened, refusing to break. "So it is possible? You can travel through time?"

Pope chuckled at the ignorance. "Not in the least. I imagine Spoon dazzled you with everything you ever wanted to know about force, gravity and speed. Everything he said is true. The theories about bending light by moving faster than light are sound, as are the theories behind black holes. The trick is creating a manmade black hole, and Mr. Spoon incorrectly assumed that this is impossible."

"A black hole? You created a black hole?" Crandall smiled, but he was upset. This sounded like a third-grade science lesson. "A black hole like in all those low-budget A&E science-fiction movies?"

"Black holes are a reality, Mr. Cady. We figured until very recently that the creation of one would take an amount of space larger than our sun with a density greater than anything you could possibly imagine, and a temperature of about a hundred and twenty billion degrees. We calculated that a wormhole in spacetime could be held open only with the ability to exert negative pressure and create antigravity. That's the basic principle behind time travel, you see. Two black holes with a density strong enough to prevent light from escaping, and a wormhole between them that allows an object to pass through."

"Like a man?"

"Not yet, I'm afraid. The density and temperature alone would kill a man in a very disagreeable manner."

"But a disk?" Crandall asked, something in Pope's words suddenly sounding true.

"We were able to create a vessel that offered enough negative energy to keep the disk from being damaged."

"And you sent it back a month in time? Why not a hundred years?"

Pope smiled. "Remember Spoon's lessons, Crandall. A time vessel cannot travel to a point in time prior to its creation. To simplify it for you, imagine that you create a time machine today. How can you possibly send it back to yesterday before the vessel existed? You would unravel its existence and wind up with the parts and pieces you started with, and a very unusable machine."

"So how does it work?"

"You open your black hole today after completing your vessel, and four weeks from now, you open a second hole. The wormhole that connects the two becomes a channel in time, similar to a channel connecting two lakes. Drop the disk through, and it remains frozen in an area that waits for time to catch up to it. The principle is extremely simplistic, but getting the bugger to work is another story." Pope grinned. "Then again, if it was easy, then I wouldn't be able to take credit for the first evidence that time travel is possible, but it also shows without a doubt that while you and I don't know what tomorrow will bring, time already knows. The events on that disk are proof-positive that we have no choice."

"If you hadn't filmed that disk, then I wouldn't be here today," Crandall countered angrily. "I'd be at home, playing with my daughter."

"How can you know that for sure, Mr. Cady? Truth is, you can't. Who knows why you would have found yourself in the middle of this deserted park awaiting your inevitability."

Crandall was confused and irritated. He was getting nowhere. "What does this have to do with me?"

Pope shrugged. "Maybe nothing. Like I said the other day, don't flatter yourself and think that you are one in a million. ZayRhran is a big company. A huge company, in fact. One with a budget half the size of your state, and ZayRhran is only a subsidiary of a larger parent company. You think that with that many dollars absorbed into the economy we don't have the power to pull some strings and do what we want with who we want and when we want?"

"But why me?"

"Why me? Poor me? It'll never happen to me." The doctor chuckled. "It's always someone else until it happens to you. Then it's 'why me' and 'what did I do to deserve this?'"

"And?"

"Why are people singled out in an earthquake, or a tornado, or a car accident for that matter? Why do they always think they are being picked on?"

"With all due respect, Pope, ZayRhran is not a natural disaster," Crandall argued. "A disaster maybe, but a manmade one. Somewhere along the line, my name was drawn along with a million others, or so you say. How did that happen, and why?"

Pope shook his head. "You're a poor listener, Cady. I'll bet your school teachers marked you down for that, didn't they?"

Crandall frowned. As a matter of fact they had, but what had he missed? What had Pope said that was so significant? He glanced at his watch. 5:20. Time was running short.

The doctor shook his head with disappointment. "An earthquake, a tornado…" He shook his head.

"Who's the old man that shoots me?" Crandall demanded. "I'm entitled to that."

Pope took a step closer. "Does the name Alex Carter mean anything to you?"

Crandall shook his head. "No. Nothing. Why?"

"How about Alexis Carter?"

The blood in Crandall's veins froze. All of his confidence suddenly fled his body as though he had exhaled it.

God saw you do it, you little shit…

"I figured it might," Pope went on, irritatingly calm. "To you it was a bad dream; an episode that you learned from and regretted, but an accident. You say some prayers, go to church, act like a good little boy, and all sins are forgiven in God's eyes. After all, you're not sinner, right? Time to move on, but that accident that you caused as a child stole the life of another man's daughter." The doctor grinned, and there was something ugly about it. "Tell me, Crandall, how easily could you forgive God for taking the life of little Angela Cady? Would you let it go, telling yourself that it had just been an unfortunate accident caused by some kid playing a stupid prank, or would you allow the rage and sorrow to manifest itself over the years, your life ruined, your mind mush." Pope was pacing back and forth. Back and forth. "And what would you do if you were given the chance to come face to face with the man that killed your daughter? How would you react?"

Crandall felt the horror of that autumn day flooding back, his confidence lost, his fears returning, the guilt suffocating him the way it had on that fateful day when the car slammed into the tree, the sickening sounds of metal rolling back vivid and real.

"Revenge is a very powerful motive," Pope whispered happily. "It enables a man to volunteer himself for all sorts of strange experiments in exchange for one tiny little moment in time."

Crandall looked around, feeling exposed, but the empty buildings showed him nothing.

5:24 p.m.

The old man was out there somewhere. He was probably watching, waiting for that tiny little second Pope had spoken of to open up where he could slip through and right the terrible wrong Crandall had committed as a child.

"Now I understand your fear," the doctor said almost sympathetically. "To be confronted with your forgotten past so suddenly has to throw you off guard, and that is a very precarious position considering what happens in the next few minutes."

"Where is he?" Crandall demanded, his voice scratchy.

"Who? Alex? Oh, he's around, I'm sure. After all, the disk doesn't lie."

"You son of a bitch," Crandall hissed. "You're fucking twisted, do you understand that? I was just a kid!"

"I am not emotionally involved, Cady. There are thousands more out there like you, but you should take solace in the fact that we didn't specifically choose you simply because of your childhood errors. Like I said before, you were an interesting subject, bur the events of that autumn morning were only a symptom."

Crandall was panicking, his eyes darting back and forth, all around the open arena, searching for movement, searching for an angry father who'd lost his daughter.

"I didn't kill my wife," Crandall snarled. "Any more than I killed my dog. You've been playing with my mind, but I didn't do it."

"You don't know that for sure."

"I do." And suddenly he stopped, because he felt fate closing around him. Dropping his eyes to his watch, the minute rolled over.

5:28.

Drawing a deep breath that smelled heavy of moisture, Crandall felt himself returning. Not just returning in terms of his confidence, but in terms of his soul. All along he had been waiting to uncover the mystery behind this meeting when there was no mystery. Standing where he was, it made sense in a grotesque way, the last chapter of his horrific life coming to a grateful conclusion. "I do," he repeated. He reached into his pocket and pulled out the orange bottle, popping the lid and draining the contents to the dusty ground as thunder rolled overhead. "I cannot prove my memory in court, but I can prove it in my own mind. I loved Emily despite her illness, and I love her still. I'll go wherever your recorded future wants to take me, but I know that I had my moment here to defend myself, and I'll know that I saw through your scheme."

A tear rolled over his cheek, and he even managed to smile, a strange sensation drifting over his body, bringing a sense of calm to his mind that he had never known. The truth was in front of him. The truth was scattered all over the ground, it was sleeping with his departed wife and it would live within his daughter. "We were a family, the three of us. I loved them both, and I always will. I didn't kill my wife, and the truth will prove me innocent."

At the back of his mind, Crandall felt relief that his camera was recording, because this moment, this tiny little moment in time would be remembered forever. It would be viewed, reviewed, scrutinized and argued over for years to come. ZayRhran would fall, and the belligerent little Dr. Pope would wonder how things had gone so terribly wrong when they had been prepared so right.

5:29:00

The doctor was smiling. "You were my favorite," he whispered, standing straight. "People, as a whole, are too lazy to try and learn 'why', but you were brave enough to fight back. You never gave up, Mr. Cady, and you saw it through in a way that was only good enough for you."

Crandall nodded, even as he saw movement from the corner of his eye.

"I'll make sure that your daughter is granted every opportunity afforded to a child. It will be my honor to ensure her success as a human being."

The old man that could only have been Alex Carter came from the shadows, his eyes slanted with anger, a gun in his hand, lowered by his side.

Crandall accepted the peace offering. "I appreciate that, and I believe you."

Carter lifted his pistol, his knuckles going white as he clenched the weapon, the years of frustration appending themselves into a wad of revenge, and his gift in time was granted.

Pope stepped back, and flinched slightly as the gun went off. A yellow flash, and a string of gray smoke. Crandall's body whipped backward, red splattering across his chest as he fell, colliding with the ground, a plume of dust rising around him that settled as he did.

Alex Carter stopped, his gun lowered over his victim, his hands shaking as his moment had come and passed, the years playing and replaying this exact moment over so fast that he felt empty in the stomach. The dead man at his feet seemed different than he had expected. He wasn't a monster. He was just a man.

"Hello, my friend," Pope said, drawing closer.

Carter stood, the barrel of his pistol pointed at his victim. It felt wrong. He had killed a man to offset the death of his little girl, but it didn't bring her back. The world remained, the clouds overhead the same, the breeze unchanged. Killing this man didn't change anything.

"You've finally made it," Pope continued.

The statement meant Carter had become that person he never wanted to be, and he felt sick as he stared down at Crandall's body, feeling fearful and faint with dread. What had he done? Why had he done it?

"How does it feel?"

How did it feel? Felt terrible. Nothing like he had imagined. His revenge had been wasted on a man who had made no effort to protect himself. He looked up, confused, and he began to walk back and forth, his emotions running like the blood on the dead man's shirt. This wasn't what ZayRhran had promised. They had promised something better.

"What just happened?" he asked as he paced, his mind wrought with confusion. "Everything's different."

Pope chuckled, crossing his arms. "This was your doing. Enjoy it."

Another shadow closed in at Carter's back and he looked over to see a man holding a camera that was trained directly on him. "It's not my fault," he whispered, and suddenly he was enraged that this was what he had been reduced to. The whole thing was a staged production to capture how he was supposed to feel after taking another man down, and it sickened him. The camera was an insult, and he felt like the lead role in a reality television series. "Turn that fuckin' thing off."

5:29:59

* * * *

The cameraman lowered the device, but he was still grinning.

Pope reached into his pocket and pulled out a piece of gum, unwrapping it and shoving it into his mouth, chewing aggressively.

"That's a wrap, ain't it, boss?" the cameraman asked.

Pope lifted his eyes to the man and smiled. "For you it is."

Carter felt the sickness becoming him, feeling a pawn in a game played at his expense. His eyes were red, brimming with tears as the regret of who he'd become manifested from his consciousness, and the regret made him hateful. He'd killed a man to bring back his daughter, but the joke was on him, his emotions being studied as he stood. He was nothing more than a monkey in a cage.

The cameraman was shrugging. "Okay, doc. See ya." He lowered his camera and turned his back.

Pope winked. "On the other side." He turned to Carter whose face was contorted with rage, the gun pointed at the cameraman's back, his thumb pulling back on the hammer.

CHAPTER 23

27, August. 5:33:03 p.m.

"Gets easier, doesn't it," Pope asked. His face was solemn, even sad. Spitting his gum, he pulled a cigarette, licked it's end, and pinched it between his lips as he flicked the Bic and pressed the flame against the dry end, dragging deeply. He exhaled the smoke and looked directly at Carter. "After you've killed one, the rest just seem to fall into line." He sighed softly. "Like puppets."

Carter looked at his smoking gun, the clumsy thing in his hand more like a toy for adults.

"I'm all that stands in your way for wholesome redemption," Pope said, stepping forward. "Why don't you finish what you started?"

Carter felt sick to his stomach, the idea of who he was repulsive. Tossing the gun away, the first heavy drops of rain fell from the clouds overhead, the sound heavy as they splattered against the wooden stands, metal rides and dry ground. He shook his head.

"Aren't we sentimental all of a sudden?" the doctor mocked. He was confident as he sighed. "Look at what you've become, Carter. Everything you dreamed of came true, and you're moping around like it's the end of the world."

Alex shrugged. "I guess I just suddenly realized that it wasn't his fault, and I feel bad."

A soft smile. "Well, as they say, what's done is done."

Carter nodded. "Guess so."

"You know what? That choice you just made, that split second when you decided not shoot me was all your own. The footage ended with his last statement, so you should take solace in the fact that your future, from this moment on, is an open road, my friend."

"I am not your friend."

"Have it your way." Pope smiled as the rain began to fall steady, shrouding the world around him in moisture. "It's a funny thing though. I survived it all. The one who's hated more by most. The engineer behind the whole damn thing."

Carter's head was lowered in shame, his breath coming in short gasps. "What about the man's daughter?"

Pope shrugged, tossing his soggy cigarette to the muddy ground. "That's a tough question, but it's none of your concern."

The thunder was a slow, long rumble, that went on and on.

"But you said you'd take care her."

"What, and have him panic? Did you see how relaxed he looked while he let you walk right up to him and blow a hole through his heart?" Pope wiped the rain from his face. "She's now a threat to ZayRhran, Carter, so she's now a threat to me."

Lightning flashed overhead, and the two stood on top of the mud, Carter's head lowered in shame. The rain came harder, the sound like a constant hiss as it splattered against the aged rooftops, the painful drops a venomous torture upon the land.

"You think I'm a demented bastard, don't you?" Pope asked.

The old man huddled in the rain, diminished by the strength of nature, the guilt breaking him down, yet Pope failed to notice the shadow rising upward behind Carter's back.

"You've got a gun," Pope continued. "Why don't you shoot me then? Save that little girl and adopt her as your own. Try and justify the two men you killed here today and convince yourself that you're still a good person."

Carter was trembling, his emotions revealed as he cried into the storm.

Pope shook his head. "You've got a weak soul," he murmured. "If there was a God, I'd think He'd be awfully disappointed right about now."

It was then that Pope noticed the rising shape over Carter's shoulder. A shape that materialized into the form of a man, straightening as it grew, the mold becoming a figure, complete with shoulders and a head that raised itself, the eyes glinting through the downpour. The doctor's smile faded, the rain suddenly cold, the sounds around him drowned beneath the splattering cry of drops attacking drops. He blinked to see, his eyes not believing what they saw.

Carter recognized the fear in the doctor's eyes, and he frowned, whirling to see a man standing only a few feet behind him, his eyes leveraged with confidence and determination—the ghost of a man who shouldn't be standing.

Pope took a step backward as Crandall Cady took a step forward, lifting his shirt and revealing a steel plate with a small dent over the heart, several packets of burst catsup packets falling out and slapping the muddy ground. And there was something else.

Crandall's fingers closed around the grip of the Glock, and he drew the weapon, moving forward, his eyes crazed with animosity.

Thunder cracked overhead, lightning flashing as the rain fell in torrents.

"It's a funny thing though," Crandall murmured through the rain. "You didn't survive any of this, Dr. Pope."

"You can't..." The doctor was lost for words. "You can't be standing there. You can't be. You were killed."

Crandall clicked the safety to 'off', and lifted his gun, the barrel aimed at the good doctor. "It seems that I just seriously fucked with your theories on predictability, doesn't it?" He grinned. "You're whole experiment was a waste of time, Pope."

The doctor backed into a barrier, his retreat ended.

Carter looked on, his soul relieved, though terrified. The man had returned from the dead, and he had come full circle, any fear he might have had replaced with the idea of closure.

"Jesus Christ, Crandall, I'll give you whatever you want," Pope pleaded.

Crandall smiled, his finger slowly pulling back on the trigger. "All I want is the fear to go away," he answered.

"I can give you tha-"

The gun went off, Pope's body slamming back against the wall, tumbling through, boards cracking and crumbling, the small building sagging and collapsing inward, the sounds muffled under a thunderous rumble overhead.

Crandall stood from behind his gun, his hands calm. "You just did."

Carter stood uncomfortably, awaiting his fate, but Crandall lowered the Glock and turned to the man. The moments dragged on, the rain pounding them both, each unwilling to give an inch.

"Do you still want to kill me?" Crandall asked. He tossed his gun into the mud, his aggression spent.

Carter eyed the weapon and then the man. Slowly, he shook his head.

"I'm sorry for what I did," Crandall said. "I never meant to hurt anyone."

Alex nodded. "I know."

Crandall waited a moment then walked away, leaving the scene, the pounding rain slowly washing mud over his gun. He disappeared into the haze of mist. Carter watched the gun disappear, transfixed in time, unable to forget who he'd become. Several minutes passed until he too turned and drifted away, the bloody scene cleansed by the rain.

All that was ever found were two skeletons, months later, the flesh eaten away by nature and her wild.

No one ever found the guns or the ruined camera.

The day light returned...

28, August

Angela came running from the house, her face shining under the sunshine, her small footfalls tapping the sidewalk as she raced toward her father, arms outstretched.

Crandall lifted her up, twirling her around, his arms holding her tight. He could feel her small heart beating against his, and he was unable to control his tears of delight as they ran along his cheeks.

He'd thrown away all of his orange bottles that morning, dumped them down the garbage disposal, promising himself that from this day forward he was going to deal with life as it came, and he was unafraid.

"Grandpa and me fished this morning," Angela was saying as she pulled away from his hug, her little face beaming with pride as she met his eyes. "I caught one too."

God, how he loved her. Nobody would ever take her away, not now, not ever—and he nodded. "That's good, honey."

She frowned slightly. "Dad?"

"What is it?"

She reached out, her finger gently touching one of his tears. "Are you crying?"

He considered her question, and with a smile, he nodded. "Yes," he said, realizing that he wasn't embarrassed. "I guess I am."

> (AP) ZayRhran, a pioneer in the advancement for leading cancer detection and treatment has filed chapter eleven bankruptcy. After the disappearance of its leading physician and CEO, James Pope, the company closed its headquarters and discontinued all practices.
>
> Mr. Crandall Cady filed a lawsuit against ZayRhran last month, claiming a conspiracy to "isolate and exploit private citizens for personal gain", but there wasn't enough evidence to pursue his allegations to trial, and he settled out of court for an undisclosed settlement. The lawsuit's allegations, though unproven, were enough to "mortally damage ZayRhran's future," according to Cady's lawyer, Jeff Brown.

ZayRhran spokesman Dr. David Swisher claims that the settlement was reached to bury a "ridiculous rumor that might be taken as gospel by the average consumer." He went on to further state: "ZayRhran could have prevented life-threatening illnesses for millions of unsuspecting cancer patients, but the paranoia of one man has ruined it for us all."

Cady could not be reached for comment.

* * * *

Ben Spoon dropped the newspaper, and it fluttered silently to the floor. He rolled over, curling into a ball, the sounds of the crazy old farts around him enough to make him scream.

Instead, he laughed.

0-595-30053-7

Printed in the United States
16306LVS00004B/181